P9-CQP-275

HAROLD ROBBINS

The Storyteller

PUBLISHED BY POCKET BOOKS NEW YORK

This novel is a work of fiction. Names, characters, places and incidents are either the product of the author's imagination or are used fictitiously. Any resemblance to actual events or locales or persons, living or dead, is entirely coincidental.

POCKET BOOKS, a division of Simon & Schuster, Inc.
1230 Avenue of the Americas, New York, N.Y. 10020

Published by arrangement with the author
Library of Congress Catalog Card Number: 85-27720

ISBN: 0-671-62740-6

First Pocket Books printing January 1987

10 9 8 7 6 5 4 3 2 1

POCKET and colophon are registered trademarks
of Simon & Schuster, Inc.

Printed in the U.S.A.

For
GRACE

The Storyteller

THE NEWEST, PASSION-FILLED NOVEL FROM AMERICA'S MASTER NOVELIST...

HAROLD ROBBINS

"HAROLD ROBBINS IS A MASTER!"

—*Playboy*

"ROBBINS' BOOKS ARE PACKED WITH ACTION, SUSTAINED BY A STRONG NARRATIVE DRIVE AND ARE GIVEN VITALITY BY HIS OWN COLORFUL LIFE."

—*The Wall Street Journal*

HAROLD ROBBINS IS ONE OF THE "WORLD'S FIVE BESTSELLING AUTHORS...EACH WEEK, AN ESTIMATED 280,000 PEOPLE...PURCHASE A HAROLD ROBBINS BOOK."

—*Saturday Review*

"ROBBINS GRABS THE READER AND DOESN'T LET GO..."

—*Publishers Weekly*

HAROLD ROBBINS

The Storyteller

Books by Harold Robbins

The Adventurers
The Betsy
The Carpetbaggers
Descent from Xanadu
The Dream Merchants
Dreams Die First
Goodbye, Janette
The Inheritors
The Lonely Lady
Memories of Another Day
Never Love a Stranger
The Pirate
79 Park Avenue
Spellbinder
A Stone for Danny Fisher
The Storyteller
Where Love Has Gone

Published by POCKET BOOKS

PROLOGUE

FEAR IS THE surrogate for pain. It comes first. You look out the rear window, then the side window. You're traveling at thirty miles an hour, in the correct lane, heading for the Wilshire turnoff on the San Diego Freeway. Everything is in order. Then you see the big trailer truck barreling alongside you, cutting in front of you from the left lane, racing you to the turnoff.

"Stupid!" I said, hitting my brakes to allow the truck to move in. It was then the fear began. The truck was still beside me. I hit the brakes even harder. The fear began clutching into my gut and throat. The trailer was tilting toward me, looming above me like a gray prehistoric monster. I turned the wheel away from it.

It appeared as if in slow motion that it was falling toward me. I think I screamed in fear. "You're going to kill me, you son of a bitch!"

The truck jackknifed, turning its six headlights, glaring and blinding. Then the fear was gone, replaced by an agony of pain and I screamed again as a million pounds of steel tumbled down, pushing me into the dark.

I opened my eyes to the fluorescent ceiling lights of the

intensive care unit. A nurse was staring at me. "How did I get here?" I asked.

"The paramedics," she said shortly. "Your personal doctor was also here." She turned and called to one of the doctors, "He's awake."

There were two doctors on duty, one man and one woman. The man glanced at me, then turned away, leaving the woman to stand next to me. "What did the goddam truck do to me?" I asked.

"You have a hip fracture, but it could have been worse," she said consolingly. "It shouldn't keep you from working, it's not your writing arm."

She was a young doctor, very pretty, pretty enough to be starred in the television medical soap programs. I looked at her. "Okay. So I can write," I said. "But, what about fucking?"

Her face expressed her shock, then she answered quite seriously, "That will be a problem. You see, the fractures are located so that you cannot move your hips for that form of activity."

I smiled at her. "Then oral sex?"

She looked down at me. "You're sick."

"I know that," I said. "But that has nothing to do with the broken hip."

She placed a reassuring hand on my arm. "You're going to be all right. We're getting ready to transfer you to a private room."

I was curious. I felt that I had been there only a short time. "What time is it?"

"Almost ten in the morning," she said. "You were brought in here about eleven last night."

"I was out that much?" I asked.

"Just as well," she answered. "You were in a lot of pain.

4

We shot you up with enough dope so that you could get through the examinations and the X rays, then brought you back down here and put you on the life systems and monitors."

"It was that bad?" I asked.

"Not really," she said. "But we have a reputation to protect. We don't want a patient with even a minor problem to sneak up and die on us."

"That's reassuring," I said sarcastically.

"You were really in no danger," she said.

She blushed. I looked up at her. "What made you so sure of that?"

"The moment we shot you with some Demerol, you got an erection and began talking dirty."

"Like how dirty?"

Now she was laughing. "Pretty dirty." She looked around to see if anyone was close. "Like in your books. You wanted me to play with you, suck you, fuck you and a lot of other things I don't care to say."

"Really," I said. "And what did you do about it?"

"Nothing. Just worked together with the orthopedist to rig up your leg traction. By then you were asleep and it was over."

"Don't feel bad," I said. "I'll give you another chance when I have my private room."

"I'm in IC," she said. "I never go up to the private rooms."

"Ever?" I asked.

"Only sometimes," she said. She looked down at me. "I have several copies of your books at home. Would you mind signing them for me?"

"Of course," I said. "But only if you bring them up to my room."

She didn't answer. I watched her turn as two attendants rolled a gurney over to my bed and stopped beside me. She turned back to me. "We're going to transfer."

I pointed at the traction hanging over my right knee and under the ankle. "How do you manage it with that?"

"We know how," she said. "Just relax and let us do the work. We'll try not to hurt you too much."

"You don't have to be so honest," I said. "I'd rather you lied a little and gave me another shot of dope."

"Don't be a baby," she said, the attendants helping me across to the gurney with the sheet under me.

I felt the stab of pain racing through and caught my breath. "Shit!"

"It's over," she said. "It wasn't that bad."

"Promises, promises," I said.

She bent over me, wiping a cool washrag across my face. "You're okay," she said.

"You're okay, too," I said as the attendants began to wheel the gurney away.

I felt stupid as they pushed me through the corridors, lying flat on the gurney looking at my leg hanging on the traction over me and beyond that the ceiling. Out of the corner of my eye I saw people moving aside to allow me to pass; I felt embarrassed even though I realized that most people paid no attention to me. This was normal living in the hospital. I closed my eyes. I didn't feel like looking at any people looking at me. I had had enough.

Strangely that clicking of the wheels of the gurney crossing the stone floors of the corridors brought memories of the subway wheels on the tracks many years ago. I didn't know. Maybe I dozed. I always dozed standing up on the subway, my back to the door, the crowd pushing against me holding me up. Then I woke up as the crowd moved off at Forty-second Street, and I would follow them to the station and up to the street toward the office where I worked.

July and August were always a bitch in the subway. The heat and sweat mixed, swirling the peculiar air down from the fans. I would always travel in my shirtsleeves, my jacket and tie folded across my arm. I was seventeen at the time and had a summertime job as a copy boy on the *Daily News*. The day I met her it was extraordinarily hot.

The crowd behind her pushed more tightly against me. She looked up at my face. "If you could turn your arm off your chest to the side, I would have a little more room."

Silently, I nodded, moving my arm carefully against the post so that I didn't lose my jacket and tie. She smiled her thanks to me, then turned around, her back pushing against me. The train began moving out of the station and the normal swaying of the cars began speeding up. I think it took less than thirty seconds and I was raising a hard.

I felt the sweat beginning from my face down to my shirt collar. I glanced down. She had her buttocks jammed into my groin. I began trying to think of other things but nothing worked. My hard kept getting more confined in my shorts. Trying not to let her learn of my predicament, I managed to slip my hand into my pants pocket and carefully moved my prick into a more comfortable position straight up behind my fly. I glanced down at her again. I began to feel better. I guessed she hadn't noticed anything.

The train came to a stop in the tunnel between stations and the regular lights went out and the emergency lights pushed out a dim yellow flicker. The girl looked back over her shoulder up at me. "Are you comfortable?" she asked.

I nodded. I had to concentrate. I couldn't talk too much. "Fine," I said.

She smiled up at me in the flickering lights. "I can feel you against me."

I looked at her. She didn't seem angry. "I'm sorry," I said.

"That's all right," she said. "You wouldn't believe how many men do that on the subway." She waited for me to answer her but I didn't know what to say. She nodded. "You're the fourth man this week. I don't like most of them though, they're pigs. But I don't mind you, you seem nice and clean."

"Thank you," I said.

She looked at me. "Did you come yet?"

I shook my head, no.

"Would you like to?" she asked.

I stared at her, but before I could answer I felt her hand reach behind her back and cup my testicles through my pants crotch. That did it all.

At the same time, the train lurched into motion, the regular lights came on as it moved into the station. My knees seemed to turn into jelly as my orgasm kept my prick slamming against my belly. I hung on to the post to keep from falling as I felt the hot viscous ejaculation spreading over my underwear.

Then the train doors opened on the opposite side and she turned to me and looked up smiling. "That was fun," she said and walked through the open doors.

I watched her, still hanging on to the post, as she went out with the crowd onto the station. I would have followed her to call and try to make a date but I couldn't walk. Then I felt the damp soaking through my pants with my jacket in front of my arms.

I tried to catch her eye as she walked along the platform as the train began to move again. But she was gone as the windows moved quickly away from her.

"Shit!" I thought. I was really stupid. I had it all in my hand and I blew it. All I had to do was talk a little bit more instead of being a dummy. I blinked my eyes to look back at the station but when I opened them, I looked up at my leg hanging over me in the traction.

I looked around the room. It was the private room. Washed-out blue walls and ceiling. I heard shoes on the floor and turned to see a nurse coming to me with a wet washrag.

She was a comfortable lady in her forties. She held out the washrag toward me. "Wash your private parts."

"What for?" I asked, taking the washrag.

"You had a dream while you were sleeping," she said. "But don't worry about it. It's quite normal when you have a few shots of pain killers."

"I only remember being put into the gurney downstairs."

"You were asleep when they transferred you here."

"I remember the gurney reminded me of the subway," I said. "That's strange."

"Clean yourself up and forget it," she said. "You have been sleeping over three hours and your doctor should be coming in almost any minute now."

Less than five minutes later, Ed came into the room. Looked around at my traction device and then pulled a chair next to me in the bed. "You're pretty lucky, sport," he said.

"Glad you think so," I said sarcastically. "It hurts like a bitch."

"It could have been worse. Your fractures will heal in

time, but I've known of some others that would have put you into a wheelchair for life."

I looked at him. For the first time I saw his weariness in his watery blue eyes lined with red from lack of sleep. "I'm sorry," I said. "I guess I screwed up your dinner date."

"That's okay," he said. "You're going to be out of action for a while so you can send over some of your reserve stock."

"How long will it take me to heal?"

"It's not easy to say. It all works in steps. First step, you stay in this traction in the hospital for about a week until we make sure that the various bones are lined up in place. Then you can go home. You start very slow. Walk carefully, with a walker, later with crutches, always slow and a little bit at a time, get a lot of rest and bed time. After a month of that we shoot a few more X rays. If that goes well then we can let you move around a little more but still on the crutches. A month after that, more X rays, and the fractures should be healed. Then working with one crutch or cane you walk slowly for another few months until we're sure that your cartilage and the articulation in your hip socket are cool. Then you can get into your usual routine."

I added up the time. "Six months?"

"About," he said.

"Can I work?" I asked.

"I suppose," he said. "But you'll be in constant pain so you'll have to go slow."

"How much time will it take for the pain to go?"

"At the scale of ten being now, three months will bring you down maybe to five, and when you're completely healed you'll go down to two or one, but that is something that you will learn to live with. It won't interfere with any of your activities."

I looked at him. That was one thing I respected about him—he told the truth. No pie in the sky. "Really fucks up my schedule," I said. "This weekend I was supposed to turn in the bible for a television series. A week after that an article for a British newspaper. Then I was supposed to begin my new book and have the first part of it in three months."

"I don't think you can make that schedule," he said seriously. "But what do you have to worry about? Your last book is still on the best-seller list and it's been there more than a year."

"It's also about more than that year that I spent the money I received for it. I have a big machine to keep running."

He was silent for a moment, then he nodded. "I guess that's true. Life in the fast lane is not cheap. Just with homes here in Beverly Hills, on the Riviera in France, a villa and a yacht, and a winter place in Acapulco, how do you manage?"

"The same way you do," I said. "I keep working."

"You also piss out a lot of money on booze, parties, dope and girls. Cut out some of that and you'd save a lot of money."

"You're beginning to sound like Paul, my lawyer. What neither of you understands is that it's the icing on the cake that binds it all together and makes it worthwhile. Just putting money in the bank doesn't bring you any fun. At least I spend my money on a lifestyle that brings me pleasure and enjoyment."

"But you still have to work," he said.

"So? Don't you?"

"Yes," he said. "But people don't think like that about you."

I laughed. "They think about my books and it makes them think of me that the books and I are the same thing."

"Do you mean you always worked like that? Even when you were beginning?"

"Always," I said. "Maybe even more so."

PART I
1942

=1=

"JOE!" HIS MOTHER'S voice echoed faintly through the closed bedroom door. He rolled over slowly and peered at the alarm clock next to the bed. It was eleven in the morning. He turned back and covered his head with a pillow.

This time his mother's voice sounded louder. He peeked out under the pillow. The bedroom door was open and his cousin, Motty, was standing outside in the hall. He stared at her. "What the hell are you doing here?"

"Your mother wants you," she said.

"I heard her," he said truculently. "I'm still tired."

"You better get up," Motty said. "It's important."

"It can wait another half an hour," he said, ducking back under the pillow.

A moment later, he felt the blanket pull away from him. "What the hell are you doing?" he said, covering his genitals with his hands.

Motty laughed at him. "You've been jerking off again."

"I was not," he said angrily, sitting up.

"Bullshit," she said. "I see the come stains on your sheet."

He looked down at the sheet. "I was sleeping."

"Yeah," Motty said sarcastically. "You always say that. I know better. I've known you since you've been a kid."

"What makes you such an expert?" he asked. "You're only a little older than me."

"I'm twenty-five," she said defensively. "That's old enough. I remember when I used to give you baths when you were practically a baby."

"And you were playing with my prick most of the time," he replied.

"I was not!" she said emphatically.

He took his hands away from his genitals. "I got a hard on now," he said. "Would you like to give me a bath again?"

"Pig!" she snapped. "You have a perverted mind. I read all the stories you write for those magazines. Spicy love stories, spicy detective stories, spicy adventures."

He looked up at her. "You don't have to read them."

"I was curious what you were doing," she said.

"Did they turn you on?" he asked.

"They disgust me," she said. "If you want to call yourself a writer, why don't you write for some decent magazines? *Saturday Evening Post, Collier's, Ladies' Home Journal*."

"I tried," he said. "I can't write their kind of stories." He sat silent for a moment. "But it's not too bad. I'm averaging about fifteen dollars a week from them."

"That's not much," she said. "I get thirty-five a week writing ad copy for A and S."

"I don't call that writing," he said. "Besides you also work at the sales counter in the store."

She ignored his remark as she walked to the door. "You better get downstairs," she said. "Your mother is upset."

He waited until he could hear her footsteps going down the staircase to the entrance hall before he got out of bed. He stretched and breathed deeply in front of the wide-open window. It was October, but the air was still warm and humid. It seemed as if the summer never wanted to let go.

He leaned against the windowsill and looked down at the small driveway that separated their house and the house next door. He saw Motty coming out the side door.

"You're going to be late to work," he called.

"It's Thursday. The store opens late on Thursday."

"Oh."

She looked up at him. "Are you working late tonight?"

"No," he said.

"Maybe you'll come by the store and pick me up. I don't like the idea of coming home alone by myself. That's a scary area at night."

"I'll call you," he said. "I'll try."

"Okay," she said and walked along the driveway to the street.

He turned back into his room. Motty was all right even though sometimes she was a pain in the ass. She had been living with them since she was ten years old. Her mother and father had been killed in an automobile accident and since his mother was the only relative she had, it was only right that his mother would take in her sister's child.

He turned back to the room. His brother's bed was still on the other side of the room as if he was expected home every night. Steven was his older brother, seven years older, and was in his third year in medical school in Oklahoma, and he made it home only about two weeks a year around the holidays. Sometimes he wondered if Steven was really his brother. Steven was always very serious, always studying, and ever since he had been a child he knew he wanted to be a doctor. He used to tease Steven that the reason he wanted to be a doctor was so that he could talk Motty into taking her clothes off and examine her. But Steven had no sense of humor. He never laughed.

Joe took a cigarette from a package on the dresser, lit it,

and took a drag. The taste wasn't that great. He really preferred Luckies but even though Luckies Green had gone to war—as the slogan put it—they still cost more than Twenty Grands, so that was what he smoked. He pinched the cigarette until it went out, then carefully left it in the ashtray so that he could relight it later. He put on his bathrobe and went out into the hallway, past his parents' room next to the bathroom.

His mother had her back to him as he came into the kitchen. She didn't turn to him. Still paring and scraping carrots over the sink, she spoke over her shoulder. "Would you like some breakfast?"

"No, thanks, Mama," he said. "Just a cup of coffee, please."

She still hadn't turned to face him. "Coffee on an empty stomach is not good for you."

"I'm not hungry," he said, sitting at the kitchen table. He sat there holding and rolling the clincher between his fingers until the burnt end of the cigarette had tapped off.

His mother stared at the cigarette as she brought him a cup of coffee. "Cigarettes are the worst thing for you," she said. "It will stunt your growth."

He laughed. "Mama, I'm already five ten. I don't think I'll be growing anymore."

"Did you see your letter?" she said suddenly.

He put down his cup of coffee before he tasted it. "What letter?"

It was on the kitchen table. She pushed it toward him. It looked like an official envelope. It had also been opened. He picked up the letter. It was official. It was from his draft board. Quickly he took the letter out. All he had to see was the first line: "Greetings."

"Shit!" he said, then looked at his mother.

She was already crying.

"Cut it out, Mama," he said. "It's not the end of the world."

"One-A," she said. "In three weeks they want you to report to Grand Central for your physical."

"That doesn't mean anything," he said. "I've been One-A for over a year. And, besides I saw in the papers that only forty percent of the draftees pass their physicals. I may not even pass."

"You should be so lucky," she said snuffling.

He laughed again. "I'm sure we can do something. Papa's a very close friend of Abe Stark. And there's some others too we can talk with." He didn't want to tell her that Papa was very big with the Brownsville boys. She knew it but never wanted to mention it. She wouldn't even acknowledge that her husband was loan-sharking as well as running his chicken market off Pitkin Avenue.

"With the draft board nobody has any influence," she said. "You really have to have something wrong with you."

"Maybe they'll find out I have the clap," he said.

She peered at him. "You have it?" She didn't know whether she should be happy or angry.

"No," he said.

"What happened with your job at the *Daily News*?" she asked. "They don't draft newspaper people. You shouldn't have quit it."

"I didn't quit it," he said. "I told you many times, they fired me. They didn't want anyone working for them in One-A because they couldn't depend on it that he could keep the job."

"Your girlfriend, the big writer on the paper—she could have done something about it."

He was silent for a moment. There was no way he could

tell her that it was because he was fucking Kitty that he got fired. He lit the clincher and blew out some smoke, then lifted his coffee to his lips. "At least you don't have to worry about Steven, Mama," he said. "He has to be safe for another four years."

"You would have been safe too," she said, "if you had taken the job at your Uncle Izzy's machine shop."

"We weren't in the war then," he said. "Besides, you know I couldn't do that kind of work. I'm a writer."

"You should have gone to City College," she said. "Maybe that would have gotten you a deferment."

"Maybe," he answered. "But I didn't pass the tests."

"The trouble was, you were never serious," she said. "You were always running around with those little whores."

"Come on, Mama," he said. "The next thing you'll tell me, that I should have gotten married."

"For a deferment," his mother said, "I wouldn't have complained even if you married one of those whores."

"What would that have gained me?"

"Three-A," she said. "And if you had a baby, maybe more."

He shook his head. "But that's all over. I never did any of those things so let's forget about it."

She looked at him and the tears began to come again. "I spoke to your father. He wants you to go down to his place and talk to him."

"Okay," he said. Then he smiled. "Maybe I'll sleep at the chicken market for three or four nights before I go to Grand Central. Maybe I'll be so covered with chicken lice that they'll throw me out."

"Don't make fun of your father," she said.

He was silent. She had had a special shower built in the

garage so that his father could leave his clothes there and wash up before he came into the house after work.

She went back to the sink. "Go upstairs and get dressed," she said. "I'll get you some breakfast before you go out."

He walked slowly through the lunch-hour crowd on Pitkin Avenue. Looking through the windows of the Little Oriental restaurant, he could see every table already filled and a line of customers waiting for their turn to eat. Across the street, Loew's Pitkin theater was taking down the sign advertising the early-bird matinee; now until six o'clock admission would be twenty-five cents. He wasn't interested in the double feature they displayed. He liked it more when they used to have a stage show and a movie rather than the double features. They used to have great masters of ceremonies then—Dick Powell, Ozzie Nelson, all were wonderful. There were others too, but now all of them had gone to Hollywood to get into the movies.

He had walked four more blocks. Now there were no more expensive shops; the stores were plain and less decorated. Even Rosencrantz's five-and-dime didn't have the pizazz that Woolworth's, just five streets before, had. He turned to the corner near the street where his father's chicken market was located.

It was near the middle of the side street, in a large lot with a wire fence that completely enclosed it. In the corner of the lot was a small building about twenty feet square, then, next to the building, the wire fence continued, and in the middle two long wire gates that allowed the farm trucks to enter and bring the fowl from the country. Through the gate at the far end of the lot there was a long shed where the chickens and other fowl ran back and forth in narrow pens, adding to the noise of the street with their cackling and honking. He stood across the street and looked up at the painted sign across the whole front of the wire fence.

PHIL KRONOWITZ—ALBERT PAVONE
LIVE CHICKENS—GALLINE VIVE
KOSHER KILLED—RESTAURANTS SERVED
RABBINICAL SUPERVISION
WHOLESALE and RETAIL

The sign was painted with bold white lettering on a shining Italian green background. He stood there on the sidewalk while he finished his cigarette. His father didn't like him to smoke.

He dropped the cigarette into the street and crossed to the small building. He turned the door knob. The door was locked. "Damn," he said to himself. He hated to walk into the market through the open area. He disliked the smell and the noise and the blood of the fowl screaming their disaster.

Behind the building, he walked past the long shed. The first half of the shed was devoted to the kosher fowl. In front of it were a dozen triangular iron scoops, the bottom of each attached to a pipe that went into a pail. This was where the *shochet* slit a chicken's throat and then thrust its head down into the scoop until the blood had been drained from its body. Then the *shochet* mumbled a prayer and gave the chicken to the customer—or, for an extra nickel or dime, handed the chicken to a "chicken-flicker" who plucked the feathers from its body, then passed it quickly over a fire to get rid of the lice and quill ends of the feathers. This was his father's part of the market.

Al, his father's partner, was a fat, smiling Italian. He sold many more fowl than Phil Kronowitz—not only because they were sold for less, but because there was no ritual to slow down the work. His workers just slit the fowls' throats, then let them run crazy, splattering blood around the pen; and when they were dead, they were thrown into a vat of boiling water so that the feathers could be taken off with the large wire brush.

There were no customers in front of his father's side. Two chicken-flickers and the *shochet* were sitting against the wall of the office building. The *shochet* was smoking a cigarette. He was a tall man with a long black beard and *payess* covering his cavernous face.

Joe spoke in English. "How are you, Rabbi?"

"How should I be?" the *shochet* answered. *"Ich mach a leben,"* he added in Yiddish, even though Joe knew he spoke English as well as he did.

Joe nodded. "Where is my father?"

"Where should he be?" the *shochet* replied.

"There's nobody in the office," Joe said. "What about Josie?"

Josie was the big lady who was the cashier and the bookkeeper. "She went out to lunch," the *shochet* said.

"With my father?" he asked. He always had a feeling that his father was screwing Josie. She was a busty, big-assed lady—the kind his father liked.

The *shochet* seemed to think the same thing. "I mind my own business. I don't know what anybody does on their own lunchtime."

"Shithead," Joe said to himself and walked across to where Al was standing near the boiling vats. *"Buon giorno,* Tio Alberto," he said, smiling.

"Vass machst du, Yussele?" Al laughed. "Not bad for a *luksh?"*

Joe laughed too. "You speak better Yiddish than I do, Uncle Al."

Al didn't have to be asked. "Your father is having lunch at the Little Oriental. He told me you should go over there right away."

"Little Oriental?" Joe asked. "I thought that Jake wouldn't let him in the restaurant because he was afraid my father would bring some chicken lice into the place."

"Your father took a bath and has a real suit on," Al said. "And besides, even if he didn't, Jake would let him in. Your father is having lunch with Mr. Buchalter."

"Gurrah?" Joe asked. Al didn't have to answer. Joe knew who they were. Lepke and Gurrah owned Brownsville and East New York. Even the Mafia wouldn't fuck with them.

"Okay, Uncle Al, I'll get right over there. Thanks."

"I'm sorry about the One-A," Al said. "I hope everything will be all right."

"Thank you, Uncle Al," he said. "It'll be okay, whichever way it goes."

=== 2 ===

LOUIS BUCHALTER WAS about five feet seven, with a pudgy face and expressionless eyes hidden by the broad-brimmed fedora that sat squarely on his head. There were two other men seated beside him at the round table as Joe sat down next to his father.

"So you're the writer?" he said to Joe in a surprisingly thin voice.

"Yes, sir," Joe said.

Buchalter looked at Joe's father. "He's a good-looking boy, Phil. So what's the problem?"

"He's One-A and his mother is going crazy."

"He's being called up for his examination already?"

"Yes," Phil said. "In three weeks."

Buchalter was silent for a moment. "Grand Central?" he finally said. "That's going to make it expensive. It would have been easier if we had heard about him at the local draft board."

"But you could do it?" Phil asked anxiously.

"Everything can be done," Buchalter answered. "But like I said, it'll be expensive."

"How expensive?" Phil asked.

Buchalter's eyes were inscrutable. "Two grand cash and twenty-five percent of the bank profits instead of ten."

Joe looked at his father. "It's not worth it, Papa. I have a forty percent chance that I can get a Four-F."

"Grosser k' nocker!" his father said angrily. "What makes you such an expert?"

Joe was silent as Phil turned to Buchalter. "There's no other way, Louis?" he asked.

Buchalter shook his head, then paused a moment. He looked at Joe but spoke to Phil. "Does he have a job?"

"No," Phil said. "He works at home. He has a typewriter up in his room."

"Could he work in a store?" Buchalter asked.

"What kind of a store?" Phil asked.

"It's clean," Buchalter said. "All he has to do is answer telephone messages, and once in a while deliver some packages."

Phil was silent.

"And it will make it easier for us to change his classification. The store is in Manhattan, and if he gets a room near there, we could lose his draft papers and give him a whole set under another name." Buchalter looked at Joe. "Do you mind if you work with a shvartzer?"

Joe shook his head. "I don't mind."

"You'll get twenty-five a week."

"That makes it even better," Joe said. "But will I have time to write?"

"You'll have all the time you want," Buchalter said. "No customers come into the store."

"I don't want my kid to wind up in the clink," Phil said.

"Phil, would I do a thing like that to you?" Buchalter said.

"I know you wouldn't," Phil said. "But sometimes things go wrong."

"I'll guarantee it," Buchalter said. "And if you do that for me, you can forget about the twenty-five percent of the bank and we'll go back to the old figures."

"And the two grand?" Phil pressed.

"That you have to pay," Buchalter said. "The money is not for me. It's for the guys who have to handle the paperwork."

Phil thought for a moment, then held out his hand. "It's a deal."

Buchalter shook his hand, then turned to Joe. "Do you have your draft card and notice with you?"

"Yes, sir," Joe said.

"Give them to me."

Joe took them out of his pocket and handed them across the table. Buchalter looked at the papers for a moment and handed them to one of the men sitting next to him, who put them in his jacket pocket.

"Kronowitz," Buchalter said. "We have to change that name. Do you have any ideas?"

"Joseph Crown is the name I write under," Joe said.

"That's good enough," Buchalter said. He turned to the man next to him. "Make a note of that."

The man nodded.

Buchalter turned again to Joe. "Write down this name and address. Tomorrow morning at ten o'clock, you go there." He waited until Joe took out a pen and a small notebook. "Caribbean Imports, Fifty-third Street and Tenth Avenue. The man's name is Jamaica. You can get the telephone number in the book."

"Yes, sir," Joe said.

"Anything else, Phil?" Buchalter asked.

"Nothing, thank you, Louis," Phil said. "I'm really grateful to you."

"That's what friends are for," Buchalter said. He rose to his feet, the two men with him. "I'll go out through the kitchen," he said, then looked down at Joe. "Good luck, kid."

"Thank you, Mr. Buchalter," Joe said.

His father waited until Buchalter and his friends had gone, then looked at his son. "If it weren't for your mother," he said bitterly, "I would have let you go in the army and get yourself killed."

Joe was silent.

Phil looked at him and shook his head sadly. "You want some lunch?"

"No, thanks, Papa," Joe said. "Mama made me have breakfast just before I came down here."

His father rose to his feet. He was a big man, almost six feet tall. "Let's go then," he said. "This is Thursday afternoon and we'll be very busy."

Jake came running from the front of the restaurant to the table. "What is this, a meeting hall?" he complained. "Nobody ate."

Phil looked at him contemptuously. He threw a ten-dollar bill on the table. "This should take care of it," he said and walked out.

Joe stopped outside the restaurant with his father. "I have an appointment at the magazine."

His father looked at him. "You have nothing else to say?"

Joe looked up at his father, then reached up and kissed him on the lips. "Thank you, Papa."

There was a glint of tears in Phil's eyes. "I'll see you tonight, *tateleh*."

* * *

He came out of the IRT subway station at Canal Street. The clatter of the trucks coming and going from the Holland Tunnel was deafening. He stood on the corner waiting for the traffic light to change so that he could cross to the opposite corner to the building where the magazine offices were located.

It was a renovated loft building, and the old freight elevator was used for passengers as well. The elevator operator pulled up the wire grill to let him on. He got out on the fifth floor and walked through the opaque glass doors to the magazine. The simple black paint lettering read: "Searchlight Comics."

He walked down the long corridor. Alongside the windows was the art department. There the illustrators and artists were working on their drawing boards and easels. Along the corridor on the inside wall were the offices that held the editorial staff and the business department. The cubelike offices without doors were lined up like glass-walled prison cells. He paused and entered one of the open offices.

Mr. Hazle, the editor of the magazine group, was almost hidden behind a pile of manuscripts and artwork on his desk. He looked up over them and gestured for Joe to come in.

"Come in, Joe," he said. "I was just thinking about you."

Joe smiled. "Hello, Mr. Hazle. I hope you have a check for me."

"In another day or so," Mr. Hazle said, his owllike eyes peering behind his round glasses under his bald head. "The reason I wanted to talk to you, was that we liked your story for *Spicy Adventure* very much."

"That's good," Joe said, still standing. There was no room for another chair in the tiny office.

"I was talking to the boss," Hazle said. "He liked it too, but he said that twenty-five hundred words is too much for

29

the story. With illustrations it would take up ten pages, and we haven't enough space for it. Five pages a story is our limit."

"So what do we do?" Joe asked.

"The boss said he liked it so much he wants you to turn it into a serial, maybe twenty chapters, one in each issue."

Joe looked at him. "Twelve hundred words a chapter at a penny a word, that's only twelve dollars a story. I know the illustrators are getting more than that. They're getting twenty-five dollars a page."

"That's the kind of magazine it is," Hazle said. "Our customers don't read, they want to look at drawings of tits and ass."

"Still, I should get more money," Joe said.

Hazle stared at him. "I have an idea. The boss liked the story, especially the character of the girl, Honey Darling. Maybe I can talk him into you turning it into a feature every month, a different adventure with Honey Darling in it. That way he will pay two cents a word, and feature stories run seven hundred fifty words. That will give you fifteen dollars a month and wouldn't stop you from writing other stories for us."

"Do you think he'll buy it?"

"I'll go right in there and ask him," Hazle said. "Just give me the word."

"You got the word," Joe said.

"Grab one of those chairs in the corridor," Hazle said. "I'll be back to you in a few minutes."

Joe sat down in the corridor as Hazle walked to its end and entered the only closed office on the floor. Joe reached for his pack of cigarettes and lit one up. He took a deep drag and looked across the corridor to a girl sitting at a typewriter. She glanced at him for a moment and then turned back to her typewriter. He kept watching her type as he dragged on his cigarette.

After a moment she turned toward him and called out, "Are you Joe Crown?"

He nodded.

"I thought so," she said. "I've read most of the stuff that you sent in. You're good, maybe the best writer that comes in here. Hazle himself said that."

"That's good," he said.

"You're too good for them," she said. "Maybe you should try some better magazines."

"I haven't got the contacts," he said. "You need contacts; otherwise they don't even read your stories."

"You should have an agent then."

"I need a contact for that too. Agents don't want to waste their time with beginners."

She looked at him. "I'll give you the name of an agent that I know," she said. "But don't let Mr. Hazle know that I told you."

"I won't, I promise," he said.

She looked over her shoulder to make sure that Hazle wasn't returning. Then she quickly typed the name on a sheet of paper, and handed it across the corridor to him. "Put that in your pocket—quickly," she said nervously.

"What's your name?" he asked, doing as she said.

"I put my name and telephone number on the paper, too," she said. "But you can only call me on Sundays. That's the only day I have off."

"Okay," he said. "I'll call you. Thanks a lot."

She nodded and turned back to her typewriter as Hazle came down the corridor. Joe looked up at the bald man.

"Mr. Kahn wants to see you," Hazle said.

Joe followed the editor to the closed office. It wasn't

large, but one corner had four windows. The walls were mahogany veneer and there was a fake mahogany desk. On the wall were paintings of various magazine covers.

Mr. Kahn was a big, jovial man with a bushy head of hair and large tortoiseshell eyeglasses. He came from behind his desk and held out his hand. "Joe," he said in a deep baritone voice, "I like to meet writers of talent, and I consider that you are one of our best."

"Thank you, Mr. Kahn," Joe said.

"I told Hazle that we'll make that deal. You get the two cents a word. Like I said, we like to reward talent."

"Thank you, Mr. Kahn."

"Nothing at all, Joe," the publisher said. "You just come in anytime you want to see me. We're all one family here." He went back behind his desk. "Too bad we can't talk some more but there's so much work to do."

"I understand, Mr. Kahn. Thank you again," Joe said, and followed Hazle out of the office.

Hazle walked into his small cell-like office. "I knew he would go for it." He smiled.

"What made you so sure?" Joe asked.

"You remember that last scene in your story where the Arab cuts open Honey Darling's brassiere with his scimitar and her jutting breasts burst out?"

"I remember," Joe said.

"Mr. Kahn said the imagery from that scene gave him the biggest hard on he had since he read Pierre Louÿs *Aphrodite*."

"Maybe you should have asked him for three cents a word then." Joe laughed.

"Just give him time," Hazle said. "Now you have to get to work. First, you have to edit the twenty-five hundred words into three seven-hundred-fifty-word stories."

= 3 =

HE WAITED UNTIL he was in the street outside the office building before looking at the sheet of paper the typist had given him.

> Laura Shelton
> Piersall and Marshall Agency
> 34 East 39th Street
> Tele: Lexington 2200

Underneath was the typist's name. Kathy Shelton. Tele: YOrkville 9831. P.S. Don't call my sister until tomorrow so that I can tell her about you tonight. K.S.

He felt good. That was a stroke of luck. He had heard about that agency. It was one of the best literary agencies in the city. Several times he had tried to make an appointment with them but the operator or the receptionist would never let him through.

He walked along Canal Street. Traffic was building up as rush hour began. He checked his watch; it was almost five o'clock. He went into a candy store on the next corner and ordered an egg cream. The counterman looked at him. "Small or large?"

He still felt lucky. "Large," he said.

"Seven cents," the counterman said, placing a large glass of the white-topped chocolate drink in front of him.

He left a dime on the counter and took his drink over to the pay phone opposite the counter. He heard his nickel tinkle down the box and then dialed the number. It was one of the new pay telephones, and it seemed strange not to hear the operator's voice answer. He sipped his drink as the ringing of the telephone sounded in his ear. A voice answered, "Hello."

"Lutetia?" he asked. "Joe."

Her voice was thin and tinny through the receiver. "How are you, Joe?" She sounded as if she was stoned.

"Is Kitty home?" he asked.

"Yes. But she's asleep."

"Smashed?" he asked.

"Out of her mind," Lutetia answered.

"Shit," he said. "She told me that she'd give me the five bucks for the work I did. She said she'd have it for me today."

"If she said she had it for you, she probably had it," Lutetia said. Then she laughed. "But you'd have to wake her up first."

"I was counting on that money," he said.

"Come up anyway," she said. "Maybe you'll get lucky and she'll wake up."

He thought for a moment. There wasn't anything else he had to do. "Okay," he said. "I'll be over there in about a half-hour."

Lutetia stood in the open doorway as he came from the staircase. The light in the entrance hall behind shone through the sheer chiffon dressing gown, revealing her naked body beneath.

"She's still out," she said as he walked through the door.

He turned to her as she closed the door. He saw the glass of red wine in her hand. She seemed to be moving in slow motion, her long sandy brown hair falling to her shoulders, the large black pupils vague in her soft blue eyes. The scent of marijuana hung in the apartment. "You seem pretty gone yourself," he said.

"Not like her," she said. "Vodka and tea don't mix."

He followed her into the combination living-and-dining room. She sprawled onto the couch, the dressing gown falling from her legs up to her waist where the gown was fastened by a soft belt. She looked up at him. "There's a bottle of wine and some glasses on the cocktail table," she said.

"Not for me," he said. "I walked up from Canal Street. The heat and the humidity got to me. I'd like a cold drink."

"We've got Canada Dry and Coca-Cola in the icebox," she said. "You know where to get it."

When he returned from the kitchen with a glass of ginger ale, she was lighting another joint. The acrid scent of the marijuana wafted into the room. Her hair fell forward as she bent over the cocktail table. Now the upper part of her gown opened, revealing her breasts. She held the joint toward him. "Want a drag?"

"Not right now," he said, sitting in the easy chair opposite her and sipping his drink.

She took two more drags on the joint, then put it in an ashtray and lifted her wineglass. She leaned back against the couch. "I'm bored," she said.

He smiled. "What else is new?"

"I'm horny," she said.

"You can take care of that," he said.

"I've been masturbating all afternoon," she said. "But it's not that much fun alone."

"Masturbation is a solo sport," he said.

"Doesn't have to be," she said.

He sipped his ginger ale without answering.

Still leaning back against the couch, she spread her knees wide apart and, turning her index and middle fingers into an inverted "V for Victory," opened her blond-haired pussy until the pink, moist lips seemed to be shining at him. She watched him looking at her. "Getting a hard on?" she teased.

"I'm not dead," he said, feeling the throbbing in his phallus.

"How'd you like to eat that hot juicy pussy?" she asked.

"Wouldn't mind," he answered rubbing himself through his pants. "But what's in it for me?"

"I'll jerk you off," she said.

"I can do that better myself," he laughed. "Suck it or fuck it, either will be okay with me."

"You know I'm not into cock," she said. "They're all ugly."

He unbuttoned his trousers and took out his penis. He could feel the juice already dripping. He looked at her. "It's right here," he said. "Just sacrifice yourself a little."

"Prick!" she said.

"That's where it's at," he laughed. "No suckee, no eatee."

She stared at him for a moment, then she nodded. "Okay, come over here."

He stood up and let his trousers fall off, then went over to her. He held her head between his hands and pulled her face to his phallus. She kept her lips clenched. "Open your fucking mouth, you bitch!" he said angrily.

Stubbornly, she was turning away from him, moving her

face from one side to the other. Finally, he was able to hold her face still, but by then it was too late. His orgasm swept through him, spurting his semen wildly over her. He stared down at her.

She lay still, looking at him. "It's disgusting," she said trying to control her voice. "Disgusting."

"Dyke bitch!" he said, wiping himself with the corner of her dressing gown. He put on his pants, then turned to her.

"Where are you going?" she asked.

"Leaving," he said.

"You can't go now," she said. "You said you'd give me some head."

"That was only if you gave it to me," he said.

"I was going to," she said. "It's not my fault that you couldn't hold it long enough until I was ready."

He stared at her for a moment and then began to laugh. "Okay, you bitch," he said. "Wipe off my come and get out of that stupid kimono. I'll eat your cunt until your ass falls off."

Two hours later, Kitty was still asleep. He looked at Lutetia. "It's almost eight o'clock," he said. "I guess there's no chance that she'll get up now."

"That's right," Lutetia said. She smiled. "You know, you don't give such bad head for a man."

"Thanks," he said dryly. "Can I use your phone?"

She nodded. She watched him call his cousin and arrange for her to meet him at the main entrance of the store on Fulton Street. He put down the phone. "I have to get going now," he said.

"Okay," she said. "What do you want me to tell Kitty?"

"I'll check her tomorrow."

"Okay," she said, picking up her wineglass. "You're not angry with me, are you?"

He smiled. "No. But next time, I'd like equal time."

As he waited in front of the main entrance of Abraham and Straus, the hands of the big clock on the iron post in front showed five minutes to nine. A special policeman took his place at the inside doors; in a few moments a second policeman came to guard the outside doors. First to come out were the customers; by the time the closing bells began to ring at nine o'clock, most of them had gone and the policemen locked all the doors except the single double door in the center. The last customers straggled out and the first of the employees began leaving the store.

Motty was late; she didn't come out until it was almost nine-thirty. She smiled as she saw Joe. "I'm sorry I took so long," she said. "But the ad manager wanted some changes in Sunday's ads at the last minute."

"It's okay," he said. He took her arm and they walked across the corner and passed Gage & Tollner's restaurant. The restaurant was busy.

"A lot of our executives have dinner there on Thursday nights," she said.

"Are they good?" he asked.

"They're expensive," she answered.

He took her through side streets to the Atlantic Avenue subway station. It was a shortcut, almost three blocks shorter than staying on Fulton. The streets were dark and gloomy, lined with old tenements filled with colored and Puerto Ricans, all on relief. The people they saw didn't seem friendly. Hurrying past them, Motty held on to his arm unconsciously. He heard her sigh of relief as she saw the lights shining brightly at Atlantic Avenue. The subway entrance was on the corner.

He had the nickels ready and they went through the turnstiles. They walked quickly to the head of the platform. The first car was usually less crowded; it also was just opposite the exit at the New Lots Station where they would get off.

They were lucky. The first train rumbling into the station was an almost empty New Lots Avenue express. They sat down on the long, hard straw bench. He looked at her. "Okay?"

She nodded. "Thank you for picking me up. Last week one of the girls from the store was raped on the side street."

"She probably wanted it," he said.

"That's not true," she said angrily. "I know her. She's a nice girl. Why do you guys always think that a girl wants to get raped?"

"They do," he said. "Just look at the way they dress, even the way you do. Your dress is so low-cut that your tits are sticking out and so tight across your ass that every wiggle seems like an invitation."

"You really have a dirty mind," she said.

"It's normal," he laughed. "Tits and ass. Every guy gets a hard on."

"You have a hard on all the time," she said. "Even when you were a kid."

He didn't answer.

"Did you meet with your father?" she asked.

"Yes."

"What happened?"

"Nothing," he answered. "Everything's okay."

"Was your father angry?"

"You know Papa," he said. "But everything worked out.

I wound up getting a job at an importing company in New York."

"What about the draft?" she asked.

He was annoyed. "I said everything was taken care of."

She was silent for a moment; then, looking down at her handbag on her lap, "I got a letter from Stevie," she said in a low voice. "He wants me to marry him when he comes home for the holidays."

Surprise sounded in his voice. "My brother?"

Now *she* was annoyed. "You know any other Stevie?"

"I don't understand it," he said. "How did you get the letter before my mother?" His mother opened everybody's mail before she passed it on.

"He didn't mail it to the house," she said. "I got it at the store when I came in this morning."

"He's been writing to you?"

"Now and then," she answered.

"Ever said anything about it before?"

"No."

"Sneaky bastard," he said. He looked at her. "What are you going to do?"

"I don't know," she said. "I'm afraid of what your mother will think about it. After all, we are first cousins."

"That don't mean shit," he said. "That's very normal in Jewish families. You know the saying, the family that marries together stays together."

"It's no joke," she said.

He looked at her. "How do you feel about it? Do you want to marry Stevie?"

"I like him," she said. "But I never thought about marrying him. In his letter he said that he had always thought about me. And if we could get married we would have a good life. First of all, this next year would be his last year in medical school and if we were married he wouldn't go right into the army, he would take his residency in a regular hospital for three years instead of the medical corps. He already has been offered positions from eight hospitals across the country. We could live wherever we wanted. There's a big shortage of doctors."

He stared at her. "That sounds good. Even Mama wouldn't argue about that. I don't think you have to worry about her."

She was silent.

"What's bothering you?" he asked.

"I don't know," she said huskily, her voice close to tears. "You know, it seems so cut-and-dried. I used to dream of love and romance. Maybe I'm being stupid. I'm twenty-five already. There's a war on and there are no men around. Another couple of years and I'll be an old maid."

He reached for her hand and held it gently. "Don't feel like that," he said. "You're a wonderful girl."

There were tears in the corners of her eyes. "But he never said in the letter that he loved me."

"Not at all?" he asked.

"Maybe at the end of the letter. He signed it, 'Love, Stevie.'"

"Then what are you complaining about? He said it." He smiled. "That's Stevie, my brother. He's a doctor, not a writer."

In spite of herself, she began to laugh. "Then you think it's all right?"

"Great!" he answered. "And just remember if he doesn't give you enough, you can always call on me. That's what brothers-in-law can be counted on for."

41

=4=

THE PUSHCARTS WERE stretched out along the sidewalks between Fifty-second Street and Fifty-fourth Street on the west side of Tenth Avenue. The vendors were mainly Italian, and that was the language Joe heard as he walked along the sidewalks. He looked at the carts piled high with fruits and vegetables; others had Italian cheeses wrapped in gauze or shaped in a ball and hanging in thin ropes. There were pushcarts that displayed cheap housedresses and underwear, and others that sold housewares, knives and forks, plates and sundries. The sidewalks were crowded as women and men argued and bargained with each other as the shopping day began in earnest. It was almost ten o'clock when Joe crossed between two of the pushcarts to the other side of the street to the small store window that was lettered "Caribbean Imports."

The window was dusty and probably had not been washed in months. There was no way he could have seen into the store. He opened the door, which was as dusty as the windows. If it had not been for the small card that read "Open," the store would have seemed closed.

Inside there was a counter, and a single light burning dimly over it. He looked around. There were some shelves

on which were displayed an assortment of knives and forks
of various sizes held by wooden and steel holders. On the
counters were several wooden dolls, also in various sizes,
in different native costumes. On the walls behind were paintings, square, oblong and rectangular, in bright colors and
representing scenes of people and villages indigenous to the
Caribbean Islands.

He stood there for a moment. The store seemed empty—
no one there and no sound. He knocked on the counter and
waited. There was no answer. Then he glanced to the back
of the store where there was a door in the rear wall behind
the counter. In amateurish lettering was painted "Private."
He hesitated a moment, then knocked on the door softly.

A few seconds later a faintly British-accented black voice
came through the closed door. "That the new boy?"

"Yes," he called. "Joe Crown."

"Mon!" the voice called. "Ten o'clock already?"

"Yes, sir," Joe answered.

The sound of chain locks rattled and a tall black man
peered out through the crack of the door. "Anyone else here
with you?"

"No," Joe answered. "I'm alone."

"Lock the front door and turn the sign. Then come back
in here." The man watched through the crack of the door
as Joe locked the store and returned to him. Then the big
man opened his door. He stood in the doorway completely
naked and held out his hand. "I'm Jamaica," he said in a
resonant Island voice.

Joe shook his hand. "Joe Crown."

"Come in," Jamaica said. "I'll jump into a pair of pants."

Joe followed him into the back room. There was a dim
lamp resting on an old-fashioned roll-top desk. A faint scent
of marijuana hung in the air. Jamaica pulled a pair of shorts

43

and his pants from behind the desk chair and climbed into them. There was a sound against the far wall. Joe turned toward it.

A three-quarter sofa bed stood in the middle of the room. His mouth fell open in surprise. Three very pretty black girls, also naked, were on the bed.

Jamaica glanced at him and smiled, his teeth white and large. "Don't pay no attention to them," he said. "They all wifes."

"Your wives?" Joe felt stupid.

"Sort of," Jamaica said. "They my girls. They work for me. I have six more of them. I'm their sweet man."

Joe stared at him. "How can you take care of all of them?"

Jamaica laughed. "It's easy. I never take on more than three of them at the same time."

"How do you remember their names?" Joe asked.

"That's easy too," Jamaica answered. "They all have the same name. Lolita." He turned to the girls on the bed. "Now git your asses dressed an' ready for work," he said. "I got big business with this man."

He pulled his shirt from the chair and began to slip into the sleeves, then looked at Joe. "I'm forgetting my manners," he said. "Would you like a fuck off'n one of them before'n they get dressed?"

"No, thanks," Joe said, staring at them.

"Well, any time," Jamaica said. "They available. An' that's free for you. Jes' one of the extras on this job."

Joe nodded.

"Then let's go out into the store," Jamaica said. He looked back at the girls. "One of you Lolitas get your ass out to the coffee shop down the corner an' get us some coffee an' sweet rolls."

Jamaica followed Joe into the store and sat behind the

counter opposite him. He looked at Joe. "They told me that you a writer."

"That's right," Joe answered.

"What do you write?"

"Stories. For magazines—you know," Joe said.

"I don't read much," Jamaica said. "But I have respect for writing."

"That's okay," Joe said.

Jamaica looked at him. "You know them girls are not part of your job," he said. "They a sideline of mine."

"Not bad." Joe smiled.

"Keeps me a little busy but it's okay," he said.

Joe nodded.

"Your job is mostly to stay in the store an' answer the telephone because I'm mostly outside. Sometimes you have to make some deliveries after the store closes. You'll get extra for that." Jamaica looked at him. "That okay?"

"It's fine," Joe said. "But I still don't know what I'm doing or what we're selling here. I don't know anything about these things I see on the shelves and walls here."

Jamaica shook his head. "Mr. B. never told you?"

Joe shook his head.

Jamaica met his eyes. "Gumballs, ganch an' happy dust."

Opium, marijuana and cocaine. "Mr. B. never told me," Joe said.

"There's nothing to worry about," Jamaica said. "I have a very high-class clientele. All musicians and high-society people. An' Mr. B. has an agreement with the syndicate. They have a big blanket on us so there's never any trouble."

Joe was silent.

"It's a good job," Jamaica said. "Most of the time you don't do nothin' here an' you can write all you want. And along with the twenty-five dollars, you'll probably pick up twenty or thirty a week extra on deliveries."

"That's fine," Joe said.

Jamaica looked at him shrewdly. "You scared?"

Joe nodded.

"Look at it like this," Jamaica said. "Jes' figger you're better off bein' scared here than being scared shitless with your head bein' shot off in the army."

Joe was silent. That was one way of looking at it. The rear door opened and one of the girls came out. She was dressed in a cheap print housedress wrapped tightly over her big breasts and her big muscular buttocks. She looked at him curiously with her dark eyes, then, tossing her black hair ironed into soft curls around her face, turned to Jamaica. "Kin we get coffee an' danish for us too?"

He looked at her. "The work tables set up?"

"Almos' finished," she answered.

He peeled a five-dollar bill from a big roll in his pocket. "Okay," he said. "But make it fast, we have a lot of work to do."

She took the money and looked at Joe. "Cream an' sugar in your coffee?"

"Just black, thank you," Joe said.

She smiled. "If'n you like black, you jes' my kin' of man."

"Get goin'," Jamaica said sharply. "Save your cock-teasin' for after we finish working." He watched her as she left the store and then turned back to Joe. "Gals are a pain in the ass," he said. "Have to keep showin' them all the time that you in charge."

Joe was silent.

"Your hours will be noon to seven," Jamaica said. "I'll be out from one to six."

Joe nodded.

"Come on," Jamaica said. "Let's see how the gals are doin'."

Joe followed him into the back room. It had suddenly been changed into a workroom. Two fluorescent ceiling fixtures gave a harsh blue light. The sofa bed had been made up and turned into an imitation-leather couch. Two tables, each covered tightly with a black oilcloth cover, were placed together to form a T-square. The two girls still in the room were also wearing cheap print housedresses.

Jamaica pulled a key chain from one of his pockets. For the first time Joe realized that one of the walls was covered with tall, locked metal closets, and at the far end were two new electric refrigerators. The refrigerator doors were also fitted with locks. Quickly Jamaica began to unlock the closets and the refrigerators.

Quickly and expertly he and the girls began to remove the equipment from the closet and set up their sections on the table. The T end of the tables held a hand-operated mill grinder and a large electric flour mixer with two rotating blades that fit into a mixing bowl, and next to it was a large sifter that emptied into another bowl. In the center of the table was a balance scale, the small weights against it measuring from a half gram up to two ounces. At the other end of the T-square were small leaves of paper, one side waxed, the other side either pink or blue; beyond that were brown glass bottles already labeled. Joe looked at one. They were counterfeit-labeled, "Merck," then "COCAINE. Flaked Crystalline Snow. Seven (7) Grams."

The long rectangular table was divided into one small section and one longer section. The small section held a small hand press that made ten pills at a time. The larger one, another kind of a roller for marijuana, with small teeth like spikes, was used to strip leaves from the branches, which then were placed into another sifter that allowed the leaves to fall into a tray without the seeds. Next to that was a large, hand-operated cigarette roller.

Jamaica took several boxes from the refrigerators. Two gray boxes were placed on the T tables. He opened the boxes, which held ten brown bottles each. This was the real thing, original bottles of prescription cocaine. Next to the bottles he placed a large round tin labeled "Lactose" and a small little bottle labeled "Strychnine." He looked at Joe. "Prescription coke is seventy percent pure. It could blow your head off," he said. "We cut it into equal parts of coke and lactose, then a pinch of strych to give it the bitter taste that hides the sweetness of the lactose. That way everyone is happy."

Joe didn't answer. That it made a better profit was not even mentioned. He continued to watch while Jamaica placed a large square brownish-black block of pressed gum of opium in front of one girl, and then a large box filled with stems of marijuana before another.

Jamaica looked over at him. "Do you use any of this stuff?"

Joe shook his head. "A joint now and then. But I'm really not into it, gets me crazy."

Jamaica smiled. "Just as well. If you can't handle it, you're better off leaving it alone."

There was a knock at the door and the girl he'd sent out for coffee stuck her head into the room. "Coffee's on the counter out here," she said.

Jamaica smiled. "Okay," he said. He looked at the girls. "Let's go."

The girl standing behind the T-square tables spoke to Jamaica. "Kin we all have a toot?" she asked. "We have to get ourselves up. Don' forget we didn' git much sleep last night. It was seven in the morning by the time we got in here."

Jamaica stared at her for a moment, then nodded. He took out a small vial and a tiny silver spoon. "Okay. But on'y one toot each," he answered. "Don' forget we got a lot of work to do this morning. This is the weekend coming up."

The girls clustered around him like a little flock of sparrows begging for bread crumbs. Jamaica looked at them and then at Joe. "They all Lolitas." He smiled again. "All cunts."

Jamaica rose from his chair behind the counter. He placed his empty coffee container down and looked at the girls. "Party time's over," he said. "Let's get back to work."

He watched the girls as they went into the back room, then turned to Joe. "Kin you start tomorrow at noon?"

"I'll be here," Joe said.

"I'll have more time to explain what you have to do," he said. "Right now, I have to keep my eye on those girls. If I'm not there, they'll steal my ass off."

"Okay," Joe said.

The telephone rang and Jamaica picked it up from under the counter. "Caribbean Imports," he answered in a guarded voice. He listened for a moment. "Need it right away?" he asked. Another moment passed before he answered. "I'll take care of it."

He put down the telephone and looked at Joe. "Can you do me a favor?"

Joe nodded.

Jamaica gestured for Joe to follow him into the back room. The girls were already working. He took out two brown paper bags, putting one into the other, then very

49

quickly filled them and closed them. His movements were so fast that Joe couldn't even figure out what had been put into the bags.

Jamaica tied the bags with a brown cord and handed them to him. He scrawled an address on a piece of paper.

Joe looked down at it. "25 C.P.W. Penthouse C $1000.00."

"Got it?" Jamaica asked.

He nodded.

Jamaica gave him a five-dollar bill from his roll. "Give this to the doorman," he said. "He'll let you in." He walked into the store with Joe. "This is a big customer," he said. "He's a big Broadway composer, so make it fast. He said he's making the Twentieth Century to California at two o'clock."

"COD?" Joe asked.

"That's the only way we do business," Jamaica said.

It took less than ten minutes for Joe to reach the apartment house. The doorman peered at him, then pocketed the five-dollar bill and took Joe to a closed elevator and up to the apartment. He waited in the open elevator door and watched Joe deliver his package and receive an envelope. Joe checked the envelope and before he could nod his thanks the apartment door had closed. He returned to the elevator.

It took approximately another ten minutes for Joe to return to the store. It was empty. Joe knocked at the rear door. Jamaica came out into the store.

Joe gave him the envelope and Jamaica went behind the counter and counted the bills, then stuck them into his pocket. He came up with a ten-dollar bill in his hand and held it out to Joe. "The customer just called me and told me that he was in such a hurry he didn't have time to give you a tip."

50

"It's okay," Joe said. "I can wait for it."

Jamaica smiled. "Keep it," he said. "I'll see you tomorrow."

"Thanks," Joe said. It was not until he was outside in the street that he realized that he had just passed the first test.

=5=

HE CLOSED THE door of the telephone booth that shut the outside noise away. "Miss Shelton? I'm Joe Crown," he said into the phone. "I'm the writer that your sister asked to call you."

Miss Shelton's voice was educated, self-important and cool. "Yes, Mr. Crown." She seemed to offer no encouragement.

"Can I have a moment of your time for an appointment?"

She answered, still cool. "You're the writer?"

"Yes, Miss Shelton."

"What have you had published?" she asked. "Besides the stories in the magazines I already know about."

"None," he said. "But I have written a number of short stories and novellas."

"You have submitted them to magazines?" she asked. "What has been their reaction?"

"Only rejections from those who read them," he answered. "Usually they came back unopened with a note that they do not read a manuscript unless submitted by an agent."

"Kathy thinks you could be a good writer," she said.

"Your sister is very encouraging."

"Can you send me several of those stories so that I can

appraise your work? Try to select some of those you think are among the best."

"I'll do that, Miss Shelton," he said. "Shall I mail them or deliver them to your office?"

"Mail will be all right," she said. "I'll contact you as soon as I have time to read them."

"Thank you very much, Miss Shelton," he said.

"Not at all, Mr. Crown," she said formally. "I have a great deal of respect for my sister's opinion and will look forward to seeing your work. Goodbye, Mr. Crown."

"Goodbye, Miss Shelton," he said. There was a click in the receiver against his ear. The nickel tinkled down into the box as he hung up the phone. Automatically he put his finger into the return slot. This was his lucky day. He looked down at his palm. There were four nickels in his hand.

He invested one of the coins to call his cousin. Motty came on the phone. "What did my mother say?" he asked.

"I didn't talk to her," she said. "She left the house before I woke up."

He nodded. He had forgotten Friday morning was the busy time at the chicken market and his mother helped his father out on Friday. That was the only day they needed two cashiers to handle the rush. "When are you going to tell her?"

"I think Sunday would be the best. Saturday is too hectic. With the morning at the *shul*, then rushing home to make dinner."

"Okay," he said. "If you need any help with her, call me."

He put down the telephone and placed another coin in the slot and dialed. Lutetia answered the ring. "Kitty there?" he asked.

"Wait a minute, I'll put her on the line."

A moment later Kitty came on the phone. "Joe?"

"Yes," he answered. "I stopped by yesterday afternoon but you were sleeping."

"I know," she said. "I really tied one on."

"You okay now?"

"Perfect," she said. "I have your money for you if you want to stop over now."

"I'll be right there," he said. He waited until the coin had tumbled down. But this time there was no jackpot.

Marta turned from the cashier's window that looked out over the chicken market. Phil was turning the lock in the deep drawer of his desk. She saw him strap on the shoulder holster, then check his Colt Police Positive .38-caliber revolver and slip it on. She looked at her husband. As she said every Friday that he strapped on the gun, "Why is it so important that you have to carry a gun just to collect lousy five-dollar bills?"

"That's not just five dollars," he answered as he usually did. "It comes to one thousand or two thousand dollars in the afternoon. There's a lot of *meshuggeners* that try to grab it."

"And you're going to kill them?" she asked.

"And you want them to get away with it?"

"What if they kill you first? You're such a sharpshooter, you'll be faster?" she retorted.

"You don't understand it," he said. "I don't wear a gun because I expect to use it. It's because if they know that I wear a gun, they won't bother me."

She dropped the subject as she collected a bill from a customer in front of the window. Then she watched him stuff his billfold with five-dollar bills. "Where's the *shiksa*?" she asked. "She's always late after her lunchtime."

"It's only twelve-thirty," Phil said. "That's only a half-hour since she's gone. She's allowed an hour for lunch."

"She knows that Friday is our busiest day. She should have more consideration and take only half an hour. But what do you expect from a *shiksa?*" Marta said sourly.

"She has to make lunch for her two kids when they come home from school," he said.

"She should make an arrangement," she said.

Phil didn't answer her. Josie already had an arrangement. He started to leave. "I'll be back by four o'clock."

"So be careful," Marta called after him as he walked out the door. She turned back to the window where several customers began lining up before her.

Josie's apartment was only two blocks from the market. The door was open. He walked into the living room. Josie came in from the kitchen. "What took you so long?"

"We got busy," he said, taking off his jacket and placing it over the back of a chair.

"You mean your wife was yakking about me," she said, annoyed.

He didn't answer her as he slipped off his gun and shoulder holster. He began unbuttoning his shirt, then realized that she was still completely dressed. "What's bothering you?"

"Your wife doesn't like me," she said.

"So?"

"She knows," she said.

"She knows shit," he said. He dropped his pants to the floor and opened the fly of his BVDs. He took out his already erect phallus and held it toward her. "Feel these fucking balls," he said. "They feel like fucking rocks."

"We've only got twenty minutes," Josie said. "I'll be

late. You know that your wife will be pissed off at me and give me a hard time the rest of the afternoon."

"The only hard time you're goin' to get this afternoon is my prick in your hot wet pussy," Phil said angrily.

"By the time I get undressed and out of my girdle and then dressed again, it will take over an hour," Josie said.

"Then don't get undressed," Phil said. "Bend your ass over the side of the couch and I'll shove it into you from the rear."

She stared at him for a moment. "You got your rubber ready?"

"What the fuck are you doing to me?" Phil said half shouting at her. "You trying to make me crazy?"

Silently she turned away from him and bent herself over the arm of the couch as he had told her. She slipped the back of her skirt up and flipped it over her back. Then she pulled up the bottom of her girdle to the top of her buttocks. He didn't give her the time to drop her panties, just enough to allow them to drop down against her garters to her stockings. She felt his strong hands gripping her by her hips as he slammed himself inside her. "Oh, Jesus!" she half-screamed. "You're sticking that fucking thing all the way up to my goddam throat!" He felt like a triphammer slamming into her. A groaning animal sound came from him. She turned her face to look at him. His face was contorted purple with the blood rushing into his veins.

She reached underneath herself with one hand and cupped his testicles, squeezing them gently. "I love your balls, Phil," she said, catching her breath. "You got the biggest balls I ever saw on a man." She began squeezing them hard. "Oh God, Phil!" she said. "Why do we always have to make it so fast? Why can't we spend more time together?"

"Fuck, don't talk, you cunt!" he said harshly. Then he caught his breath. "Oh, shit!" he yelled. "I'm coming!"

She reached for his phallus. "You got the rubber on?" she asked in a frightened voice.

"Fuck the fucking rubber!" he yelled.

Angrily she pushed him off her with an elbow and turned around to look at him. "My God!" she said. "You son of a bitch. You're still shooting your jism all over my damn couch."

He stared at her silently until he could recover his breath. "Get me a washrag for my dripping cock," he finally said.

"Fuck your cock," she snapped. "Look what you did to my couch! You ruined it!"

Suddenly he felt drained. "I'll get you another fuckin' couch," he said. "Just get me a washrag and get yourself dressed. You're already late for work."

She looked at him, then smiled. "Come to the bathroom with me," she said. "I'll clean you up. It won't take long to get to work."

He followed her into the bathroom and stood there as she knelt cleaning him. She looked up at him. "Can't you come over tonight instead of going to *shul?*" she asked.

"I wish I could," he said seriously. "But tonight I'm one of the *minyan.* That's one of the ten men that take out the Torah. Maybe, next Friday night."

She stood and watched as he began to put on his clothes. "Okay," she said.

He was ready to leave. "I have to go," he said.

"I know," she said sadly. She lifted her face to his and kissed him. "You know, Phil, I really love you."

There was a strange sadness in his voice. "I know, Josie," he said. "I know."

It was almost five o'clock when he returned to his office

at the market. From the window outside he could see the market was already cleaned and closed. "How did it go?" Marta asked.

"How should it go?" he said. "It goes." He didn't look at Josie, as she sat counting the cash at her window. Neither did she turn to him.

"Josie will have the night deposit finished in a few minutes," Marta said.

Still not looking at Josie, Phil called to her. "How much?" he asked.

"A hundred and fifteen dollars, Mr. Kronowitz," she answered.

Marta looked over at Josie. "Try to hurry," she said softly. "Mr. Kronowitz might be late for *shul*."

"I'd better go and get the car," Phil said. "I have to hide it two blocks away from the *shul* or the rabbi will see it."

Josie looked at him as he went out. "Have a nice weekend, Mr. Kronowitz," she said.

"You too, Josie," Phil said, looking back at her. "Have a nice weekend."

Marta got into the car beside him. "She doesn't work on the weekend?" she asked.

"She works on Saturday. Al pays her extra to help him," he said.

"Then she doesn't work on Sunday?" she asked. "Why not?"

"*Goyim* are entitled to a *Shabbes* too," he said.

= 6 =

KITTY BRANCH WAS seated behind the typewriter with her usual coffee mug on one side and the deep ashtray filled with cigarette butts on the other. Her short curled pepper-and-salt hairstyle was attractive with her black-rimmed eye-glasses. Despite the warmth of the apartment she wore a gray linen skirt and a soft cotton long-sleeved shirt. She looked up from the desk as Joe entered the room. Her voice was raspy from whiskey and weariness. "Want a coffee or a cold drink, Joe?"

"Coca-Cola is fine," he answered. He looked down at her. "You look tired."

Despite her ladylike appearance she spoke like a truck-driver. "I'm fucked. I have to dry out. Too damn much booze. It's going to kill me."

Joe dropped into a chair opposite her. "You know what's best for you."

"I know," she said. "But I never do it."

Joe didn't answer.

She called to the other room. "Lutetia, bring Joe a Coca-Cola." She turned to Joe, taking five singles from her desk, and handed them to him. "You were very helpful, thank you," she said.

"Thank you," Joe said. "I was glad to do it."

Lutetia brought the bottle of Coca-Cola and a glass with ice cubes. "Anything else you want?" she asked Kitty sulkily.

Kitty stared at her. Lutetia was wearing the same sheer chiffon dressing gown that she had worn yesterday. "For Christ's sake!" Kitty snapped. "Don't you ever put on clothes?"

"What the hell for?" Lutetia retorted. "We don't go out anymore. For the last week all you've done is drink and pass out, drink and pass out. I'm getting tired of it."

"Why don't you get a fucking job?" Kitty snapped.

"Doin' what?" Lutetia asked angrily. "The only job I can make money at is modeling over at the New School, and you don't like me doing nude modeling."

"You used to be a good secretary," Kitty said.

"Sure. For twenty a week. Modeling I could make fifteen dollars a day, twenty-five a day for private sessions. And at least I get to talk to some people." She glanced at Joe and then back to Kitty. "The only one I saw yesterday was that asshole friend of yours who thinks that the sun shines out of his prick!" Angrily she stalked out of the room.

"What's getting into her?" Joe asked.

Kitty looked at him. "I think she's getting ready to leave me."

He filled his glass. "Don't worry about it. Let her go."

"You don't understand," Kitty said, a hint of tears in her voice. "I love her."

Joe sipped at his glass without speaking.

Kitty looked across at him. "She told me that you tried to rape her."

He met her eyes. "Do you believe that?"

Kitty hesitated, then shook her head. "No. I know her.

She gets pissed off even if I want to get a stiff cock inside of me once in a while."

Joe was silent.

"What did happen yesterday?" Kitty asked.

"She wanted me to french her," he answered.

Kitty looked at him. "And you did?"

"Yes," he said.

"What did she do for you?" she asked.

"Bullshit me," he replied. "She promised to suck me but she faked it until I came off in her hand."

Kitty began to laugh. "She's a real bitch."

"Yeah," he said sarcastically.

"But she's got the sweetest pussy I ever tasted," Kitty said.

"Sweet pussy is not enough," he said. "That's not the only thing in life."

"She's still a kid," Kitty said. "She doesn't know any better."

"Okay," he said. "But she's goin' to screw you up, I'll bet on that."

Kitty looked at him for a moment, then reached for a cigarette. "I know that," she said sadly. "But what can I do about it? I love her."

"I'm sorry," Joe said.

She shrugged her shoulders. "I'll manage," she said. "I've been through it before." She looked up at him. "I heard that the front desk wants a five-part story on the Gould family. You know, they built the New York Central with the Astors. If it comes through I'll have about twenty hours of work for you."

"That's okay," he said. "I have an afternoon job in a store meanwhile and I have a deal for several stories for the magazine."

She smiled. "I wish you could connect with one of the decent magazines."

"Maybe I'll get lucky," he said. "Meanwhile I'm not complaining. It may not be much money but I'm being paid for writing."

"That's right," she said. "That's the name of the game." She squashed out her cigarette. "You'll keep in touch? Maybe we'll have dinner one night?"

"Right," he said, rising to leave. "I hope things work out okay for you."

She took him to the door. "So do I," she said.

Motty walked through the driveway between the houses. The garage was open. Uncle Phil's car was not there. She opened the side door of the house and entered the kitchen. The house seemed empty. The wall clock in the kitchen read six o'clock. That was normal for Fridays. She left work early and her aunt and uncle spent the evening at the synagogue. Usually they didn't get home until ten or eleven at night.

She walked to the two pots standing on the stove's gas burners and looked. Pot roast and small round potatoes in the large pot and *tsimmes*—carrots and peas cooked with either honey or brown sugar—in the smaller pot. All she had to do was heat them slowly. She hesitated for a moment. She really was not hungry so she decided to go up to her room and have a shower before dinner.

The tap, tap sound of the typewriter came from Joe's room as she started up the staircase. She stopped in front of his door. The typewriter was really rattling, he was speeding along. She knocked on the door. "It's me," she called.

"I'm working," he shouted through the door.

"I know," she said. "I'm taking a shower before dinner. Call me when you're ready and I'll heat the dinner for us."

"Okay," he called back.

The sound of the typewriter began again and she walked into her room. Slowly she closed the door. Suddenly she felt tired. She took off her dress and stretched out on the bed in her slip. She closed her eyes and began to doze. Half asleep, she began to dream.

It wasn't a dream, it was a nightmare. Her aunt Marta was screaming at her. "No, over my dead body you'll marry my Stevie! You have to be crazy! What money have you got to help him? So could he open an office? Get an apartment and furniture to live in? My Stevie is going to be a doctor, a professional man. He has to marry a girl from a family with money. Not a girl we had to bring up, who we had to take care of so that she wouldn't grow up in the street!"

She felt the tears running down her cheeks. "But, Tante, we love each other. We always loved each other, even when we were kids."

"Love, shmove!" Aunt Marta shouted at her. "Out! Out of my house, you whore, you Jezebel! Out!"

Motty turned to Stevie, still crying. "Stevie, tell your mother! We love each other. Tell her!"

Stevie stared at her through his horned-rimmed glasses with the solemn look he always had. "We have to think about it," he said nervously. "Maybe we're acting too hastily. Mama is only trying to do the right thing for us."

Then all she could do was cry until the tears blurred her eyes and she could barely see. Still crying, she felt strong hands gripping her arms. "Stevie!" she cried. The tears still rolling down her cheeks, she looked up. "Joe."

HAROLD ROBBINS

"You were crying out loud," he said. "I could hear you from my room."

She sat up in bed. "I'm sorry."

"Don't be," he said. "Everyone has bad dreams sometimes."

"This was stupid," she said. She looked up at him. "I guess I'm really afraid of your mother. You know how she feels about Stevie."

Joe laughed. "I know. She thinks that there's no girl good enough for him. Her son the doctor."

"She doesn't feel that way about you," she said.

"I'm a nogoodnik," he said. "What's a writer who doesn't work?"

"It's a different kind of work," she said.

"I know it. You know it. But she doesn't," he said wryly.

"Let me change," she said. "I'll heat up dinner."

"No rush," he said. "I'll be working. Just call me when you're ready."

She sat on the edge of her bed until she heard the sound of his typewriter. Slowly she took off her slip and looked at herself in the mirror over the dresser. There were dark circles under her eyes. She turned the light on in the room. Daylight was fading quickly. She switched on the bedside lamp and turned back to the mirror. The circles under her eyes seemed even darker. Slowly she unfastened her brassiere and her girdle. In the mirror she could see the red lines on her flesh where her undergarments had compressed it. She rubbed the marks on her thighs and hips, then cupped her breasts. They felt heavy in her hands and she wondered whether they were becoming bigger and softer. She hoped not. A 36 C cup was big enough. She always felt embarrassed about the size of her breasts. At work, the men were always looking at them, trying to grab a feel of them or talking about them. She felt an aching in them.

Quickly, she checked the date. She was only a few days away from her period. Maybe that was why she felt so heavy. She tended to gain a few pounds before her period, and maybe that was also why she now felt so blue and down. Automatically she touched her pubis. It, too, felt heavy and swollen. Quickly she fingered her clitoris, but the moment she felt the pleasure and excitement she stopped. She always felt very horny just before her period, but nice girls didn't do the things she wanted to do. She turned to the bathroom. A quick shower would make her feel better.

Joe's door was standing open as she walked past it in the hallway on her way to the staircase. The sound of the typewriter went clackety-clackety, faster and faster. "I'm going down to the kitchen," she called in to him.

The typewriter kept clacking; he seemed not to have heard her. She hesitated a moment, then went into his room and stood behind him looking down at the page in the typewriter.

The razorlike scimitar slit her brassiere and suddenly her naked breasts leapt forward. [Motty read the words on the page.] *Quickly, she tried to hide her beautiful globules with her hands but without avail. Her breasts were too big to hide and they overflowed her small graceful fingers. Then she felt the Arab's hot lips and breath moving down her throat and neck, down and down, the heat growing more intensely as he moved toward her breasts. Honey wanted to scream for help but there was none available. She was completely in the savage's power and no one to save her. With one hand she tried to push him away but he only laughed and slipped the scimitar under the belly band of her harem pants and slowly began to cut them away from her beautifully rounded curvy hips and legs. "No!" Honey cried. "Please, no. I'm a virgin!"*

Haroun Raschid smiled, leering. "Of course," he said in his fascinating sexy voice. "Only a virgin's blood is pure enough to mix with a sheik's love."

The scimitar flashed. She moved quickly, running toward the entrance of the tent before she ever realized she was completely nude. The tent flaps opened and two giant Nubian slave warriors pinned her arms.

"Bring her here," the sheik ordered.

They brought her to the center of the tent, still squirming and trying to escape. "Bind her wrists and her ankles to the two center poles."

Instantly, they obeyed, and turned silently from the tent. Honey tried to move but it was impossible. They had tied her securely. She shook the blond hair around her face. She stared at him as he slowly moved around examining every tiny secret corner of her nude body. Now she couldn't see him because he was completely behind her. She felt his hands touching her back, the soft curves of her buttocks. "What are you going to do to me?" she cried.

"You will see," he said softly and came out from behind her and stood unmoving. Then raising his right hand he uncovered the soft silk strands of a cat-o'-nine-tails whip.

Her eyes were wide and frightened. "You're going to hurt me and beat me!" she cried.

"No, my love," he said softly. "Believe me, you will never feel any pain, only pleasure. The pleasure

that will bring a passionate excitement into your body
that only the magic of our love can satisfy."

As if hypnotized, Honey stared as the whip in his
hand raised up and up, before her. She held her breath
as it began falling toward her . . .

The typewriter was suddenly still. Joe looked up at her
beside him, his eyes glazed as if he had been far away.

She felt a strange heat inside her as she looked down at
him, then, "Jesus!" she exclaimed, suddenly realizing that
he had been seated in nothing but his undershorts. "You've
got a hard on!"

He blinked down at himself, then up at her. "That's
right."

"How can you write with a hard on?" she asked.

"When I write like that, I have a hard on," he said. "I
feel everything I write. When I write tears, I cry, when I
write fear, I'm frightened. Whatever I write I feel. I even
feel what other people feel when I write about them."

"Even real people?" she asked.

"Even about you or Mama and Papa. Stevie, everyone."

"Does your feeling come from writing or do you feel
and then write?"

"I don't know," he said. "Sometimes one comes first,
sometimes the other."

She looked down at him. "You still have your hard on."

He opened his fly and held his penis in his hand. "Yes."

"What do you do about it?"

"You know, jerk off or take a shower—and there's always the real thing. I could get laid." He looked up at her.
"You read it over my shoulder. Didn't it get you horny?"

She didn't answer. The truth was, it had. The heat in her
loins felt like fire. "No," she answered huskily.

"Touch it a little," he urged. He remembered a phrase from his childhood. "Kiss it and make it better."

She was shocked. "I'm going to marry your brother."

"You're not married yet," he said.

She let out a deep breath. "You are a shit!"

"That's right," he said.

She stood next to him for a moment, then smiled. "I think that you're not as bad as you like people to believe you to be."

"I still have a hard on," he said.

"That's your problem," she said. "I'm going downstairs to get supper ready."

= 7 =

THE BELL OVER the store door rang for the first time in the two weeks he had been working there. He rose from behind the narrow counter aisle in which he had jammed the typewriter table where he worked. A flashily dressed, pretty black girl walked toward him. "Hello, Joe," she said in a soft southern voice.

He looked at her blankly.

She smiled. "You don't remember me, do you? I'm Lolita."

He still drew a blank. But he did remember there had been three girls the first day he had come to the store. "I remember," he said. "But which Lolita were you?"

She laughed. "I was the one who went out for the coffee."

He nodded, but really did not recognize her. "Lolita?" he said questioningly.

"My name is not really Lolita," she said. "But that's what Jamaica calls all of us. My name's Charlotte. Charlie for short."

"Nice to meet you, Charlie," he said, holding out his hand. Her hand was small and warm in his palm. "What can I do for you?"

"I was just in the neighborhood," she said. Her hand still rested warmly in his clasp. "What are you doin'?"

"Working," he said, gesturing to the typewriter behind the counter.

She glanced at it. "Writin'?"

"I'm trying."

She withdrew her hand. "Jamaica around?"

"Not until six o'clock," he said. He glanced at his wristwatch. It was only a quarter to four.

"I was hopin' I'd find him here," she said. "I wanted to make a little contact."

"Sorry," he answered. "He doesn't leave me with any. That's his department. All I do is take telephone messages."

"I can always find up some scrapins in the back room," she said.

"The back room's locked," he replied. "And he keeps the key on him."

"Shit!" she said. "I'm really feelin' down." She looked up at him. "You don' know how bad it is out there on the street. I must have been up and down Broadway from Columbus Circle to Times Square three times and never scored."

He felt disappointed for her. Then he remembered. "I have a small clincher of a joint. I don't know how good it is because I have had it a long time."

"Anything will be a help," she said.

He took out his pack of Twenty Grands and tapped out the small piece of cigarette. She took it in her fingers and held it under her nostrils.

"It's not bad," she said. She opened her purse and took out a bobby pin. Carefully she clipped the joint in the pin, then lit a match. She inhaled slowly and deeply. She looked at him through the curl of smoke. "This is a godsaver!"

He lit a Twenty Grand for himself and stood there without

speaking. The pungent smell of the marijuana was overriding the tobacco in the cigarette. He began to feel it in his head. He stared down at her breasts swelling over the square-cut decolletage of her blouse.

She smiled at him. "Like them black beauties?"

"Unbelievable!" he said.

With her finger she pulled down her blouse. "Ever see such purple nipples?" she asked. "They stick up like little black pricks."

He stared silently. He could feel the surging in his penis. Still smiling, she placed her hand on his fly. She laughed. "You have a real friend there."

"We better cut it out," he said. "The front door is open."

"It don't mean a shit," she said. "Nobody ever comes in here. Like french?"

"I'm not crazy," he said.

"I give the best french in the world," she said. "Let's get in the back corner behind the counter. Nobody can see us back there."

She followed him behind the counter. Carefully she pinched out the joint and knelt in front of him and opened his fly. Expertly she cupped his testicles with her hand and, resting the shaft of his penis on her palm, gently began to lick her tongue in a slow circle around his glans as her teeth sharply touched him in unexpected tiny bites.

He felt his legs becoming weak, the sensation running through himself under his groin into his anus. Suddenly the telephone began ringing. "Jesus H. Christ!" he exclaimed. Picking up the receiver, he spoke into it. "Caribbean Imports."

A very formal woman's voice came to him. "Mr. Crown?"

He could hardly answer. "Yes." He looked down at the

black girl. She was really into her work, her eyes smiling at him, her large white teeth nipping at him.

"Laura Shelton," the voice came into his ear. "I have good news for you."

He leaned on one arm so that he would not fall from the counter. "Yes, Miss Shelton," he managed to say.

"I'm sorry I haven't called you before, but I have been very busy. But despite that I have been working for you. You know that story you sent to me, 'The Shoplifter and the Store Detective'?"

"Yes," he gasped.

"I just sold it to *Collier's* magazine for one hundred and fifty dollars," she said.

"Oh, my God!" he shouted, no longer able to control himself. His orgasm was tearing throughout the whole of his body. He looked down at the black girl; his semen was overflowing from the corners of her mouth to her chin and onto her cheeks. "Oh, my God!" he yelled.

She must have sensed a strangeness in his voice. "Mr. Crown?" she asked quickly. "Mr. Crown, are you all right?"

"Yes," he gasped. "I was just overwhelmed."

"You must be very excited," she said with self-satisfaction in her voice. "Especially since we've never even seen each other face to face."

He looked down at Charlie, still kneeling before him, her hand holding his erection tightly, her tongue still licking him as if he was a popsicle. "Yes," he said more calmly. "I never felt anything quite like it."

"We have some details to work out," she said. "Could you come into the agency tomorrow morning? I'll have the agency contract ready for you, and the magazine check."

"Ten-thirty okay?" he asked.

"That will be fine," she said.

"Thank you very much, Miss Shelton," he said. "And also pass along my thanks to your sister for bringing us together."

"I will do that, Mr. Crown," she said. "I'm looking forward to meeting you at last. Goodbye, Mr. Crown."

"Goodbye, Miss Shelton," he replied and placed the telephone on the counter. He looked down at the black girl, whose fist still held him tightly. "What the hell are you trying to do?" he asked. "Break it off?"

She wiped the semen from her cheek and chin with the back of her other hand and licked it off. "One good come deserves another." She smiled. "There's still a lot of juice in your balls."

He stared at her as she brought him into her mouth again. Her cheeks went concave as she drew him in tightly. Then a sharp knifelike pain tore into his anus as she forced two long-nailed fingers inside him. He almost fell as the pain ricocheted through his groin. He yelled in agony and almost automatically hit her across the face with his open hand, knocking her to the floor. "Bitch!" he snapped angrily.

She held her hand against her cheek, a peculiar expression on her face as she looked at him. "I was jus' tryin' to pleasure you," she said.

The back-room door opened behind her. Joe had forgotten the secret alley door that Jamaica used to the back room. Jamaica glanced at him, then down at the girl. His voice was cold. "You tryin' to put a hurtin' on that boy, Lolita?"

The sound of fear echoed in her voice as she tried to grovel toward him. "No, sweet man. I was jus' foolin' with him."

"Bitch!" he snarled. With his heavy boot, he kicked her in the ribs and she rolled sidewise across the store. "How many times done I tol' you never to come into the store less'n I ask?"

She curled herself into a ball, crying. "I didn' mean nuthin'," she said. "I jus' was so horny for to see you."

"Lyin' bitch!" he said coldly, drawing his belt from his trousers. "You were lookin' for some dope." He slashed the belt across her back and buttocks until she slumped half-unconscious on the floor. Then he picked her up with one hand under her armpit, and half-dragging her across the floor threw her into the back room and closed the door behind her. He turned to Joe, the leather belt sliding back into the loops of his trousers.

"I'm sorry, Jamaica," Joe said.

"It's not your fault," Jamaica said. "She a schemin' bitch. She know the rules."

"I didn't mean for her to get beat up like that," Joe said.

Jamaica looked at him as if he were stupid. "You hit her, didn' you?"

Joe didn't answer.

"Don' you know that was what she wanted?" Jamaica smiled. "That's the way she gets her kicks. She's happy now. Now she knows she's really loved."

"I don't get it," Joe said.

"You're young yet." Jamaica smiled. "You'll learn." He glanced at the telephone still on the counter. Usually it was on the shelf underneath. "Who was on the phone?"

"It was my agent," Joe said. Then it suddenly dawned on him. He was now a real honest-to-God writer. "*Collier's* magazine just bought a story of mine!"

"First time?" Jamaica asked curiously.

"With a real classy magazine," Joe said.

"That's great," Jamaica said. "Congratulations."

"Thanks," Joe said. "I still can't believe it. I bet she

thought I was crazy. Lolita was still frenchin' me while I was on the telephone."

Jamaica laughed. "Not too bad," he said. "You were gettin' it both ways."

Joe shook his head. "I still don't get it."

Jamaica sniffed. "Thought I caught a smell of ganch when I came in."

"Yes," Joe said. "I had a half a joint. I gave it to her."

"No shit for any of those girls unless I okay it. *Capish?*" Jamaica's voice was emphatic.

"*Capish,*" Joe said. "I'm sorry."

"Now you know, forget it." Jamaica opened a small notebook. "I have several extra deliveries. Have the time for them?"

"That's my job," Joe said.

=8=

THE PIERSALL AND Marshall Agency was located in a renovated brownstone house in the middle of the street between Fifth and Madison Avenues. A square plaque attached to the iron-spike railing indicated that the offices were on the fourth floor. He entered down the steps to the basement entrance and into a small hallway with an old-fashioned grilled elevator. The elevator was empty and he went into it, closed the gate and pressed the button. The elevator screeched and ground to the fourth floor.

He left the elevator and walked into a small reception area where the receptionist sat behind a desk and a telephone switchboard. She looked at him.

"Miss Shelton," he said.

"Your name?" she asked officiously.

"Joe Crown."

"Do you have an appointment?"

"Yes." He nodded.

She pressed two keys on the switchboard. "Mr. Crown is here for Miss Shelton," she said. She listened for a moment, then put down the telephone. "Take a chair," she said. "Miss Shelton is in a meeting but she will be with you in a few minutes."

There were a two-cushion couch and two chairs, all in old worn leather, gathered around a small coffee table covered with magazines. He looked around. The walls were covered with tired, peeling tan paint and several ancient equally tired framed prints. He glanced at the receptionist. She ignored him, her eyes staring into space.

The telephone switchboard buzzed. "Piersall and Marshall Agency," she singsonged. A sound of excitement came into her voice. "Yes, Mr. Steinbeck, I'll put you right through to Mr. Marshall." She turned to the switchboard keys, then turned to Joe. "That was John Steinbeck, the author," she announced importantly.

Joe nodded.

"I'm sure you've heard of him," she said. "He's one of our clients."

He resented her snobbery. "I'm one of your clients too," he said.

Her nose turned up. "I never heard of you."

"You will," he said, getting up from his chair. "Which way is the men's room?"

"It's downstairs on the main floor behind the elevator," she said. "But Miss Shelton should be ready to see you any minute now."

"Then she'll have to wait," he said walking to the elevator. "Unless you want me to take a piss in the pot holding that rubber plant in the corner." Then before she could reply, he pressed the button for the main floor and the elevator went down.

"The second office on the left beyond the glass door," the receptionist said grudgingly as Joe came from the elevator.

"Thank you," he said and walked through the glass door. Miss Shelton had her name on the office door. Joe knocked.

"Come in," she said through the door.

He went inside. It was a small office, the desk covered with manuscripts, yet everything was neatly in place. She was a tall girl in her middle twenties, her sandy hair wrapped tightly in a bun, her fair skin faintly shining with the warmth of the office, her blue eyes clear behind her eyeglasses. She rose and held out her hand. "Mr. Crown," she said pleasantly.

"My pleasure, Miss Shelton," he said.

She gestured to the chair opposite her. "You were surprised at my call?" she said, smiling.

"More than that," he replied. "I couldn't believe it."

"I could tell that from your voice," she said. She met his eyes. "I have some papers for you to sign."

"I understand," he said.

"Only three things," she said. "First, an agency contract that will give us authorization to represent you for a period of one year from each sale we make for you. The period is not cumulative—the period is only from the last sale."

He nodded.

"The second is that we would develop a small bio about you so that we can help with publicity and supply information to publishers and reviewers who might be interested in you and your work. And several snapshots would also be helpful for that purpose."

"What kind of bio?" he asked.

"Age, where you were born, education, hobbies. Things like that."

"That's easy," he laughed. "I never did very much. Born in Brooklyn, age twenty-five [a lie—he was twenty-two]. Graduated Townsend Harris High School 1938 [also a lie]. CCNY, majored in literature and journalism but did not graduate because I left in the third year in order to help out with family finances." Lies, all lies.

She looked at him. "Any hobbies? Sports, games, chess?"

"None like that," he answered.

"But you do have other interests?" she asked.

"Yes," he said. "But I don't think they're relevant."

"Let me be the judge of that," she said.

He hesitated, then shrugged. "Sex," he said.

She laughed, faintly blushing. "You have a delicious sense of humor, Mr. Crown."

"Call me Joe." He smiled. "You said there was a third item."

She was slightly flustered. "Oh, yes. I have the acceptance agreement and the check for the *Collier's* story. You will notice that the agreement is for one hundred fifty dollars. From that we deduct our normal ten percent and expenses, phones and mail, etcetera. The net check is for one hundred and twenty-eight dollars."

Joe looked down at the check, then at her. "Miss Shelton, I could kiss you," he said.

She laughed. "Not yet," she said. "Let's wait until we have a few more contracts under our belts. Now, I want you to make sure you send as much material to me as you can, so that we can begin mining the market. You are a good writer, Mr. Crown. I feel you will do very well."

Jamaica was standing behind the counter as he came into the store. "I have good news for you." He smiled.

Joe was puzzled. "Good news?"

Jamaica nodded. "You're movin' uptown to a better job."

"I don't get it," Joe said. "I'm happy with this one."

Jamaica looked at him. "You don't have any choice," he said flatly. "Neither do I. This is from Mr. B."

Joe was silent for a moment. "What is it?"

"I'll explain it to you in the car," Jamaica said.

Joe followed him into the back room. It was empty. The work tables had been put away, the girls already gone. Quickly Jamaica locked the cabinets and the refrigerator. "Lock the outside door," he said. "And meet me in the alley."

A moment later, Jamaica pulled up behind the driver's wheel of his black shiny 1940 Packard 12. He gestured and Joe climbed into the seat behind him.

"Who is going to look after the store?" Joe asked.

"It'll keep," Jamaica said. "This is more important." He turned the car up Eighth Avenue, then around Columbus Circle and uptown along Central Park West before he spoke. After a moment, he glanced at Joe. "You know about the Lolitas I take care of?"

"Yes."

"I have another group of Lolitas," he said. "These are high-class girls. Ofay girls, real society types. It's a big operation and Mr. B. and the Italians have a fifty percent cut."

Joe watched him as he moved the big Packard expertly through the traffic. "What's that got to do with me?" he asked.

"I own four brownstones on Ninety-second Street off Central Park West that I joined together and turned into a furnished apartment house. It comes to about seventy apartments, and almost half of them are rented by the girls. We supply maid service and a janitor and handyman to take care of repairs. The girls pay us between two hundred and four hundred a week depending on their business. Our former resident manager cut himself a piece of our action."

"You fired him?" Joe asked.

"In a kind of way," Jamaica said. "But that wasn't my department and I don't ask my partners what they did. This morning Mr. B. called me and told me to send you up there."

"What if I don't want the job?" Joe asked.

Jamaica glanced at him. "That wouldn't be smart. Mr. B. is doing a big one for you and your father. He does one for you, you do one for him."

Joe was silent.

"It won't be permanent," Jamaica said gently. "Two or three months, just until they can move in a professional. They know you're a writer and you got no stomach for that kind of thing. But Mr. B. said you could take care of this for a while, and he'll consider your marker paid off."

Jamaica slowed the car and then cut into Ninety-second Street between oncoming traffic. He pulled to the curb in front of a yellow-canopied entrance. He turned off the ignition.

Joe looked at the entrance. The white lettering on the sides of the canopy, spelled out UPTOWN HOUSE. FURN. APTS. The entrance was a wide glass double door. "Is there an office for me here?" he asked.

"You could kind of call it that," Jamaica said. "But actually it will be your apartment."

"Why an apartment?"

"You'll be living here," Jamaica said. "That's part of the deal. Mr. B. already told that to your father. He said you have to stay away from your house. Something about the neighbors might squeal to the draft board if they see you around."

"They haven't anything to squeal about yet. I haven't got a new draft card."

Jamaica took a small envelope from his pocket and handed it to him. He watched Joe open the envelope and read the card. JOE CROWN. Classification: 4-F. Dated Oct. 22, 1942.

"Now you do," he said without expression.

Joe stared at him.

Jamaica smiled. "It's really not the end of the world. Actually, if you really love pussy like you say you do, you might even think you're in heaven."

=9=

His mother looked suspiciously at him. "What kind of a janitor's job pays one hundred dollars a week? With a three-room apartment also? Janitors are lucky if they get a room in the cellar of an apartment house for free, not also with getting money. It's something wrong, you'll probably wind up in jail or worse."

"Jesus! Mother," he said. "First, I'm not a janitor. I'm a resident manager. I manage seventy apartments that make maybe seven, ten thousand dollars a week. And I have enough time to write. That's the most important thing. This first check for a hundred and fifty dollars for the story from *Collier's* magazine is only the beginning."

"First of all, you didn't get a hundred and fifty, you got a hundred and twenty-eight, second of all, how do you know you can sell any more stories? You got guarantees?"

"Shit!" Joe said. He rose from the table and looked down at his father, who had been unusually quiet. "Papa, would you explain to her why I have to take that job?"

He stared at Joe for a moment, then turned to his wife. "It's a good job, Marta," he said softly. "Believe me, my friend wouldn't do anything to get him into any trouble."

"Your friend's a lowlife gangster!" Marta snapped.

Phil's face turned purple with anger. "Gangster!" he shouted. "It was you who wanted her baby to get out of the draft, not my friend. But it's my friend that did what you wanted. Now, Joe has a Four-F draft card. And he's got to pay for it, and I have to pay for it whether you like it or not!"

"So my son has to go to jail or get killed or something even worse!" she yelled at him.

"Your little baby boy will go to fucking jail if they ever find out about his goddam draft card!" Phil was almost out of breath. "So shut up already or I'll have another fucking heart attack!"

Marta felt frightened. "Phil, calm down. Quiet, I'll get you a pill." She looked up at Joe. "See! See what you made your father do?"

"I'm all right already," Phil said. "Just let's have some peace and quiet."

"I would like to look at the apartment before he moves in. You know how dirty people are, the place might be covered with cockroaches and mice. How do I even know the sheets are clean?"

Phil spoke calmly. "Okay. You can see it. But not right now. Wait until he gets settled down. Then nobody will bother him."

"Okay," Marta said finally. "But what do I tell the neighbors when they don't see him around here?"

Phil shook his head in amazement. "The whole neighborhood knows he was going for his physical. Tell them he went into the service. That's why we had to get him away from here."

"And what about Stevie and Motty's wedding? What will the neighborhood say when he doesn't come home for his brother's wedding?"

Joe looked down at Motty, still seated at the table. She had never let him know she had told his parents about her and Steven. Motty didn't meet his eyes. He turned to his mother. "Maybe by the time that happens, I'll be able to come home for it."

"No," Phil said emphatically. "You're supposed to be in basic training by the time they get married around the holidays, and everybody knows they don't give leaves during basic training."

"I'd better get up to my room and begin packing," Joe said.

Phil rose from the table. "I have to go out for a couple of hours," he said. "I'll be home by ten-thirty."

"Every Monday and Wednesday night you go out for a couple of hours to make some collections," Marta complained. "Why don't they pay on Friday afternoon like they used to all the time?"

"We're doing more business," Phil answered. "If I don't chase after them, we'll never get our money back." He walked toward the door. "I'll be back by ten-thirty," he repeated.

"Don't forget to keep your pills in your pocket," Marta said.

Phil held up a small bottle. "I have them, I have them," he said.

Joe had just finished his packing and closed his valise when he heard his father's car come up through the alley between the houses. Then he heard the side door open, and his father walked heavily up the staircase and into his parents' bedroom. A moment later he heard sounds from their bathroom; finally, the noises subsided and Joe noticed the light had gone out from under their door to the hallway.

Joe pushed some of his manuscripts off the bed. Then one of the stories caught his eye and he sat down on the side of the bed to reread it. It was a story he had written in pencil on a lined yellow paper pad about five years ago. He had written it to impress his high school English teacher, who was the first person ever to tell him he had talent and should become a writer.

The fact that the square-cut decolletage of her dress gave him a completely exciting view of her exquisite full breasts and pink nipples had nothing to do with his decision to become a writer. But it had helped. That was basically what this story had been about. A young high school student had fallen in love with his English teacher because he thought that the view she had afforded him of her decolletage was especially for him. His dreams had been shattered when he took her a bouquet of flowers, and her door was opened by her husband. Almost a full year she had been in his thoughts and dreams, almost ten jars of vaseline had been wasted on his sore, irritated penis and stained bedsheets. Now, as he reread the story, he realized that the last year of his frustration should have been the story—not the one he had written. He threw the manuscript on the floor and undressed and got into bed. For a moment, he thought about brushing his teeth but he was too bored with it and turned off the bed lamps. He looked into the dark and the faint light from the streetlight at the end of the alley made patterns on the ceiling. The shadows were beginning to blur when a soft tapping sound came into the room.

He sat up in bed. The sound was strange. It was not coming from the door or from the hallway. The soft tapping sound echoed again. Motty's voice whispered from the wall against Stevie's bed on the far side of the room.

Kneeling on the bed, he pressed his ear to the wall. "Motty?"

"Yes," she whispered. "Pull out the bolts of the old sliding doors between our rooms."

Then he remembered—the sliding doors between the two rooms had been closed when Motty had been given Stevie's room. He pulled the bed slightly away from the doors, then opened the bolts. It was difficult. The bolts had been closed for many years. Finally, with a small scraping sound, they gave. He managed to open the doors slightly.

She held her face between the open doors. "Are you awake?" she asked.

"Of course not," he answered sarcastically. "I always do things like this in my sleep."

"Don't be shitty," she said. "I want to talk to you."

He was still kneeling on the bed, and his face was even with her own. "Then why didn't you come through the regular door?"

"I didn't want your parents to see me in the hall," she said. "You know how they are. Especially your mother."

He nodded. "I know. Come in then." He began to move off the bed.

"You'd better come in here," she said. "Your room is right next to theirs."

Silently he moved across the bed and then squeezed himself through the narrow opening into her room. He found himself against the back of a chest of drawers. As he slipped out from behind it, he scraped his shoulder. "Shit!" he exclaimed, rubbing his shoulder.

"Did you hurt yourself?" she asked.

"It's nothing," he said, looking at her. "Now what was so important?"

She stared at him. "You're naked!"

"I was fucking asleep," he said shortly. "I wasn't planning to go visiting."

"I'll get you a towel," she said.

He watched her walk across the room and get a towel from the closet. She was wearing a cotton nightgown under her bathrobe. She held the towel to him, her eyes averted. He wrapped it around himself. "Okay," he said.

She looked up at him. "I didn't congratulate you for selling a story to *Collier's*."

"Thank you," he said. He smiled. "I should really congratulate you. Remember that story you told me about the store detective who caught that girl shoplifting and took her into a dressing room to take her clothes off and raped her?"

"That's the story that *Collier's* bought?" Her eyes were wide.

"I changed it a little," he said. "I turned it into a love story. That he tried to protect her and wound up losing his own job."

"That's beautiful," she whispered. "Really beautiful." She was silent for a moment, then her eyes began to overflow.

"Now, what the hell's the matter?" he asked.

"I'm frightened," she whispered.

"What about?" he said. "Everything's okay. You and Stevie are getting married. Mama's happy for you and she's happy that I got a Four-F. What's there to be frightened about?"

"Everything's changing," she said. "You're moving out. You won't be in the next room anymore."

"It don't mean a shit," he said. "You'll be able to meet me in New York. It's only across the river, not across the world."

"But I have no one to talk with here at home."

He put his arm around her and brought her head to his shoulder. "Don't be a crybaby," he said softly. "We can talk all the time on the phone."

"It's not the same," she whispered.

"Soon you'll get married and it'll be better," he said. He stroked her hair softly, he felt her shivering against him. "It will be better, you'll see."

"No," she cried, turning her face to him. "It won't be the same."

He looked down at her face, his eyes searching deep into hers. Slowly he moved his lips to her forehead, then to her cheek, finally to her mouth. He felt the heat from her body pressing heavily against him. His phallus sprang wildly toward her. He tried to push her away from himself. "This is crazy," he said hoarsely.

She didn't move, just falling even more heavily against him, her groin moving toward his searching need. Silently they moved to the bed, the towel falling from him to the floor. Quickly, he removed her robe, then the nightgown, and bent over her. "Motty!" he said.

"Don't talk!" she said. "Just tear me apart and fuck me!"

$=10=$

THE SOUND OF the engine came up from the alley as Uncle Phil's car backed into the street. Quickly she moved from her bed to the window. In the faint gray of morning she saw the car turning and moving away. Quietly she went back to the bed.

Joe was fast asleep, lying naked on top of the blankets. She stared at him. It was strange. It was as if he had always been there in her bed with her. She had always thought that if they ever did it she would feel upset and guilty. But it was not like that. Instead she felt annoyed at her stupidity. Why had she denied herself her desires for so many years? She touched him lightly on the shoulder.

He turned on his side slowly, still asleep. She felt the excitement beginning to move inside her as she saw his erection, full and strong in the morning. Gently she held his phallus in her hand. His eyes opened, sleep disappearing from his dark pupils. He looked down at her hand holding him, then up at her face. He was still silent.

A soft, quiet smile came to her face. "It's beautiful," she said.

He didn't answer.

"Why did we wait so long?" she whispered.

He shook his head. "I wanted to but you—"

"I was stupid," she interrupted him. "But I was afraid."

"But now that we did it, we'll find a way to manage it," he said.

She shook her head slowly. "No," she said softly. "It was beautiful, and I want to keep it that way. If we try to make it any more than it has been, we'll turn it into something sordid and it will destroy all of us. All of us in the family."

He felt the beating in his pulse. "I'm beginning to juice."

"I'm soaking wet too," she said and looked down at him. "Damn!" she said in surprise. "The sheets are covered with blood!"

"What happened?" he asked nervously. "Beginning your period?"

She stepped from the bed. "No, you stupid jerk, I was a virgin."

He stared at her, his mouth agape.

"Now I have to strip the sheets from the bed," she said quickly. "If your mother finds out, she'll know what has happened and she'll kill me!"

Despite himself he felt a sense of pride. Even in high school he had never copped a cherry. "Mother doesn't have to know. Just tell her you were surprised with the period."

"Not your mother," she whispered. "She watches my cycles better than I do."

Jamaica had already brought his typewriter and the boxes of manuscripts and typing paper from the store before Joe had arrived at the apartment. Quickly Joe began to unpack.

The apartment was not bad. The furniture was slightly

tacky but serviceable. The living room contained an imitation-leather three-seater couch with a matching easy chair placed in front of a coffee table and lamps placed on end tables on each side of the couch. In one corner of the room was a small dining table with two chairs placed in front of one of the windows that faced the street. The kitchenette was a closet angled from the table. The bedroom was painted dark green; a three-quarter wooden bed in a lighter shade of green matched the dresser and a chest of drawers. A yellow imitation-satin bedspread covered the sheets and pillows. The bathroom was American Standard white fixtures, with a yellow curtain hanging from the shower rod and a matching curtain covering the small window. There were two lights in the bathroom, one on the ceiling, the other attached to the medicine cabinet over the sink.

In less than two hours, Joe had put away his clothing and placed the two valises on a shelf over the bedroom closet. He carefully placed the typewriter on the dining table so that the light from the window shone over his shoulders onto the typewriter, and placed paper and manuscripts on either side of it. He was still looking down at it when he heard a knock at the door. He crossed the room and opened it.

Jamaica was smiling. "How is it?"

"I'm unpacked," he answered.

Jamaica came into the apartment. "I have a few more things for you. Fred's bringing them up."

Fred was one of the two handymen that worked in the apartment house. "What?" Joe asked.

"We're bringing in a new combination electric refrigerator and tabletop stove. The one here is fucked. The telephone will be installed this afternoon. We have our own switchboard downstairs. All calls go through it."

"Including the girls?" Joe asked.

"Especially the girls," Jamaica answered. "The switchboard monitors them, and each morning will give you a list of their bookings."

Joe nodded. "I understand that. Now who collects the money?"

Jamaica answered. "The girls have to turn in the money to you each morning. The switchboard service will let you know how much money each of the girls owes us."

"Complicated," Joe said.

"Not really," Jamaica said. "The girls average about five hundred a night, that's five tricks a night at one hundred a pop. Special services like group parties, shows and S and M are at the girls' discretion for extra charges."

Joe looked at him. "What are the girls like?"

Jamaica laughed. "The best-lookin' chicks in the world. You'd think that each one of them came right out of Billy Rose's Diamond Horseshoe. These kids are not Lolitas. Real ofay society class. You'll probably fuck yourself to death in less than a week."

"Not me." Joe smiled. "I have to work. Writing and fucking don't mix. Each takes too much time."

"That may be." Jamaica smiled. "But that's your problem, not mine." Another knock came from the door. "That's probably Fred with the furniture," he said.

But Jamaica was wrong. A young girl stood in the open door. Long straight brown hair, horn-rimmed eyeglasses, loose tan sweater over a brown skirt. She seemed more like a college student than a hooker. She looked at Jamaica. Her voice was soft and cultured. "I thought I'd drop downstairs and meet your new man and see if there's anything I could do to help him."

Jamaica nodded and gestured. "Joe Crown, Allison Falwell."

Allison held out her hand. "Nice to meet you, Joe."

Jamaica stopped Joe's hand. "Mr. Crown," he said disapprovingly to the girl.

Allison stared at Jamaica. "But he seems so young."

Jamaica's voice went cold. "Mr. Crown," he repeated.

Allison turned to Joe. "Nice to meet you, Mr. Crown. Is there anything I can do for you?"

"No, thank you," Joe said coolly but politely, taking his cue from Jamaica. "But if there is anything, I will call you."

Jamaica closed the door behind her. "Bitch!" he said. "You'll see more of them soon. All trying to get an edge."

"So?" Joe asked.

"You can't let them," Jamaica said. "If you want to be a good pimp you treat all of them the same way. You don't like what they're doin', just belt them."

"I don't know if I can do that," Joe said.

Jamaica stared at him. "Jes' think that every one of them wants to tear your ass out with their fuckin' fingernails like Lolita did. Then you'll fin' it easier to belt them." He paused a moment before adding, "Jes' remember, no matter how great they look, they nuthin' but whores."

His mother answered the telephone. "It's already eight o'clock," she said as she recognized his voice. "Have you had dinner?"

"Not yet, Mama," he said. "I've just been straightening up. And I had to learn all the details about the job."

"You have a kosher restaurant near you?"

"There's two good delis within blocks of here," he answered.

"The apartment is clean? Is the bed good?"

"Everything's okay, Mama," he said reassuringly. "Don't worry, I'm a big boy." He changed the subject. "Papa home yet?"

"No," Marta answered. "This is one of his nights he has to make collections."

"Motty there?"

"Yes," she said. "You want I should call her to the phone?"

"Please, Mama."

His cousin's voice came through the receiver. "Joe?"

"You okay?" he asked.

"I'm okay," she said. She lowered her voice almost to a whisper. "The house seems empty."

"I know what you mean," he said.

"How's the job?" she asked.

"It's a job," he said noncommittally. "It'll be okay. Jamaica told me it's only temporary. I should be out of this in about three months."

"And then what do you do?"

"I don't know. But this takes off my marker and I'm a free agent. I'll keep on writing and looking around."

"Your mother seems down. I think she misses you."

He didn't answer.

"I miss you too," she said.

"Maybe we can meet one night," he said. "I'll take you to some chinks."

"I don't think so," she answered. "I don't think I can handle it if we spend some time together. Believe me, it will be better if you just stay away."

He was silent for a moment, then sighed. "I guess you're right."

"But you will call me, won't you?"

"Of course," he said. "Take care of yourself."

"You, too," she said and hung up the phone.

He stared down at the telephone. He hadn't said it, but he, too, felt lonely. This was really the first time he had ever lived away from home. There was a knock at the door and he rose to open it.

Allison was standing outside the door. "I tried to get you on the phone," she said. "But the switchboard said that your line was busy."

He nodded. "It was."

She held out a bottle of champagne. "One of my johns gave me this. I thought it would be fun if we shared it. Sort of like a welcome home party for you."

He looked at her. "But I haven't had time yet to get glasses."

She smiled and with her other hand held out two champagne glasses. "I thought of that too."

He hesitated a moment, then stepped back. "Come in." He closed the door as she walked to the table.

"You open the champagne," she said. "I'll go into the bedroom and make myself comfortable."

It was the first time he had ever opened a champagne bottle and finally the cork popped out and he quickly caught the champagne in the glasses.

"Bring the champagne in here," she called from the bedroom.

He walked into the open doorway. One small light shone from the bed table. She was stretched out nude over the bed cover. She held her hand out for a champagne glass. She saw him staring at her. "Like what you see?"

He laughed. "What am I supposed to say? That you're ugly?"

She sipped from the glass and then smiled. "Then why don't you get out of your clothes?" He stood there silently. Quickly she reached and opened his fly. "What's taking you so much time?" she asked. "You're ready."

"I'm always ready," he said.

"So am I," she laughed, then guided his erection to her mouth.

=11=

THANKSGIVING EVE AND the first snowfall of the season. Joe stood at the window looking down at the street. The snow was swirling down but the gutters were already muddy and brown from the traffic. He lit a cigarette and checked his Ingersoll—three-thirty in the afternoon. He knew the offices would be closing earlier. The holiday and the snowstorm would be an unbeatable combination. By nightfall the streets would be deserted.

The telephone next to his typewriter rang. He picked it up. "Crown."

He recognized the voice. "Happy Thanksgiving," Laura Shelton said.

"Happy Thanksgiving, Miss Shelton," he replied. Then he asked curiously, "Are you still in the office?"

She laughed. "I've been working and I wanted to pass along some good news to make your holiday a really happy Thanksgiving."

"You sold another story?" he asked excitedly.

"That, too," she said. "But also something even more exciting."

"Don't make me crazy." He laughed.

"*Collier's* bought your story 'Coney Island Holiday' for two hundred and fifty dollars."

"That's great," he said. "What could be better than that?"

"Universal Pictures read 'The Shoplifter and the Store Detective' and want to make it into a movie. They want to make it with Margaret Sullavan and James Stewart. You remember they were a big success in *The Shop Around the Corner.*"

"I don't believe it!"

"It's for real," she said. "They offered twenty-five hundred for the movie rights and they want to give you five thousand to go to Hollywood for twenty weeks to co-write the screenplay and pay all your expenses to go out there."

"I don't know anything about screenplays," he said. "Do they know that?"

"They know it," she said. "But they do it all the time. That's why they put a screenwriter to work with you. But that's only the first offer they made. I'm sure I can bring it up a little. Thirty-five hundred for the rights and seventy-five hundred for the screenplay."

"Don't scare them off," he said nervously. "Maybe they won't think it's worth it."

"I won't scare them off," she said reassuringly. "I've been through this before. We can always grab their offer and run."

"You're the expert," he said. "I'm with you."

"Thank you," she said. "I appreciate your confidence."

"No, Miss Shelton," he said. "I thank you."

"Don't worry about it," she said. "We'll have this sewed up over the weekend. I'll talk to you on Monday for sure."

He looked down at the telephone, and the news finally seeped in. "Hot damn!" he shouted into the empty room. He picked up the phone and called home. Maybe now they would believe that he really was a writer. But there was no answer at home.

He felt himself exploding with the news. He had to talk to someone. He called his cousin at work. "I'm just going into a meeting," Motty said hurriedly.

"I won't take a minute," he said. "I have news for you. I just sold another story to *Collier's* and Universal wants to make a movie out of 'The Shoplifter and the Store Detective.'"

"Congratulations," she said, but she didn't sound excited. "I have news for you too."

"What news?" he asked.

"I think I'm pregnant," she whispered into the phone. "I'm three weeks late."

"Shit!" he exclaimed. "Are you sure?"

"I'm afraid to check with the doctor," she said. "Stevie is coming in next week. What can I tell him?"

"Tell him nothing," he said. "The marriage is scheduled for the weekend. Five weeks means nothing. Many first babies are born early."

"You're a shit," she said angrily. "Stevie is your brother. Doesn't that mean anything to you?"

"Sure it does," he said. "That's why I'm telling you to sit tight. Open your mouth and everybody gets hurt. The whole fucking family."

She was silent for a moment. "Do you think it will work?"

"Sure it will," he said positively. "You won't even be showing until three months."

"My breasts feel heavy," she said.

"That could be premenstrual too," he said. "You told me many times that your tits swell before your period."

"I'm nervous," she said. "Stevie is a doctor. What if he figures it out?"

"Doctor or not," he said, "Stevie is still an asshole. You just do as I tell you."

"I have to run," she said. "I'm late for the meeting."

"We'll talk later," he said. "Just stay calm." He heard the click of the phone as she put it down. He stared at the telephone still in his hand. "Balls!" he said to himself. "Who the hell was it that said a virgin never gets knocked up on the first time?"

Phil cut a big slice of the *brust flanken* on his plate and smothered it with red horseradish. He looked across the table at Marta and Motty, speaking through his full mouth. "We sold a hundred and twenty-one turkeys today."

"That was good," Marta said approvingly.

"The *luksh* sold over four hundred," he grumbled.

"Don't complain," his wife said. "I remember five years ago we were lucky to sell twenty or thirty. Who knew about turkeys in those days? Chickens or capons we knew, but turkeys were for *goyim*."

He wiped his sour rye bread in the gravy on his plate. "It's good, Mama," he said, tasting it.

"You're lucky you're in the business," she said. "Or, maybe you'd be eating turkey instead of *brust flanken* with the way meat stamps are given out. And with capon and chicken so high and hard to get, that's why our people are buying turkeys."

"I'd starve first," Phil said. "Turkey meat is dry with no *shmaltz* and without no *shmaltz* there's no flavor."

"Stop complaining," Marta said. "You make more money with turkeys than anything else."

"You're such a *k'nocker*," he said. "Why don't you go into the market like you used to? You have nothing to do all day in the house."

"Al's wife doesn't come to the market," she said.

"She never did," Phil said. "She never had the time, she was too busy having another baby every year."

"It doesn't matter," she retorted. "How would it look if I stayed in the market and she didn't? Everybody would think that you were not doing as well as he did."

"It's nobody's business what I do," he said. He cut another slice of meat on his plate. "Jews get in trouble if people think they are doing too well. How do you think those Nazis started on them? Because they were too jealous of us."

"This is America, not Europe," she said.

"Don't be stupid," he retorted. "We have plenty of Nazis right here, so we should be smart and quiet. Don't give any of them a reason to be envious of us."

"Maybe Uncle Phil is right," Motty said suddenly.

"What do you mean?" Marta asked, looking at her.

"A big wedding at the Twin Cantors might not be the right thing to do just now. There is a war on and everyone knows how expensive the Twin Cantors are."

"You mean you don't want a wedding at the Twin Cantors?" Marta asked in surprise. "Every girl in the world should be so lucky to get married at the Twin Cantors."

"Wait a minute," Phil said. "The girl might be right. Not only because of the money, but remember that we have two sons and none of them are in the service. There would be many people that won't like that."

"Stevie is a doctor and everyone knows that married doctors don't have to go into the service," Marta said.

"Sure they know, but everyone will think that's why he's getting married," he said. "And there are those who think that Joe is a draft dodger. Why give them a chance to prove it?"

Marta was silent for a moment, then turned to Motty. "Then what kind of a wedding would you have?"

Motty looked at her aunt. "Just us, the family. At Borough Hall where no one would know us."

"Without a rabbi?" Marta was shocked.

"They don't have rabbis at Borough Hall," Motty said. "But it's just as legal."

"Maybe just us here at home with a rabbi?" Marta asked. "Somehow without a rabbi and a *chupa* it doesn't seem like you're married."

Motty nodded. "We could do it here, but remember then that Joe couldn't come. We can't take the chance that someone would see him and ask questions. At Borough Hall nobody would know who he is."

Phil looked at his wife. "The girl has *saichel*. Smart and quiet. That's the way to do it."

Marta's eyes began to fill with tears. "All I want for my children is *naches*, not problems."

Motty went quickly to her aunt's side and put her arms around her. "Please, Tante Marta," she said softly, her own eyes beginning to tear. "Please."

"Why, God?" Marta cried, "did it have to happen at a time like this?"

"Don't blame God," he said rising from the table. "Fuck Adolf Hitler!"

Marta's tears turned to anger. "Then I don't give a damn. No rabbi, no wedding. I will not allow my children to live in sin!"

The telephone rang and Phil picked it up. "Hello." He listened for a moment, then called to them over his shoulder, "It's Joe." Then back into the receiver, "Yes, Joe?"

Joe's excited voice crackled through the phone. "I sold another story to *Collier's* and Universal Pictures wants to buy my first story for a movie in Hollywood. They want to pay me seventy-five hundred dollars!"

"Seven thousand five hundred dollars?" Phil asked incredulously. "What's the catch?"

"No catch, Papa," Joe answered. "It's on the up and up. They want me to go to Hollywood to write the screenplay."

"When?" Phil asked.

"Right away, probably next week."

"So soon?"

"It doesn't matter, Papa," Joe said. "This is an opportunity of a lifetime!"

Phil turned from the telephone to his wife. "Marta," he said proudly, "our Yussele is a real writer. He's going to Hollywood to make a movie. I guess that means you can have a wedding with a rabbi after all."

$=12=$

JAMAICA SAT DOWN and put his long legs up on the table. He looked at Joe, who was staring down at his typewriter. "You don' look happy?" he asked.

"I'm fucked," Joe said morosely.

"I don't get you," Jamaica said.

"I have this job to write a movie in Hollywood," Joe said.

"That sounds good." Jamaica smiled. "For good money?"

"Yeah," Joe said. "But there's a problem. They want me in Hollywood next week and Mr. B. wanted me for three months. I still have six weeks to go."

"Tell Mr. B.," Jamaica said. "He's not an unreasonable man."

Joe looked skeptically at Jamaica. According to the newspapers, Mr. B. was accused of at least half the murders in Brooklyn and was head of all the rackets. He remained silent.

Jamaica read his mind. "You kin talk to him. He's not as bad as all that."

"Could you talk to him for me?" Joe asked.

Jamaica shook his head. "I didn't make this deal, an'

something I learned about is not to butt into somebody else's business. That's how you get hurt."

"You can tell him that I'm really no good at this job," Joe said.

"Even though that's the truth," Jamaica said, "he the boss. I don't say nuthin'."

Joe met his eyes. "You're afraid of him?" he accused.

"You betcha' yo' white ass," Jamaica answered honestly. "I'm jes' a little nigger baby tryin' to make out in a cruel cold world." Then he laughed. "But you have nuthin' to worry about. Only thing he kin say to you is that you have to stay on the job. An' then, he might say okay. But if you don't ask, you don't get."

Joe stared at him for a moment—then his ego began to bother him. "Am I really as bad as that on this job?"

Jamaica smiled. "The worst," he said, without rancor. "But that's not your first love. You a writer, not a pimp. A good pimp has to be born, not taught."

"Writers have to be born, too," Joe said defensively.

"I don't know about writers," Jamaica said. "But the fac' is that business here has gone down more'n twenty percent since you come in. The girls have been layin' on their ass on the job, not trickin'. Not once even have you beaten up on one of them. An' remember I tol' you about that. That's how you get respect."

"I also said I didn't think I could handle it," Joe said.

"That's right," Jamaica said easily. "That's why I'm not complainin'." He paused for a moment, then got to his feet. "I really like you, kid," he said. "That's why I hope Mr. B. lets you out. That way everybody'll be happy. You'll get what you want an' we'll get back to makin' real money."

Joe looked up at the black man. "Jamaica, you're something else," he said, respect in his voice. "Thank you."

Jamaica nodded. "Then you're goin' to ask him?"

"Yes," Joe said. "I'll have to see my father before I meet with Mr. B. It was my father who made the introduction."

It was slightly less than an hour since Joe had taken the subway from the station at Ninety-sixth street and Broadway to the end of the New Lots line and walked across Pitkin Avenue to the market. The lights were bright at the stores on the avenue but the market lights were dark.

Only one lamp was shining through the locked door on the street. Joe walked to open the gate to the pens. His father's car was still there. It was a little after seven-thirty, but he knew that his father stayed after the market closed at seven o'clock to check the day's receipts. He turned the knob on the rear door. It, too, was locked.

He was about to knock at the door when a woman's scream sounded from inside. Automatically he slammed his shoulder against the door and the flimsy lock tore from the rotted wooden doorjamb.

He was just inside the door when he heard the second scream. It came from his father's small office. It was unlocked, and it opened at his touch. Then he froze in the doorway, his eyes blinking in surprise.

Josie's eyes were staring in fear as she turned to him. "Your father!" she cried. "Your father—"

Phil was lying lengthwise across her on the small couch, his pants down to his knees, his hips still embraced by Josie's fat legs, her dress high above her breasts. Phil's eyes were almost shut in pain as he gasped for breath. Slowly he began sliding to the floor.

Joe grabbed his father's coat from the chair behind the desk and pulled out the bottle of pills that were always in the breast pocket. He knelt on the floor and raised his father's head against his knees. "Get some water!" he shouted at Josie.

Shaking, she grabbed the glass of water that was always on the desk. Quickly Joe forced the pills into his father's mouth, and involuntarily his father's throat shuddered and he swallowed the pills. He looked up at Josie, who was still shaking. "Call Dr. Gitlin. Tell him it's an emergency! Ask him to call an ambulance!"

His father was gasping and spitting with difficulty. When he turned his father's face to the side, the spittle dripped from his mouth. Then he turned his head and vomited.

Josie called from the telephone. "Dr. Gitlin said he'll be here in a few minutes."

"Get me a wet towel to wipe Papa's face!" Joe said. She handed it to him. He began mopping the perspiration from his father's forehead.

"I'm sorry, Joe," Josie said, crying. "It's not my fault. I always told him to be careful. 'Screwing's too much for you, Phil,' I used to say. 'Frenchin' is easier and better for you.' But he's an old-fashioned man and he likes only the old-fashioned way."

"It's not your fault, Josie," Joe said. He looked down at his father's face. The strain was disappearing and his color began returning to normal as his breathing came more easily. "Get another towel to wipe his cock," he said. "Then help me pull up his pants. We don't want anyone to see him here like this."

She was still crying as she did everything he asked. "I'm sorry, Joe, I'm sorry," she repeated. "I'll never let him do it again."

"Okay. Don't worry. He's going to be all right," he said. "Now, you get out of here and go home. And say nothing about it to anyone. Just come in to work tomorrow like nothing ever happened."

"Thanks, Joe," she said gratefully as she ran to the door. "Thanks."

His father's head moved. Then he opened his eyes and saw Joe bending over him. "What—what happened?" he asked weakly.

"Nothing, Papa. You're okay. Rest."

"But what happened?" Phil insisted hoarsely.

"You almost fucked your brains out!" he said, his fear turning into anger. "Now lie down and rest. Dr. Gitlin will be here in a minute."

Phil took a deep breath. "And Josie?"

"She's a good girl, Papa," he said. "She was never here."

Phil looked into his son's face. "I feel ashamed," he said, staring into his eyes. "I was pretty stupid. Milton warned me, but I didn't listen to him."

"You're not stupid, Papa," he said. "You're human."

"But I love your mama, I shouldn't have done it."

"It's over now, so forget it." He heard an automobile in front. A moment later, Dr. Milton Gitlin came in, his small doctor's satchel in his hand.

He looked down at them. "What happened?"

"I came in here," Joe said, "and saw my father gasping on the floor. I shoved two of those pills you gave him into his throat."

Dr. Gitlin wasn't stupid. He saw the disarray of Phil's clothing but said nothing. He opened his satchel, took out a stethoscope and listened for a moment while he took Phil's pulse. Quickly he checked the blood pressure, and peered with a tiny light into the pupils of Phil's eyes. He nodded slightly, fixed a quick hypo of adrenaline and shot it into

Phil's arm. "You'll be okay," he said. "The ambulance will have a tank of oxygen for you on the way to the hospital."

"I'm not going to the hospital," Phil said stubbornly.

"You're going to the hospital," Dr. Gitlin said firmly. "You have had a big strain on your heart, and don't think an angina won't put you away. If everything's okay in the morning I'll let you out."

Marta was angry when she came into the waiting room at the hospital as Joe rose to meet her. He saw Motty just behind her. He kissed his mother on the cheek. "Hello, Mama."

She glared at him. "Why did they call you and not me? I'm his wife, ain't I? It's only right that I should be the one they call first."

"That's right, Mama," he said. "But I was right there in the market when it happened. I gave him his pills and called Dr. Gitlin."

"I still don't know what happened," she said. "The operators at the hospital tell you nothing."

"He strained his heart."

"How could he do a thing like that?" she asked suspiciously.

"Lifting twenty crates of chickens would kill a bull," Joe lied, thinking quickly.

"Stupid," she snapped. "He knew he wasn't to do things like that. But your father always thought he was Samson."

"How is he now?" Motty asked.

Joe kissed her cheek. "Better, much better."

"Let's go up to his room," his mother said.

"Wait a minute, Mama," Joe said. "Dr. Gitlin said he'll let us in when they have finished all the tests."

"Your father is a shmuck," Marta said. "Sometimes I feel I could kill him, he's so stupid."

Joe looked at her reprovingly. "He almost saved you the trouble," he said sarcastically.

Marta stared wide-eyed at him, then suddenly began to cry. "My Phil, my Phil!"

Joe put his arms around her. "He'll be okay. Calm down now."

"It's lucky that Joe was there with him, Tante," Motty said.

"Yes, yes," Marta said. Then she looked up at him. "Why were you there? I thought you were to stay out of Brooklyn."

"I had to ask Papa a question," he said.

"What question?" she insisted.

"If he could ask Mr. B. to let me out of the job so I can take the job in Hollywood."

Marta looked at him. Suddenly she was stronger. About this, she was in charge. "Don't you worry. That lowlife will do anything you want or I'll make him wish he was never born!"

Dr. Gitlin came into the waiting room. He was smiling as he came toward them. "Everything's all right. The electrocardiogram shows normal, no more damage, blood pressure one thirty-five over eighty-five, no fever. A good night's rest, and he can go home in the morning."

"Thank you, Doctor," said Marta gratefully. "Can I see him now?"

"You can," he said. "But remember to be very calm, don't get him excited, and stay only ten minutes. I want to make sure that he sleeps."

"We'll wait here, Mama," Joe said. He watched his mother follow Dr. Gitlin into the elevator and then turned to Motty. "You look all right," he said.

"I'm almost five weeks late," she said sarcastically. "Isn't that the time when pregnant women are supposed to look their best."

He tried to make her smile. "That should make Stevie very happy."

She didn't smile; instead she frowned. "Stevie will be here the day after tomorrow. That's Wednesday. The wedding's set for Sunday afternoon. That is, if he doesn't suspect anything before."

"He won't," he said confidently.

"I'm not that sure," she said. She looked at him. "When are you supposed to go?"

"My agent said Saturday on the Twentieth Century from Grand Central."

"I guess that's it," she said. "But I don't feel good about it."

"You'll feel better when you've gotten married," he said.

"I don't know," she said. "I'm confused. I'm worried. Maybe the marriage will be delayed because your father is sick."

"My father will be home in the morning. Everything will go according to schedule. Now, you stop worrying."

"I can't stop."

He smiled. "Normal bride's jitters."

$=13=$

MISS SHELTON HANDED two envelopes to Joe across her desk. "The first envelope holds your train tickets, first class, of course. The second is a letter of introduction to Mr. Ray Crossett, who is in charge of the story department at the studio and your immediate superior. The second envelope holds your checks, one for the story rights, twenty-five hundred less our ten percent commission, twenty-two hundred fifty net, also one hundred dollars in cash for expenses. Your weekly salary check will be sent to us here and we will send our check to you after we deduct our usual commission and expenses."

"I can't thank you enough," Joe said, glancing through the envelopes. "I've never had this much money in my life."

"Don't thank us," she said. "You wrote it, you've earned it."

"I still think I should do something special for you," he said. He looked at her. "How about we go out on the town?"

"I don't think that's such a good idea," she said. "This agency has strict rules. They don't allow personal relationships with their clients."

"What's so personal about going to dinner and a show?"

She watched him for a moment. "You asked my sister Kathy, before."

"She never called me back," he said. "I figured she wasn't interested."

"She was interested," Laura said. "But she moved to L.A. She found a better job out there—actually she is working at the same studio as you. You should give her a call when you get there; maybe she'll be able to help you."

"I appreciate that," he said. "But what about us? Nobody in the agency will know what we do on our own time."

"I'd like to go out with you but I would always worry that someone at the office would see us. And that would be a real problem for me. I don't plan to spend my whole life as an agent. I'm working to get into editing for one of the big publishers."

"That sounds pretty good," he said. "But I hear that editors need to bring along some writers."

She stared at him. "Write a novel. You're really good and that could help me."

"I've thought several times about writing a novel, but I don't know anything about it," he said.

"I can help you," she said. "Fifty percent of my work here is working with novelists. You do it—and we'll both get what we want."

"I want money," he said.

"Come up with a good novel, and the money you would get for that makes this amount look like peanuts."

"Then what happens with the agency?"

"I really don't give a damn," she said. "All I get here is thirty-five a week, while a decent editor commands a hundred to a hundred twenty-five just for starters."

"And what does a novel get?"

"A best-seller can make twenty-five thousand and more."

He rose to his chair. "I'm beginning to like you more and more."

She came around from behind her desk, holding out her hand. "I like you too."

He held her hand in his own. "And then we can have dinner?"

She laughed. "Anything you want."

He smiled. "I'm getting horny already."

She dropped his hand and went back to her desk. "You have a good trip to the Coast and keep in touch with me."

"I'll do that," he said, walking to the door. "Just remember your promise. We'll be in touch. 'Bye, now."

It was the middle of the lunch hour when he pushed his way into the Stage Delicatessen. He looked down at the tables. Stevie was already seated and waved to Joe.

Joe sat down at the table opposite him. He smiled. "I was beginning to think we'd never meet."

"I've been busy," Steve said. "I had seven interviews with various hospitals. They all offered me residencies."

"That's good," Joe said.

The waiter came up. He placed a bowl of pickles and green tomatoes and sauerkraut next to another basket of rolls. "So?" he asked.

"Corn beef on club and a celery tonic," Joe said.

"I'll have the same," Stevie said. He smiled at Joe. "Deli is one thing you don't get in Oklahoma."

Joe laughed. "Excited about the wedding?"

"Mama's making a big deal about it and probably Motty is too. The girls at the department store are giving her a luncheon shower today. I guess that weddings are more important to women than men."

"You're not excited?" Joe asked curiously.

The waiter placed their sandwiches before them and walked away. Stevie picked up his sandwich and bit into it. "This is good," he announced with a full mouth.

Joe took a bite of his sandwich. "How's things at home?"

"Papa's okay. He's back to work already. Mama's running around for the wedding. Everything's okay."

"Motty too?" Joe asked. "I thought she looked great."

"She's fine," Stevie said. "I think she's a little too heavy but that's normal. Jewish girls are usually a little heavier than *shiksas*."

Joe was silent as he took another bite of his sandwich. He wondered if Stevie suspected anything.

Stevie looked at him. "So you really did it," he said.

"Did what?" Joe asked.

"You said you'd be a writer and you did it. Now you are on your way to Hollywood. Papa said you're getting seventy-five hundred dollars for the job."

"That's right," Joe answered.

"That's a lot of money," Stevie said, a tinge of envy in his voice. "All the hospitals offer me is thirty-five hundred a year for a residency. And that's in New York. Out of town they offer less."

"You knew that before," Joe said.

"Yes," Stevie answered. "After one year I can get on staff; then I'll get between fifteen and twenty."

"That's not bad," Joe said. "I don't know whether I'll get another job. There are no guarantees in my work."

Stevie looked at his watch. "Damn it!" he exclaimed. "It's one o'clock already and I have an interview at NYU hospital at one-thirty." He finished his sandwich and stood up. "I have to run."

Joe said, "I'm sorry."

"I'm sorry too," Stevie said. "Too bad you can't join us at the wedding."

But Joe realized that his brother had other things on his mind. He shook his brother's hand. "Good luck," he said.

"Thanks," Stevie said.

"And give the bride a kiss for me." Joe smiled.

"Sure," Stevie said absent-mindedly and rushed for the door.

Joe sat down, slowly finished his sandwich and called the waiter for the check. Then he smiled to himself. Stevie never picked up a check. He had always been cheap.

Joe climbed up the stairs to Kitty's apartment. Lutetia opened the door. "She's expecting you," she said.

He walked into Kitty's small library-den. Kitty rose from her typewriter, and hugged and kissed him. "So you made it!" she said excitedly.

"I guess so."

"I'm proud of you," Kitty said sincerely. She took out a sheet of paper. "I have a list here of a number of friends I know out there. Give them a call. They'll all be happy to meet you."

"Thank you," he said.

"Have time for a drink?" she asked.

"A quick one," he said. "I still have a lot of packing to do."

"Lutetia!" Kitty called.

Lutetia came into the room with a bottle of champagne and three glasses. Quickly she opened the bottle and filled the glasses. Kitty held up her glass. "Congratulations and bon voyage."

"And good luck," Lutetia added.

"Thank you," Joe said, strangely touched. "Thank you very much."

It was eleven o'clock at night when Jamaica came into his apartment. He glanced at the packed valises. "All packed?"

"About," Joe answered.

"I have something for you," Jamaica said, handing him a small cardboard box.

Joe opened the box. The small brown vials shone up at him. "What's this for?" he asked.

"Insurance," Jamaica said.

"But you know I don't use the stuff," Joe said.

"I know," Jamaica said. "But there's fifty grams in there, and they'll get you from twenty-five to fifty dollars a gram out there. And you'll never be sure that you might not get the shorts. That's why I call it insurance. It's better than money."

Joe laughed. "Thanks. I'll remember that."

"What time are you leaving here in the morning?"

"About ten o'clock," Joe said.

"Then I won't see you before you go?" Jamaica said.

"I guess not," Joe said.

"Nervous?" Jamaica observed.

Joe nodded. "A little. I hope I can cut the mustard."

"You'll cut it," Jamaica said reassuringly. "All the stars are out in Hollywood, aren't they?"

"That's right," Joe answered.

"Then you'll do okay," Jamaica said. "Just remember, you doin' the right thing—you can touch the stars."

* * *

He called home in the morning just before he left for the station. Stevie answered. "Is Mama or Papa home?" Joe asked.

"They're at *shul*," Stevie answered.

"How about Motty?" he asked. "I'd like to say goodbye to her."

"She just left for work," Stevie said.

Joe hesitated a moment. "Then give them all my love and tell them I'll call them from California."

"I'll give them your message," Stevie said. "Good luck again."

"You, too," Joe said and put down the telephone. He checked around the apartment to make sure that he hadn't forgotten anything, then he picked up his valises and caught a taxi to Grand Central.

A redcap grabbed his valises at the Forty-second Street entrance. "Where to, suh?" the redcap asked. "Have yo' ticket handy?"

"Right with me," Joe said, following him. The big clock read a quarter after eleven. The gateway to the Twentieth Century was just to the left side of it. He was checking his ticket when he felt someone touch him on the arm.

"Remember me?" Motty said.

He stared in surprise. "Stevie told me you had gone to work."

"That's what he thought," she said. She met his eyes. "I'm not going anywhere except with you."

"You're nuts!" he exclaimed.

"I'm not," she said. "I don't love him. Now I know I never loved him. And he doesn't love me either. I'm just a convenience for him. He never once even kissed me, not even when I met him here at the station. He just shook my hand."

"Stevie never was emotional," he said.

"He doesn't think about anyone except himself. He thinks he's better than everyone, even his parents."

"But the wedding's tomorrow!" he said.

"Fuck it!" she said vehemently.

"They'll all go crazy," he said.

"They'll get over it," she said. She turned to face him squarely. "I love you. I've always loved you. And you knew that, didn't you?"

He took a deep breath, then nodded slowly.

"Then are you taking me with you, or aren't you?" she asked in a trembling voice.

He saw the tears struggling behind her eyes. Suddenly he took her in his arms and kissed her. She clung to him tightly.

"We better make it fast, sir," the redcap said. "We have only fifteen minutes till check-in time."

"Then take us to the ticket counter, we have to pick up another ticket in a hurry," Joe said. "This is heavy romance!"

PART II
1946–1947

=14=

HE LAY BACK on the bed, propped up by the pillows behind him. He watched her standing naked as she put on her makeup in the mirror. Carefully, expertly, she penciled in her eyebrows. "You've got a great ass," he said admiringly.

She watched him in the mirror continuing her work with the eyebrow pencil. "You say that to all the girls," she said without inflection.

"Not all the girls," he said, smiling. "Only those who have them."

"You're terrible," she said. "Aren't you going to work this morning?"

"Today I'm due at the unemployment line."

"You're off the payroll again?"

"Temporarily," he said. "A. J. said he'll have a project for me in a week or two."

"The last time he told that to you," she said sarcastically, "you waited two and a half months."

"This time he means for sure," Joe said. He changed the subject. "Where's the baby?"

"Caroline's downstairs in the kitchen with the Mexican. She's having *huevos rancheros* for breakfast."

Joe shook his head. "What kind of a breakfast is that for

a Jewish baby? Bagels, lox and cream cheese would be more like it."

"For thirty dollars a month you get Mexican help," Motty said. Her makeup finished, she turned to Joe. "My makeup okay?"

"Fine," Joe said. "And so are your thirty-four Bs and juicy pussy."

"It's the exercise," she said. "I owe that to the nurse at the obstetrician's office. She said if I didn't diet and exercise after the baby, everything would droop."

"I'll send her a thank-you letter," Joe said. He threw off the covers. "Look at this," he added, feigning surprise. "I've got a hard on."

"So what else is new?" she laughed, walking to the closet.

"Time for a quickie?"

She laughed again. "And ruin my makeup? Not a chance. I have an important meeting this morning."

"What could be more important than a morning fuck?"

"A new job," she said. "Mr. Marks, the executive vice president of the Beverly Hills branch of the store, wants me to be the buyer of the high-fashion department."

"I thought you were happy in the advertising department?" he asked.

"I was. But this is twice the money, and besides, with the veterans coming back from service, I don't know how long I can hang on in that department. Before the war, most of the department staff were men."

"How much will you get?" he asked.

"Could be a thousand a month but more probably eight hundred. But that's okay. There's a lot of extras with the job."

He was silent; then he looked at her. "What's the extras? You get to fuck him?"

"You've got a dirty mind," she said, annoyed. "That's all you think about. Mr. Marks is a very conservative man. Wears a striped tie and a boutonnière all the time. Besides, he's at least fifty."

He watched her fasten her brassiere and step into her panties. "The studio is loaded with fifty-year-old fuckers."

She slipped into a white silk long-sleeved shirt and began buttoning it. "It's a different kind of business. The studio is loaded with a bunch of whores who want to be actresses."

"You're beginning to sound more and more like my mother," he said.

"It's the truth," Motty said flatly. "And I've seen lipstick stains on your shorts to prove it."

He sat silently as she wrapped her skirt around her waist and then straightened the seams of her stockings. "I thought Rosa did the laundry."

She didn't answer.

"Don't you want me to explain?" he asked.

"No," she said flatly. "There's nothing to explain. It isn't as if I hadn't known you before. I've known you all your life."

He stared at her. "And you're not angry?"

She looked into his eyes for a long moment, then turned away. "I have to get started," she said. She paused at the door and looked back at him. "If all you have to do is go to the unemployment office, why don't you get back to work on your book? You can put in a lot of work in two weeks."

He didn't answer.

"Your agent, Laura, said if you could send in edited changes of the finished manuscript she could get you a good deal."

"Yeah," he said unenthusiastically. "Sure, and she becomes an editor, which is what she really wants."

"Wish me luck," she said.

He got out of bed and walked to her. "Good luck," he said, kissing her. He stood there as she walked out on the balcony that led to the stairway down to the living room, then closed the bedroom door behind him. He sat on the side of the bed and took a cigarette from the night table and lit it. "Shit," he said.

He heard the front door slam shut, then, still dragging on the cigarette, he walked out to the balcony. "Rosa," he called to the Mexican girl downstairs in the kitchen.

She came from the kitchen into the living room and looked up at him on the balcony. *"Sí, señor?"*

"Can you bring me some coffee?"

"Horita, señor." She giggled, still looking up at him.

"What are you laughing about?" he asked, irritated. She was always giggling.

"Nada, señor," she replied.

"*Nada,* shit," he said. "You're laughing about something."

She giggled again, looking boldly up at him. *"Los pantalones de sus pijamas están abiertos."*

He glanced down. The fly of his pajama pants was indeed open. He closed the button. "Don't look at it," he said. "You're too young for things like that."

"Sí, señor," she said, ignoring his comment. *"Toma usted el café en la cámara?"*

"No," he said. "I'll be in the study." He watched her as she walked slowly back to the kitchen. Cock-teasing bitch, he thought as she tossed her shining long black hair that hung just above her swaying hips as she walked. She paused in the kitchen doorway and looked back, smiling at him over her shoulder.

He turned and walked along the balcony. He passed the baby's bedroom, which Rosa shared, sleeping on a narrow bed, to the small room that was intended to be a servant's room, into which he had managed to cram a small desk for his typewriter, a typist's chair, prefabricated bookshelves and a secondhand leather easy chair.

He sat down at the desk and looked at the typewriter. There was a blank sheet of paper in it. He tried to remember what he had been working on when he placed it there. He couldn't remember. Angrily he pulled the sheet out of the typewriter, crumpled it into a ball and threw it in the waste-basket. He leaned forward without getting out of the chair and picked up the stationery box that held the manuscript of his novel. He opened the box and stared at the title page.

NOR ANY STAR PURSUE
a novel by
Joseph Crown

Quickly he riffled the pages. There were forty-five pages of notes, but only ten pages of the beginning of the novel itself. He looked at them with disgust. Only ten pages, and he was still jerking off with the first chapter, in the chicken market. It had been more than eight months since he had written it. Since then he had been working on two screen-plays. He stared at it again. It was shit. At least screenplays were more fun. You could work with other people and meet new people and bullshit your way around. Writing a novel was a lonely job. No one could help you there. Just you and the typewriter. And the only fucking you got was off the pages you wrote. It was another form of masturbation, and without the pleasure. Laura was nothing but another pain in the ass with her ideas for changes.

"Señor?" Rosa's voice came from the door.

He turned to look at her. She held a tray with a pot of coffee, a cup and saucer, a sweet roll on a plate, sugar and a spoon. He gestured to the desk. "Okay."

She bent over the desk and placed the tray in front of him. The scoop neckline of her soft cotton dress fell forward, and he could look down into her small apple breasts almost completely past her little belly to her pussy hairs. She didn't straighten up until she had filled his coffee cup, then she looked at him. *"Está bien?"*

He sipped the coffee. "Good," he said. She turned to leave, but he called her back. An idea came to him. "Did you show the *señora* the lipstick on my shorts?"

He knew she knew what he was talking about. "No, *señor.*"

"How did she find it then?" he asked.

"Each day the *señora* checks the *ropa lavada.*"

"All the time?"

"Todo," she said.

Silently he sipped at his coffee. He lit another cigarette and let the smoke curl from his nostrils while he watched her sourly.

"You are angry with me, *señor?*" she asked.

He shook his head. "Not with you. With myself." He stared down at the typewriter. Nothing was working. He knew the book was in there, but he couldn't get himself to bring it out. Maybe it was too easy here in Hollywood. In the three and a half years they had been here, he had made more money doing less work than he had dreamed in New York. Everything was easier. The girls were prettier and more available. Sex was a way of life for them. No hassle.

Fucking for writers, producers and directors was a path to getting a job in a movie. A big part or small, it didn't matter—the important thing was to get on the screen. Even the weather was easier. Sometimes it rained, but it was never really cold—never the bitter cold that he had been used to in New York.

Even Motty said that it was easier here. The only trouble was, there wasn't anything to do. That was why she went to work six months after the baby was born. In just a few months she had been promoted to assistant to the department's head of advertising. She had told him, laughing, that California girls could never make it in New York stores because the only thing they majored in at school was tennis.

He looked up from the typewriter. Rosa was still standing in the doorway. He was vaguely surprised. He had forgotten she was here. Her body was silhouetted through the thin cotton dress from the light behind her. He felt himself getting hard. "Why don't you wear underwear?" he asked angrily.

"I have only one pair," she said. "During the day no one is home so I wear only when I go out with child. Each night I must wash it."

"How much does underwear cost?" he asked.

"Brassiere, panties and slip, *dos dolares*," she answered.

He pulled open the desk drawer, where he always left some money. There were several bills—three singles and a five. He took them out and held them out to her. "Here," he said. "Buy some."

Slowly she came over to him and took the money from his hand. *"Muchas gracias, señor."*

"Por nada," he said.

Her eyes fell away from him. "You are sad, *señor*," she said in a low voice. "Can Rosa help you?"

For a moment he didn't understand what she meant, then

he realized that she had been looking at the bulging fly of his pajamas. "How do you know about such things?" he asked.

"I have five brothers and my father," she answered. "In my *casa* I have to help all of them."

He stared at her. "How old are you, Rosa?"

She still didn't meet his eyes. *"Tengo* sixteen, *señor."*

"Shit," he said. "You fuck all of them?"

"No, *señor,"* she said. *"Solamente—"* She made a fist and moved it up and down in front of her.

He smiled. "It's not necessary, Rosa," he said gently. "But thank you anyway."

She nodded seriously and left the room. He watched her go, her hips swaying. It meant nothing to her, he thought. That was the way she lived.

He ground out his cigarette in the ashtray and took a bite of the sweet roll. It was really sweet, not at all like the danishes in New York. Here they were coated with sugar icing. He washed it down with more coffee.

He stared down at the typewriter again. "How about it?" he asked. "Do you feel like writing a novel?"

The empty white page stared back at him blankly. The telephone began to ring and he picked it up. "Hello."

"Good morning," Kathy said. As her sister had told him, Kathy was working in the studio as one of A. J.'s secretaries. "What are you doing today?"

"I was pink-slipped," he said. "Today I'm registering at unemployment."

"Do it in the morning," she said. "A. J. wants to see you at three o'clock."

"He has a job for me?" he asked.

"I don't know," she answered. "He just told me to call you in. Maybe you'll get lucky."

"I'll be there," he said. "What are you doing this evening?"

"Nothing special."

"How about a happy hour?" he asked.

"At my apartment or at a bar?"

"Your apartment."

She hesitated for a moment. "My apartment," she said. "But you bring a bottle. Six o'clock okay?"

"Okay," he said.

"And bring rubbers too. I'm too close to my time," she added.

"I'll take care of it," he said. "See you at the office at three."

He put down the telephone and picked up his coffee. "You have another day off," he said to the typewriter. The typewriter didn't answer.

He sipped the last of his coffee. Thirty thousand dollars in the bank, a good apartment, two cars, a three-year-old daughter and a wife who paid her own way—what more could he ask?

He didn't have any answers. Nothing had changed. All he ever thought about was new pussy and new money.

=15=

"WE NEED A new look for the main floor of the Beverly Hills store," Mr. Marks said to her as he sat behind his large oak executive desk. "A more sophisticated look, more New York. We have to attract the new younger married now that the war is over."

Motty nodded seriously. "I agree."

"You've worked in the New York stores, you know what I mean," he said.

"Exactly," she said. "More like Saks Fifth Avenue."

"Like that," he replied. "But also like Macy's. We have to realize that our clientele is not quite ready to jump into the high price range. We have to give them the illusion that we're a classy store, but cheaper."

"Bloomingdale's," she said.

"Right on the nose." He smiled. He looked down at several blueprints spread across his desk. "We have some preliminary drawings of the main floor. Would you like to see them?"

"Very much," she said.

At his gesture she came around the desk, looking down at the blueprints as she stood beside him. The blueprints were a jumble of white lines. They were not easy to follow.

"This is the main entrance." He pointed with his finger. "Off to the right side we plan the book department. That shows class. Off to the left side we plan a great-looking fur salon, then right in front and through to the back of the store is all the better line of coats and dresses. All real class."

He looked up at her for comment. She was silent. "What do you think?" he asked.

"I don't know," she said honestly. "You have more experience than I, so I have to assume that you are right."

He swiveled his chair toward her; his shoulder brushed her breast and the faint aroma of her scent came to him. "I'm not the kind of an executive that needs yes men. The reason I wanted you for this job is because you express your own opinions."

She looked at him. He was not looking at her face; his eyes were traveling down her decolletage. She felt her nipples hardening, and she flushed, embarrassed. Now she was angry with herself for wearing a silk blouse instead of a less clinging one. She knew her nipples were pressing against it.

He looked up at her face, a faint smile on his lips. "What do you think?" he asked.

She took a deep breath. The right answer might blow the job, but she didn't know what else to say. "It really shows class," she answered, "if that's what we want. But I thought we wanted to bring in a new young clientele. One that buys rather than just looks."

Now she had his attention on business. "What do you mean?"

"You gave me the idea," she said tactfully. "You mentioned Macy's. I had a letter from a friend of mine who works for them. They're moving the book department from the main floor to the seventh floor because it doesn't bring in traffic."

"What are they replacing it with?" he asked.

"She didn't tell me," she answered. "I don't know if they have decided yet."

"What would you do then?"

She met his eyes steadily. "Cosmetics. Perfumes. Beauty accessories. On half the main floor, as soon as the customer comes in."

"That's Woolworth's," he protested.

"It's also almost twenty percent of the sales," she said. "And there's nothing wrong with that."

"But they sell cheap lines."

"We go up a step. Now that the war is over all the French companies are coming into the country. They will have cachet and are not much more expensive. We can set up a separate counter for every line. That would make it really important. And it will bring in the kind of clientele that we want."

"It could be expensive," he said.

"They want to get into the market," she said. "I'm ready to bet they will share the costs with you."

He stared at her. "You really are bright."

"Thank you."

"Do you have any other suggestions?"

"That's just off the top of my head. I haven't really thought it out," she answered. "I know what I bought the first moment they came back on the market: small appliances. Electric iron, toaster, fry pan. New dishware, pots and pans. Silk stockings, lingerie. I'd really have to study it."

"I guess we'll all have to study it more." He turned from her and looked down at the floor plan. "There's thirty thousand square feet on the main floor. We have to make each foot pay off."

She walked around the desk and faced him. "Yes, Mr. Marks."

"We can't afford any mistakes," he said.

"I realize that," she said.

"I want the Beverly Hills store to become our flagship," he said. "We'll either make our reputation or fall with it." He looked at her across the desk. "Perhaps we should take a trip to New York to see what they are up to. Their marketing techniques are years ahead of us."

She met his eyes squarely. "You want me to go to New York with you?"

"That's part of your job," he said smoothly. "You'll probably have to make at least one trip a year to Paris as well."

"I've never been to Europe," she said.

"I've been many times, before the war," he said. "It's very exciting. I could show you things you would never imagine."

"But I'm a married woman with a child, Mr. Marks," she said lamely.

"I'm a married man, Mrs. Crown," he said smoothly. "But we're talking business. Nothing more."

She wished she could believe that, but even her nipples didn't. They were tingling as his eyes caressed them. She avoided his gaze. "I'll have to talk to my husband about it."

"You do that, Mrs. Crown," he said unctuously. "You can explain to him that's why your base salary is eight hundred and fifty a month, and with bonuses you can make up to fifteen hundred to two thousand a month. And that's a very important salary."

"I realize that, Mr. Marks," she said. She held her hand

out to him, hoping that her palm didn't feel sweaty. "Thank you very much."

"Daddy going to work?" Caroline lisped from her chair as he came into the kitchen.

He bent to the child and kissed her. "That's right, darling."

"Bring me some candy?" She smiled, her soft brown ringlets shining in the light.

"Of course."

"Now," she said imperiously.

He glanced at Rosa, then gestured in surrender. He took two penny Tootsie Rolls from his jacket pocket and gave them to the child. "What does Caroline say?" he asked.

"Thank you." She smiled, already tearing the candy wrapping. She was concentrating on the candy, no longer interested in him.

The doorbell rang. He left the kitchen, crossed the living room and opened the door. The mailman looked at him. "Parcel post, Mr. Crown."

Joe took the rectangular box. The words "Returned Manuscript" were penciled several times in red crayon on the box. Silently Joe took it and signed the receipt book for the mailman.

"I'm sorry, Mr. Crown," the mailman said. "Tough luck. This is the second one you got this month."

Joe looked at him. The mailman nodded sympathetically. "That's the way it goes," Joe said.

"Maybe next time it'll be better," the mailman said. "Good day to you."

"You, too," Joe said, closing the door. He stared at the wrapped package. He'd never thought that the postman was that interested in what he delivered. Quickly he broke the string and tore the wrapping from the package. He looked down at the opened box. It was not a manuscript. Instead there were forty carefully folded paper envelopes, each holding a quarter-gram of cocaine. At twenty-five dollars per, that was a thousand dollars for him. He sent Jamaica only two hundred fifty for it. He closed the box. This time, he made up his mind—he was going to rent a post-office box. He was in luck that A. J. had called him into the studio. All it would take him was an hour on the music recording stages and he would get rid of all the envelopes. Musicians were the best customers for any kind of dope. If only he could make a connection with ganch, he would become a millionaire.

He walked back to the kitchen doorway. Caroline's face was already smeared with chocolate. Rosa was doing laundry in the deep wash basin. She looked back at him.

"Tell the *señora* that I will be at the studio this afternoon," he said.

"*Sí, señor.*" She wrung out one of the diapers. "*Tengo pollo veracruzana por comida.* Okay?"

"Okay," he said. "*A las ocho.*"

"*Sí, señor,*" she said.

It was about ten o'clock when he parked his pre-war Chrysler Airflow on the street across from the California Employment Office building in downtown Hollywood. The parking lot was already full, automobiles waiting in line at the entrance. The moment a car moved out another moved in. He glanced down the street. He parked the car a few blocks from Fountain; there were limousines with chauffeurs nearby as though hiding from the common people. He smiled to himself. The California Club, it had been called at the studios. Sometimes there were so many movie stars in the lines inside waiting for their weekly unemployment check that this had become a popular stop for the tour buses.

He walked past the public entrance to the rear of the building to the employees' entrance and went in, waving to the old man in his guard's uniform. The black lettering on the frosted glass window down the corridor read simply, "Mr. Ross." He knocked lightly and opened the door.

Jack Ross, a heavyset man with thinning hair, looked up from his desk. He smiled and gestured for Joe to come in. "How are you doin', Joe?"

Joe shook his head. "The usual, Jack," he said. "I was pink-slipped."

Ross took a printed form from a pile next to him. "Okay," he said. "We'll get right on it."

Joe nodded. "Just one problem. Christmas is coming up next month. It takes six weeks for the first check."

Ross looked at him quizzically. "That's the rules."

"Maybe we can bend them a little," Joe said.

"We're really jammed," Ross said. "It's always like that near the holidays."

"I know," Joe said. "I saw the limos hiding around the corner."

Ross smiled. "Even the stars are showing up. Ilona Massey. Richard Arlen."

"'Tis the season to be jolly," Joe said.

Ross looked down at the printed forms. "I can backdate seven weeks for you but it'll cost. Twenty-five dollars up front and ten percent of each check you collect."

"That'll be fine," Joe said. He laid twenty-five dollars on the desk in front of him.

The money disappeared in Ross's pocket. Quickly he filled out the form and pushed it over to Joe. "Sign this in the three places marked."

Joe signed it and pushed the form back to him. "When do I get the check?"

"I'll have it here tomorrow morning at nine-thirty," he said. "You'll have two weeks' checks."

"Thanks, Jack," Joe said. "I'll see you tomorrow then."

Ross smiled. "I'll be waiting for you. You take care, hear?"

"I will," Joe said. "We better make lunch sometime soon."

"After the holidays," Ross said. "Too busy right now."

"Okay," Joe said, heading for the door. "You name the day. Thanks again."

$==16==$

TRIPLE S STUDIOS were located in the valley. Although smaller in size and acreage than Universal and Warner Brothers, they were complete with four good-sized film stages and three smaller stages that doubled for filming and music recording. A three-story brick building painted a boring gray contained the executive offices just inside the studio gates. Beyond that were two two-story wooden buildings, also painted the same gray. One building housed the producers' offices. The other slightly shabbier building held the restaurant commissary on the ground level, and the upper story was crowded with cubbyholes that served as offices for writers and the script department. A number of rickety bungalows were scattered around the studio lot for directors and their staffs, and wartime Quonset huts at the far end housed the music department. Large barnlike buildings took care of the sets and the costume department. Without enough acreage to film exterior shots, the studios had an arrangement to use the Warner Brothers facilities adjacent to them.

The gray-shirted, bored studio guard leaned against the small wooden shack at the gate entrance as Joe stopped his car beside him. The guard looked at him strangely. "I thought you were pink-slipped yesterday," he said hoarsely.

140

"That's right." Joe smiled. "But A. J. called me in for a meeting."

The guard stepped into his shack and checked the visitors' list. He called to Joe. "That's for three o'clock," he grumbled. "It's only one o'clock."

"I like to be early," Joe said. "Where do you want me to park the car?"

"Use your usual place. We haven't reassigned it yet."

"Thanks," Joe said. He looked up at the guard. "Maxie Keyho around?"

"Gotta hot tip?" the guard asked curiously. Maxie Keyho was a music contractor; he was also the unofficial studio bookie.

"Not today," Joe said. "He's got a five-dollar marker of mine."

"I just saw him walking over to the commissary," the guard said.

Joe waved his hand at him and drove his car around to the parking lot in front of the writers' building. He locked the car and went into the commissary. The restaurant was a long room, its walls covered with pictures of stars and featured actors that had been in the studio's movies. It was divided into two sections: The rear section was for executives and important actors and producers, complete with tables and waitresses; the main section, the biggest part of the room, had a long counter spread with an assortment of foods, and the service was cafeteria style—you picked up your food and found a place to sit at any table that happened to be vacant. Usually the first customers entering tried to hold chairs at their table for friends. This didn't often work, especially when the commissary was busy. But no one ever bothered Maxie Keyho, who had had the same table every day for years. It was in a corner near the entrance where he could see everyone entering.

Keyho, as usual, was dressed in a black suit, shirt and tie, and sat alone. No one sat at his table unless invited. He looked up at Joe, his watery, pale blue eyes curious. "I thought you were pink-slipped yesterday," he said without greeting.

"A. J. called me in this afternoon," Joe said. The studio grapevine always worked overtime.

"Sit down," Keyho invited. "What's goin' on?"

"I don't know what A. J. wants," Joe answered, slipping into a chair. "I thought maybe you did."

Keyho shrugged his shoulder. "The only thing I heard is that he's meeting with a new banker from New York."

"I don't know what that means to me," Joe said. He lowered his voice. "Talking about New York, I just received a fresh package and thought maybe you could use it."

Keyho stared at him for a moment. "Money is tight. Everybody is getting laid off."

Joe didn't answer.

"How much?" Keyho asked.

"Forty packages," Joe said. "Usually it's a grand but I don't know whether I'll be on the lot. I'll turn it over to you for eight- fifty."

"Seven hundred," Keyho offered.

"Seven-fifty and you have a deal," Joe said.

"It's a deal," Keyho answered. "Do you have it with you?"

"In the trunk of my car."

Keyho nodded. "After lunch, at two-thirty. I'll be outside recording stage C."

Joe rose from his chair. "I'll see you there."

He walked to the counter and picked up a tray. He felt

good. Seven-fifty was a good deal. A quick five hundred profit, and he didn't have to hang around a week button-holing customers. He moved down the self-service line and looked over at the girl standing behind the hot-food table. "Salisbury steak and mashed potatoes with gravy," he said, then looked over his shoulder to see if any one of the writers he knew were there.

He opened the door and looked at Kathy sitting at her desk. "Am I too early?" he called.

She waved to him to enter while she spoke into the telephone. He closed the door behind him and crossed to her desk as she put down the telephone. "Where's Joanie?" he asked.

Joan was the number one secretary. "She called in sick," Kathy answered. The telephone rang again. "Everything's jammed up," she added as she picked up the phone again. She transferred the call to A. J. and turned back to him. "We'll have to cancel our happy hour," she said. "With Joanie out, I'll have to work late."

"Okay," he said.

She stared at him. "You're really a prick. You don't even seem disappointed."

"What am I supposed to do?" he asked. "I know when you have to work, you have to work."

"A. J. called Laura. He wanted to know if you would be okay for a project he had in mind."

"What did she say?" Joe asked.

"She said you would be good." She looked at him. "Then she took off on me. She said you were a hustler and I should stay away from you."

Joe was curious. "Why would she say that?"

"I have my own idea," Kathy said. "I think Laura has a yen for you."

"She never let me see that," he said.

"That's Laura," she said. "She covers her feelings. It's her business camouflage."

"I don't get it," he said. "Maybe she knows about us?"

"It's not that," Kathy said. Suddenly, she seemed cold. "When A. J. gets off the phone, I'll let him know that you're here," she said.

"I'm sorry," he said. "I'll leave the bottle of vodka in your car when I go out."

"You don't have to," she said.

"I'm just as disappointed as you are. It's not your fault." She didn't answer.

"How about tomorrow?" he asked.

"Maybe," she answered. The white light next to the telephone on her desk flashed on. She picked up the phone. "Joe Crown is here for you, Mr. Rosen." She listened for a moment then nodded and gestured to Joe. "He's on the way in, sir."

"Thanks," Joe said to her as he walked to the door of A. J.'s office.

She looked up at him. "Good luck," she said sincerely.

A. J. sat behind his desk like a fat, bald Napoleon. His chair was raised beneath him so that he could look down on the visitors sitting across his desk. His fat cheeks creased in a smile. "Thanks for coming in on such short notice, Joe," he said.

"It's my pleasure, Mr. Rosen."

"I might have a project for you," A. J. said importantly. "You're a New Yorker, aren't you?"

"Born and bred," Joe answered.

"Movies about New York do pretty good at the box office," A. J. said. "The Dead End Kids from Universal, then the East Side Kids from Monogram after Universal dropped it and it became a series."

Joe nodded seriously. He still didn't understand what A. J. was talking about.

"I'm thinking about a picture more important than those. More like the movie *Dead End* that Sam Goldwyn made."

"Fine film," Joe said.

"One of my New York bankers gave me the idea for it," A. J. said. "It's really not a bad idea at all. A New York gangster falls in love with a gorgeous showgirl and decides to take her to Hollywood to become a movie star."

Joe expressed the proper enthusiasm. "That's really a great idea, Mr. Rosen."

A. J. smiled. "I thought you might like it."

"I do, Mr. Rosen." Joe nodded. "Knowing you, you already have the leads in mind."

"I have the girl already," A. J. answered. "But I have been trying to decide on the leading man. It's a toss-up between Bogart, Eddie Robinson or Cagney."

Joe nodded seriously. He knew that as well as A. J. there was no chance of any of those actors doing the part. "You said you have the girl," he said tactfully.

"I have," A. J. said, picking up a publicity still photograph and pushing it across the desk to Joe. "Judi Antoine."

Joe looked down at the provocative picture of the girl in a skintight silver gown that out-Betty'd Betty Grable and put Lana Turner away. "I know her," he said.

"The whole world knows her," A. J. said enthusiastically. "She's been under contract for six months and though she's never even been in a picture we get a thousand requests a week for photographs of her. She's in every magazine and newspaper in the country."

"She's hot," Joe agreed. He didn't want to tell A. J. that on the lot she was nicknamed "The Screamer," because she shouted so loudly while fucking. She even traded him a quickie to introduce her to the director doing the movie he had been working on.

"Even my banker thinks she'd be perfect for the part." A. J. nodded, then said as if he had just thought of it, "My wife and I are taking the banker for dinner at Perino's. Why don't you pick up Judi and join us?"

Joe rubbed his chin to feel if his beard was growing. "Tonight?"

"Tonight." A. J. nodded.

"Maybe she's not available," Joe suggested.

"She's available," A. J. said firmly. "I arranged that."

"I'll have to explain it to my wife," Joe said.

"She'll understand," A. J. returned. "It's business."

Joe thought for a moment. "Okay. Now when do you want me to start working?"

"Right away. You'll get twenty-five hundred for the treatment; if we go to script, you get another twelve thousand five."

Joe nodded. "Good enough."

"Dinner will be at seven-thirty. It should be over between nine-thirty and ten."

"What do I do after that?" Joe asked.

"Drop her off at the banker's hotel and wait for her to call you at the cocktail lounge. Then you can drop her home. You should be finished by midnight."

Joe nodded silently.

A. J. looked shrewdly at him. He was in touch with the studio grapevine after all. "Just tell her not to holler too loud. Bankers are nervous by nature. He might lose his hard."

Joe closed the door behind A. J.'s office and looked at Kathy. "You knew?"

She nodded. "But not until Joanie called in sick. Usually that's her department."

"It's shit," he said.

"It's a shitty business," she replied. "But what the hell, you got a job out of it. Now you better call Laura and tell her you got the job."

=17=

HE WALKED TO the writers' building and up the rickety stairway outside the restaurant. The door opened into the steno pool, where the small desks were crowded close to each other. The head steno sat at the desk against the far wall, much like a teacher at her desk at the head of a classroom. Only two girls were typing at their desks, the head steno was proofreading a script. She looked up as he entered. "I heard you were coming back." She smiled. "I didn't even take your name off the office door."

"Thanks, Shirley," he said.

She opened a desk drawer and took out a room key. He took it from her. "Everything's in there," she said. "Pads, paper, pencils, even a typewriter."

"You're okay," he said.

"What's the new project?" she asked.

"A New York story," he answered. "I don't know too much about it yet."

"It must be a hot one," she said. "It's not often that A. J. is in that much of a hurry."

"I guess so," he said. "I just have a few calls to make. I'll be in in the morning."

"Anything I can do, let me know," she said. "Good luck, Joe."

"Thanks, Shirley," he answered and walked down the corridor to the small cubbyhole that served as his office. He opened the door with his key. The office was just big enough to hold a small desk and two chairs, one behind it and one in front of it. Any more than two people in there would have to stand in the doorway or in the corridor. He shut the door and sat down behind the desk. He stared at the telephone for a moment and just as he reached, it rang. He picked it up. "Joe Crown," he said into it.

"Judi Antoine," a girl's voice whispered into his ear. "I hear you're my date for tonight."

"That's what I hear," he answered.

"You got two Cs?"

"What are you talking about?" he asked.

"The two hundred bucks I get for the night," she said.

"Wait a minute," he said. "Nobody told me about that. I'm just the beard for A J. and his banker at dinner. I thought publicity arranged it."

"Publicity told me you would take care of it," she said. "I have expenses," she added. "How do you expect me to make out on the one twenty-five a week they pay. My apartment at the Sunset Towers costs three hundred a week alone."

"Didn't they tell you that you're getting the lead on the picture I'm writing?"

"All the time," she said. "I must have heard that at least a thousand times."

"That comes from A. J. himself," he said. "His banker who's financing the picture has the hots for you. I was supposed to drop you off at his hotel room after dinner and wait for you at the cocktail lounge. I thought it was all set up."

"Nighttime fucking is on my own time," she said flatly. "It don't say nothing in my contract about that."

"So what do you expect me to do?" he asked.

"Get me the money," she said. "Otherwise I don't show up. Let me know what's happening, I'll be at home until five-thirty."

"Come on, Judi," he cajoled. "Didn't I introduce you to Ray Stern, the director, when you wanted to meet him?"

"I don't remember," she said.

"We had a quickie leaning against the wall in my office because there wasn't enough room for a couch," he said, trying to jog her memory.

"I don't remember," she repeated. "All johns are the same to me. Just get me the money." She hung the phone up.

He stared at the silent telephone for a moment then called A. J.'s office. Kathy answered. "I have to speak to A. J.," he said.

"He's gone for the day," she said.

"I have to talk to him."

"Sorry, Joe," she said. "I can't help you. He's on his way home."

"Can we get him there?"

"Not until six-thirty," Kathy said. "Is it really important?"

"Important enough," he said. "His leading lady is an overtime hooker. She won't show up without two hundred in advance."

"Damn!" Kathy said. "I would help you but the cashier's office closes at three."

Joe thought for a moment. "Okay, honey," he said. "Don't worry about it. I'll figure a way out."

He put down the telephone and stared down at it. He

pulled his wallet out of his jacket pocket. The seven hundred fifty dollars that Keyho had given him made it heavy. Slowly he took out four fifty-dollar bills and put them in his pocket. Paying money to hookers was against his religion—even more so when it was not for himself. He was boxed in. But a job was a job and he *was* getting something out of it. He picked up the telephone again and called Judi at her Sunset Towers apartment.

Motty came into the bedroom while he was knotting his tie. "Rosa told me this afternoon that you were going to the studio."

He nodded, staring at the tie in the mirror, then untied it and began to do it over. "A. J. called me. I've got a job. A new picture."

"A good one?" she asked.

"They're all good ones starting out," he said, finishing the knot on his tie. He turned to her. "Do you like it?"

She looked at it critically. "It looks kind of big."

"That's the way it's supposed to be," he said. "It's called the Windsor knot. Sinatra uses it all the time." He reached for the dark blue jacket.

"What's with the bar mitzvah suit?" she asked curiously.

"A. J.'s invited me to dinner at Perino's with his banker."

"That's a switch," she said. "Never happened before. Just the three of you?"

"A. J.'s wife and a starlet the banker has the hots for," he answered.

She met his eyes. "Where do you fit in?"

He smiled. "I'm the beard."

"You know the girl?"

"Not really," he answered. "But it's a New York story and I'm a New York writer so I got the job. The banker wants her to play the lead so I have to pick her up and deliver her."

"What's her name?" Motty asked.

"Judi Antoine."

"Never heard of her," she said. "What movies has she been in?"

"She's never been in one yet," he replied. "But she's been under a starlet's contract for the last three months. She's the number one studio pinup photo."

"A hooker," Motty said flatly.

He laughed. "For once you're right. She's the worst." He knew the moment the words passed his lips he should have kept his mouth shut.

"Did A. J. give you the job because of your experience as a pimp or a writer?" she asked cynically.

"Hey, that's not fair," he protested.

"You could have turned him down," she said. "We don't need the job that bad. You can always work on your book."

"That will take a lot of time," he said. "Maybe more than a year. We don't have that much money to carry us."

"We could manage," she said. "Mr. Marks offered me the promotion. I'd get eight-fifty a month and with bonuses it can amount to fifteen hundred to two thousand."

"There has to be a kicker in it for that kind of money," he said.

"Of course, I'll have to go on a couple of buying trips during the fashion seasons."

"Where to?" he asked.

"New York. Maybe Paris," she answered.

"Alone?" he asked skeptically. "Without him?"

"You have a dirty mind," she snapped.

"How do you know that he doesn't?" he replied. He took the money from the dresser and put it in his pocket, then turned back to her. "If I have to pimp for a living, I'd rather pimp for strangers than my own wife."

He sat at the bar in the dimly lit cocktail lounge outside the entrance to the Coconut Grove. The faint music of the big band echoed from the show room. The bartender walked toward him as he nursed his second drink. "The show's goin' on in a few minutes downstairs," he said. "Want me to get a table for you?"

"No, thanks," Joe answered.

The bartender gestured to the drink. "Fill it up?"

Joe shook his head. "Two's my limit." He picked up a cigarette.

The bartender flashed his lighter. In its flickering flame, Joe saw the time on his watch. Ten minutes to eleven. The bartender noticed the glance. "Your date running late?"

"No." Joe smiled. "I came early."

The bartender gestured toward a table at the end of the lounge. "If she doesn't show up," he said, "there's two pretty ladies over there. I can introduce you."

Joe laughed. "You're okay," he said, placing a five-dollar bill on the counter for him.

The money disappeared. "Just tryin' to help, sir." The telephone rang on the back bar. The bartender picked it up. "Mr. Crown?" he asked, looking at Joe. Joe nodded. The bartender shook his head and put down the phone. "Your date said she will meet you in the lobby."

He made it to the hotel lobby just as she came from the elevator. "Okay?" he asked.

"Okay," she said. Silently they went outside and waited for the parking attendant to bring his car.

He gave the attendant a dollar bill and moved the car out

of the driveway into the street. "Take you home?" he asked, glancing at her.

"Mind dropping me at Dave's Blue Room?" she replied.

"Whatever you say," he answered.

Judi looked at him. "Is that guy for real?"

Joe stopped the car for a traffic light. "Mr. Metaxa?"

"Yeah," she said. "He really owns all those banks?"

"I don't know," Joe answered, starting the car again. "All I know is A. J. said the loan agreements for two million dollars will be signed in the morning."

"He said that he was putting up the money for my picture and that I'd get a new contract starting at five hundred a week instead of the hundred twenty-five I was getting. He also wants to set me up in a new apartment so that I'll be available when he comes out here every other week."

Joe glanced at her. "You must have given him the greatest fuck of all time."

"That's what I don't understand," she said puzzled. "We didn't do anything."

"Nothing?" Joe was surprised.

"Not even cop his joint," she said. "I stood there naked in front of him and he just kept talking to me as if my dress was still on. I don't think he even noticed when I put it on again."

"I don't understand it," Joe said.

She looked out the car window for a moment then back at Joe. "Do you know Mickey Cohen?"

"The gangster?"

"Who else?" she answered.

"Only from the papers," he said.

"Would you like to meet him?"

He looked at her. "Tonight?"

"Yes. That's who I'm meeting."

"I'd like to meet him," he said. "But I have to get home. My wife is pissed off enough over tonight."

"I bet Mickey will know something about Mr. Metaxa," she said thoughtfully.

A light dawned in Joe's head. "You know Mickey a long time?"

"Long enough," she said. "He was the guy who told me when I was in New York to go to Hollywood. That I had everything I needed to become a movie star."

Joe stopped the car again for a traffic light and stared at her. "Is it Mickey who staked you out here?"

She nodded. "We've been real good friends."

He had to force his attention on the traffic. It was for real. That was exactly the story that A. J. had told him. He pulled the car in front of Dave's Blue Room. For a moment he was tempted to go in with her, then changed his mind. This wasn't the time. He had to have a little more information about the banker.

The doorman opened the door to let her out. She turned to Joe. "Thank you," she said politely.

"My pleasure," he said, equally polite. "Call me at the studio tomorrow. And tell Mr. Cohen that I'd like to meet him at his own convenience whenever he wants."

He watched her walk into the entrance of the restaurant, then he moved the car into traffic and started for home.

=18=

"A GREAT SCRIPT," A. J. said into the telephone. "But we have problems."

"I don't understand," Joe replied.

"Did you ever see any of her tests?" A. J. asked.

"No," Joe answered. "Nobody ever asked me."

"Meet me in projection room B," A. J. said. "You'll see what I mean."

Joe looked down at his desk at the white bound script. He had felt good about it until just this minute. In three months he had come up with a treatment that worked and a completed script that he knew was good, maybe the best script he had ever written. For a moment he thought of bringing the script to the projection room but it would mean nothing. He left it on the desk as he walked over to the projection room.

A. J. wasn't alone. Mr. Metaxa, the banker, Ray Stern, the director, and another man Joe didn't know were there. A. J. nodded to him. "You know Mr. Metaxa and Ray. Say hello to Mickey Cohen."

Joe looked at the small heavyset man. He held out his hand. "Happy to meet you, Mr. Cohen."

The little man smiled as they shook hands. "Good to

meet you finally, Joe," he said, in a deep voice. "I have heard about you many times. Good things."

"Thank you, Mr. Cohen," Joe said.

"Call me Mickey," Cohen said.

A. J. gestured and Joe slipped into a seat as the room lights were turned down. For the next fifteen minutes they watched Judi's tests. One of them was even in color. She sang, she danced, she read lines—all badly. Only the color test was good. She was wearing a one-piece bathing suit and running on a beach. She ran toward the camera, then into the surf. She turned from the water back to the camera. The camera showed every secret of her body, the jutting nipples of her firm breasts, even the curly pubic hair straggling out of the silken swim suit. It was not a sound test and it finished on a closeup of her face. She was breathing heavily after running. The expression of her face gave the impression that she was having an orgasm. Then the screen went black and the room lights were turned up.

Joe kept silent. So did the others. They all waited for A. J.'s comment.

Finally, A. J. sighed audibly. "We fucked ourselves."

"Maybe she needs more coaching," Mr. Metaxa said.

"We've given her three months with the best teachers," A. J. said. "They've all quit her. Now we're really fucked. I signed Steve Cochran for fifteen grand as the lead and I borrowed Pat O'Brien from Warner for ten grand for the second lead. And did you see her pussy pushing out of her bathing suit? It looked bigger than a ballet dancer's cock and balls in tights. If we don't wrap her in a short skirt, we'll never get her past the Hays office."

"How much are we into, A. J.?" Metaxa asked.

"I made a Cinecolor commitment for this picture for seventy- five thousand dollars because that was half the cost of Technicolor. With that and all the other commitments, almost two hundred thousand." A. J. didn't sound happy.

"If she had an accident," Cohen suggested, "would the insurance companies cover it?"

"Not unless we were in production," A. J. answered. "Besides, we can't take chances like that."

"It was just an idea," Cohen said.

"It's too bad," Ray Stern said. "Joe wrote one of the most literate scripts I have ever read. I was looking forward to doing it. Maybe we can borrow Maria Montez or Yvonne De Carlo from Universal for it?"

"That's not the idea," A. J. answered. "We're committed to the advance sales on a Judi Antoine picture."

Joe looked at him. "We never sold them a story?"

"Never," A. J. said. "We sold them on her pinup pictures."

"Sheena, Queen of the Jungle," Joe said.

"Are you crazy?" A. J. stared at him. "You know Monogram owns that."

"Warrior Queen of the Amazons," Joe said. "Steve and Pat are pilots of a cargo plane that crashes in the jungle and get discovered by a lost tribe of Amazons. We've made that picture a thousand times and it always works. All we need is a screenful of half-naked girls, and Judi is the queen of all of them. She doesn't even have to speak a full line of dialogue. She's like a female Tarzan. You Steve, me Judi, we fuck."

A. J. stared at him, then at the others. "It just might work," he said. "How long would it take you to do a script?"

"Ten days, two weeks, if you want."

A. J. looked at the banker. "What do you think?"

"I know nothing about pictures," Metaxa said. "But I don't like losing money without a shot."

"I'm with him," Cohen said. "Let's take a shot at it."

A. J. turned to Joe. "Start writing."

"This is a new job," Joe said. "What kind of money are we talking about?"

A. J. stared at him. "How can you think about money at a time like this?"

Joe remained silent. He was not really looking for more money. What he was trying to do was collect the balance due for the present script. He had turned in the first draft; now he was at cutoff time. If he didn't rewrite and polish, the last five thousand dollars of the contract didn't have to be paid.

A. J. knew that as well as he did. "You write the new script and I'll pay off the contract and give you an extra thousand when the picture goes on the floor."

"Okay," Joe said. He looked around the room. "If you gentlemen would excuse me, I'll get right back to work."

He made notes on a lined yellow writing pad for almost an hour. He looked at them, satisfied. He had the basic story line scratched out. He reached for the phone and called the steno pool.

Shirley answered. "Yes, Joe?"

"I need some help, Shirley," he said.

"That's what I'm here for," she replied.

"Can you get me a few scripts of the tits and sand pictures that Universal and Columbia make? I have to study them for style."

"I know what you mean," she said. "Tomorrow morning be soon enough?"

"Great," he said.

Her voice lowered confidentially. The grapevine had already been working. "She tested bad?"

"Worse than that," he answered.

"I'm sorry," she said. "I liked that script you wrote."

"Thank you," he said.

"Hold on a minute," she said, putting him on hold.

She came right back on the line. "A Mr. Cohen is here. He would like to see you in your office."

"Bring him in," he said, putting the phone down and getting up. By that time Shirley had opened the door. Mickey had to step out of the way so that she could close the door behind him. Joe gestured to the chair in front of the desk.

Mickey sat down, glancing around the small room. "They call this an office?" he said. "It's more like a closet."

Joe laughed. "I'm a closet writer."

Mickey smiled. "I guess you wonder what I'm doing here?"

"It's none of my business," Joe said. "You don't have to explain anything."

"I know your father," Mickey said. "We were good friends in the old days in Brooklyn."

"My father's okay," Joe said.

"He still has the chicken market?"

Joe nodded. "The same place."

Mickey smiled again. "Give him my regards."

"I'll do that," Joe answered.

Mickey looked at him. "It's not on the record," he said, "but I'm here as Judi's manager."

"Good enough," Joe said.

"What do you think?" Mickey asked. "Do you think we can pull it off?"

"I'll have the script," Joe answered. "The rest depends on A. J."

"He's already cutting corners," Cohen said. "He got out of the O'Brien agreement with Warner Brothers."

160

"O'Brien wouldn't make this sort of a movie anyway," Joe said.

"The director bowed out too," Mickey said. "He's not doing that kind of movie anymore."

"There's plenty of directors," Joe said. "That will not create any problem."

"A. J.'s cutting the shooting schedule to twelve days instead of thirty."

"That's about right," Joe said. "The movie shouldn't take more than that."

"Metaxa's worried," Mickey said.

"I can believe that," Joe said. "It's his money and his girl."

"Wrong," Mickey said. "Not his money, not his girl."

Joe looked at him silently.

"You know about the Judge in New York?"

Joe nodded. The Judge was the unofficial arbitrator between all the Mafia families.

"Metaxa is fronting for him. The reason they loaned the studio the money is because that's good business for them. It's legitimate. Clean. I had to get Judi out here because the Judge's wife was getting pissed off."

Joe looked at him. "Does Judi know about that?"

"She knows," Mickey said. "But she doesn't give a shit. The only one she cares about is herself."

Joe was silent for a moment. "You can depend on me," he said. "I'll do the best I can."

Mickey got out of the chair. "You make this work and you have a big marker from us." He reached for the door. "You keep me informed. Leave a message for me at Dave's Blue Room. Any time, night or day. I'll get back to you."

"Okay," Joe said. Mickey nodded and left the small office. Joe took a deep breath. Nothing really changes. There's

always somebody on top somewhere. He looked down at
his scratch pad and wondered if A. J. really thought he was
the boss of his own studio.

It was almost eight o'clock by the time he got home. He
started up the steps to the bedroom and Rosa called him
from the kitchen. "A half-hour for dinner, okay?"

"Okay," he said and walked up the stairs to the bedroom.
Motty was just coming from the bathroom as she slipped
on a robe. She looked up at him as he bent to kiss her cheek.

"You look tired," she said.

"I am tired," he said.

"You need some food," she said. "I'm having Rosa make
veal cutlets."

"Fine," he said unenthusiastically.

She glanced at him. "What's wrong?"

"The picture got fucked."

"It's all off?" she asked. "You're not doing the rewrite?"

"It's off but it's not off," he said. He saw her puzzled
look and explained. "Judi's tests were garbage. She can't
do anything but look good. No acting, no dancing, no sing-
ing—just stand there. A. J. is tearing the rest of his hair
out. He said he was out two hundred grand already. There's
no way he can make this script."

"I still don't understand," she said. "What is he going
to do then?"

"I had an idea," he said. "I remembered one of those
stories at *Spicy Adventure* magazine. You know, 'The Warrior Queen of the Amazons.'"

"You told them about the magazine?"

"No, of course not," he said. "I'm not that stupid. I told
them as if it was just a new idea that had come to me. And
they bought it."

"I can't believe it," she said.

The humor of it finally came to him. He laughed. "I couldn't either. But they bought it, and I have to write it in two weeks."

"Then you're still on the payroll?"

He nodded. "Not only that, but I'm getting another grand when it begins shooting." He took off his jacket and threw it on the bed. "I'll wash up and we can have dinner."

She followed him into the bathroom. "Have you read about the new look in ladies' fashions? It started in Paris. The first important collection since before the war."

"I don't know anything about it," he answered. He turned the hot-water tap and waited for the water to heat up. "What about it?"

"Mr. Marks wants us to be the first store in L.A. to have it. Our dress houses on Seventh Avenue told us they will have the knock-offs by next week. He asked if I would go to New York to decide what would work for us."

He looked down and washed his hands without facing her. "Are you going?"

"It's part of my job," she said.

He was silent as he rinsed the soap from his hands and picked up a towel.

"I spoke to your mother," she said. "She said I could stay with them and bring Caroline."

Joe looked at her. "That's a switch." His mother had never spoken to them until the baby was born—and even then, not until they mailed a copy of their wedding certificate to verify that everything was kosher. But she was still cool to him. Fortunately, she no longer felt that way about Motty. After all, the whole thing wasn't Motty's fault—he had taken advantage of an innocent girl. "Did she ask anything about me?" he asked.

"She complained that you never call her."

"I finally gave up," he said. "She always passed the phone to my father or hung up on me. How long will you be gone?"

"About twelve days," she answered. "If I leave on Friday we'll be in New York Sunday night. That leaves the whole week to work and we'd start back home at the end of the next weekend. Mr. Marks is being very nice about it. He told me that if I took Caroline he would pay for a sleeperette for us."

"Is he leaving with you?"

She looked at him. "He's leaving before me on Wednesday. His wife is going with him."

Joe nodded. "I guess it's all right."

Motty smiled. "It will be nice, too, that your mother and Father will finally see their only grandchild." She breathed a faint sigh of relief as she went downstairs to the kitchen before him. She never told him that Mrs. Marks was leaving for Los Angeles on the Sunday that she and the child would be arriving. She also hadn't told him that Mr. Marks had reserved a room in the Pennsylvania Hotel on 34th Street for her just in case she might have to work too late to go home to Brooklyn.

=19=

NOTHING SUCCEEDS LIKE success. It was almost five months after he had finished the script of *Warrior Queen of the Amazons* that he received a telephone call from A. J.'s office as he sat at his typewriter working on the novel.

"A. J. would like to invite you and your wife to a buffet dinner at his house Friday night. Cocktails at seven, dinner will be at eight," Kathy said.

He was surprised. This was the first time he had ever been invited. "How come A. J. asked me?"

"Don't you read the trades?" she asked. "You have a hit movie. We had a PR junket with Judi to Texas and Florida. Between the Interstate and the Wometco circuits, the picture grossed six hundred thousand dollars."

"I don't believe it," he said. "The reviews murdered it."

"But the public bought it," she said. "It looks to be a blockbuster, naturally. That's what counts. The exhibitors are already calling for another picture with her. I have a feeling that's why A. J. called you."

"I'll show up," he said. "But Motty is in New York. She has to go there every three months on buying trips for the store."

"I've been to the store. They've really changed it. Is it doing well?"

"I guess so," he answered. "She's been promoted to head buyer for the whole chain."

"And what have you been doing?"

"I've already finished my novel," he replied. "I've edited about a hundred and forty pages based on Laura's suggestions, but it's hard work. Harder than a screenplay."

"Laura told me it's turning out to be one of the best novels she's ever read."

"She's prejudiced," he said. "But it's the screenplays that pay the rent. Though up to now I haven't received any offers for anything. It seems the minute I wrote *Warrior Queen* all the producers that used to talk to me, stopped returning my calls. I guess they all thought it was such a piece of shit they didn't want any part of me."

"They'll be back," Kathy said confidently. "I know this town. They don't read scripts, they read grosses."

He had an idea. "Why don't you come to the party with me?"

"Sorry," she said. "First, I moved in with my boyfriend. Second, A. J. doesn't like the cheap help at his parties."

"He's a cheap prick," he said.

"That's Hollywood," she said laughing. "Why don't you ask Laura? She's never been to a Hollywood party."

"How can I ask her?" he asked. "She's in New York."

"Didn't she call you?" Kathy seemed surprised.

"No," he said. "The last time I spoke to her was a month ago when she sent me her editing suggestions."

"She's right here," Kathy said. "Came in last night. I was sure she'd call you. She's at the Bel Air Hotel, room one twenty-one."

"I'll call her," he said. "Thanks, Kathy."

"Just one thing, Joe," she said. "Don't let Laura know that I told you she was here."

"I don't get it," he said.

"My sister is still pissed off at me because you and I went out a few times."

"Where did she pick that up?" he asked.

"This is Hollywood. Everybody talks here and she has a few friends."

"Okay, Kathy," he said. "I'll play it straight, and by the time I get finished with her, she won't believe anything they told her."

He was dialing Laura at the hotel when he realized after looking at his desk clock that it was almost five o'clock. He put down the receiver. If she was busy she would not return to the hotel until six-thirty or seven o'clock. That was the usual time that Easterners returned to their rooms.

He had an idea. She hadn't called him, so he would surprise her with a visit. Quickly he gathered together a carbon copy of the edited one hundred and forty pages and placed them in an envelope, then called the florist and ordered a dozen roses that he would pick up at six-thirty.

"Rosa!" he called from the balcony as he came out of his tiny study.

She came from the kitchen and looked up at him from the living room. *"Sí, señor?"*

"You have a white linen shirt ready for me?"

"I can iron it in a few minutes," she answered.

"I'm going into the shower," he said. "You bring it up for me."

"The *señor* is going out for dinner?" she asked.

"I'm not sure," he answered. "Probably." He turned into the bedroom and slipped off his working slacks and underwear and went into the bathroom.

* * *

It was five minutes to seven when he knocked on Laura's door, the dozen roses in one hand and a bottle of Dom Perignon in an ice bucket in the other.

Laura opened the door. He smiled. "Welcome to Los Angeles!"

She stared at him in surprise. "How wonderful," she said, taking the flowers.

"I have a bottle of Dom Perignon here also," he said.

"That's too much." She smiled. "Come in."

He followed her into the tastefully decorated room. "You can't imagine how surprised I was when I heard you were in town."

"My sister told you?" she asked.

"No," he said. "I haven't spoken to her since I went off the picture. That was four months ago."

"But somebody had to tell you," she said.

"The trade papers," he said. "They have a daily list of comings and goings from the industry."

"You look good," she said. "Very California-ish."

He laughed. "You look pretty good yourself."

She shook her head. "In this old terry-cloth robe?"

"No complaints from me," he said. "You always look good to me."

"Give me five minutes to get into something more suitable," she said. "Meanwhile you can open the wine."

"I also brought almost a hundred and forty edited manuscript pages," he said.

"That's great," she said.

"What brought you out here?"

"I had to bring a set of contracts to a client," she said. "Now give me a moment or I'll never get ready."

She went into the bathroom and closed the door behind

her. A moment later he heard the shower splashing, and he began opening the bottle of champagne. There were two champagne glasses packed in the ice bucket with the wine. He left the bottle open but didn't fill the glasses. There was a radio in the corner of the room. He turned it to his favorite station that played all the pop singers—Sinatra, Crosby, and others—then sat down on the two-seater couch.

In about fifteen minutes she came in from the bathroom, completely made up and dressed. She wore a blue silk shantung dress that clung to her figure.

He looked up at her. "You're already dressed, you must keep everything in the bathroom."

"I'm efficient." She smiled.

He poured the champagne. "Good luck."

She nodded. "Good luck." She sipped the champagne. "This is delicious."

"It's good," he agreed. "Now what would you like for dinner?"

She stared at him. "I have a date with our client and his attorney."

"Put them off until tomorrow," he said.

"I can't do that," she said. "The agency arranged it all before I got here."

"Then we'll make it tomorrow?" he said.

"I'm flying back tomorrow at seven o'clock in the morning."

"What about a late dinner, then?" he asked, refilling the champagne glasses.

"We're going to the client's house to go over the contract in detail," she answered. "I don't know what time we'll get finished."

He looked at her. "Do you have to return to New York? I've been invited to a cocktail party at A. J.'s. house. It might be fun and you would meet some important people, directors and producers."

She shook her head. "I'd like to. I've never been to a Hollywood party. But my orders from the agency are explicit. I have to go back."

"Shit," he said. "We won't even have time to discuss the pages I've rewritten."

"I'll read it on the plane and talk to you the day after," she said. She looked at him. "I'm sure you can turn up another date. From what I hear you do pretty good in the lady department."

"I want you," he said. "Not anyone else."

"I'm running late," she said. "My client will pick me up in the lobby at eight o'clock."

He rose to his feet and met her eyes. "What do I have to do to get a date with you?" he asked. "Wait until our novel is sold?"

"I think you'd better go," she said coldly.

Quickly, he put his arms around her and kissed her as he pressed his already turgid phallus against her groin. He saw her face turn white, then flush pink, as she pushed him away.

He walked to the door and turned to her as he opened it. "Just for your information—I never fucked your sister. It was always you I wanted."

He slammed the door behind him and walked down the corridor to the parking lot.

$=20=$

HE WAS STILL angry when he walked into his own apartment and up the staircase to the balcony, then to his bedroom. Quickly he took off his jacket, then his tie and shirt. "Bitch!" he said, half-aloud. "Cock-teasing cold-assed bitch!"

The telephone rang. Laura's voice echoed in his ear. "Joe," she said. "I don't want you to be angry with me."

"How do you expect me to feel when you send me away with my cock in my hand?" he snapped.

"You don't have to speak like that," she said. "You know better. I promised nothing."

"And that's what you gave me," he answered.

"Don't be a fool," she said. "First of all, you're a married man with a child. Second, we have a business relationship, and if my office ever even thought we had a personal one, they would fire me and that would be the end of our opportunities."

He thought for a moment. "Maybe you're right, but it's still shitty."

"You calm down," she said. "I'll read the new pages and telephone the day after tomorrow."

"Okay," he said. "I guess I have no choice. This is the way we have to play it."

"That makes more sense," she said. "I have to go now. Goodbye."

"Have a good flight back," he said. "'Bye now."

He stared down at the telephone. Even the sound of her voice had turned him on. Damn! he thought to himself, then walked out on the balcony. "Rosa!" he called.

"Sí, señor," she answered from the living room.

"Can I have some coffee?"

"Sí, señor."

He watched her walking to the kitchen. She still wore the thin cotton dress; underneath he could see the black brassiere and panties showing through. He wondered if she knew how whorish she looked as she moved.

He went through the bedroom to the bathroom. He flipped up the toilet seat and opened his fly. He didn't realize he still had a half-hard until he had finished and turned back toward the bedroom. She had been standing next to the bed, the coffee tray in her hands, watching him. He felt his penis growing in his hand and made no motion to conceal himself.

"Next to the bed?" she asked.

"You can leave it there," he said, still standing in the bathroom.

"Sí, señor." She placed the cup of coffee on the end table next to the bed. "Anything else, señor?"

"Nothing."

"Do you want to whip me, señor?" she asked, staring at him.

"Why should I want to whip you?" he asked.

"Sometimes my papa wants to do that to me when he is hard like that," she said.

"I'm not your papa," he said.

"But you are a man," she said. "You have four nights without the señora. It must be mucho difficult for you, *señor.* My papa comes many times when he whips me, then he feels better."

He felt his penis soften. His excitement had gone. "I'm sorry, Rosa," he said wearily. "Go away." He waited until she had gone before he stretched out on the bed.

He stared up at the ceiling. He was angry with himself. He hadn't thought about it until Kathy had called him about A. J.'s party. It had been almost four months since anyone in the business had called him. If it hadn't been for Motty's promotion they would have been dipping into his savings account just for living expenses. She had been doing well. Now she was up to twenty-four thousand a year. That was more than he had made in his best year.

He sat up and drank his coffee. This was the third trip she had made to New York. The first trip she had taken the kid with her and they stayed at his parents' house; the last two trips, she had stayed at the Pennsylvania Hotel. It was right in the garment district, she had explained. But that wasn't the only thing. Motty had changed—she was no longer that shopgirl he remembered. There was an air of decision about her. Her makeup, clearly professionally arranged, as was her coiffure, and her clothing bespoke the latest fashions. But the real change was in her eyes. Before, they were young and open, now she seemed secretive and guarded, as if she lived in a world he could not penetrate.

He wondered if she was fucking her boss, Mr. Marks. He was being stupid. Of course she was. No way would any girl, no matter how great she was at her job, get the money and promotions otherwise. Even her style of fucking had changed, more sophisticated and reserved than before. Before, she could never stop coming—now one orgasm and she stopped. Then she couldn't wait until she ran to the bathroom to douche and wash away the errant sperm that accidentally might have found its way home inside her. He really had been stupid. The cocksman had been cuckolded by a worm with a gold-plated prick. He slammed his coffee cup down on the plate and the coffee slopped onto the table. "Rosa!" he called.

She appeared immediately in the doorway, her eyes frightened. *"Sí, señor."*

He pointed to the spilled coffee. "Clean it up."

She nodded and was back in a moment with a washrag. She knelt beside him and began wiping away the coffee. Still on her knees, she turned her face up to him. "No problems," she said.

He pulled out the belt of his pants and let them fall down his legs to the floor. "You'll have to wash them. There's coffee stains on them."

She stared silently up at his genitals.

"What are you staring at?" he snapped angrily. "You want to touch it, don't you?"

Still on her knees, she remained silent.

Angrily he slapped her face. "God damn it! You wanted to touch it!"

Almost reverently, she let her fingers touch his testicles. *"Muy grandes cojones,"* she whispered. Then she clasped her hand around his penis.

He lifted her to her feet. "Not like this," he said harshly. "Undress!"

Silently, not looking at him, she took off her dress, unfastened her black cotton brassiere, and together with her panties let them drop to the floor. She clasped her hands, shielding her pubis. "No fuck," she whispered. "I am virgin."

"Ah, shit!" he said, his anger dissipating. "Get dressed."

He walked past her to the bathroom. "I'm going to take a shower and go out for a while."

"Fully let out ranch mink jackets for two hundred dollars," Mr. Samuel said. "Real dark ranch, the most popular."

"Where's the bargain? Our stores are in Los Angeles, not New York." Motty said.

"With mink jackets completely lined like this," he said, "you can put them on special sale for four hundred ninety-five dollars and they'll go like hotcakes."

"The price is right, Mrs. Crown," Marks said.

Motty looked at him. "Just remember, Mr. Marks, our fur salons always have been losers. And ground-floor space is too expensive to warrant losers."

"That's because your salespeople are not furriers," Samuel retorted. "A good furrier would make a fortune there."

"I won't argue with you, Mr. Samuel," Motty said. "But we have to work with the people we have. Maybe you have a better idea."

"If you want to keep upgrading your stores," Samuel said, "you have to have a prestigious fur salon."

Motty glanced at Marks, then at the furrier. "What if we gave you the concession? You tell us that you can do better than we do, and I believe you."

"I don't know," Samuel answered carefully. "We're spread a little thin just now. We've already got concessions at Hudson's in Detroit. It comes down to how much money you're talking about?"

"I haven't thought about it," Motty said. She turned to Marks. "What do you think, Mr. Marks?"

"I haven't thought about it either," he said. "How much does the ground-floor space cost us?"

"About ninety thousand in the Beverly Hills store," she answered.

"And the other four stores?"

"About fifteen thousand each. Beverly Hills makes up fifty percent of all our fur sales," she replied.

"It's too expensive," Samuel said quickly. "I'd have to stock a quarter of a million dollars' worth of goods just to build a volume so we could break even."

"We're damned if we do," Marks said. "And we're damned if we don't."

Samuel stared at him. "Are you serious about this?"

Marks nodded. "We're serious."

Samuel nodded. "Okay, then. I'll make you a fair offer. I'll give you fifty thousand for the concessions and twenty percent of the gross sales if you co-op the advertising and carry all the credit sales. If I'm right, we'll all make a lot of money."

"And if you're wrong?" Marks asked.

"We lose a little," Samuel answered. "But you said you always lose anyway."

Marks turned to Motty. "What do you think?"

Motty looked at Samuel. "I have faith in Mr. Samuel. He knows what he's doing."

"Thank you, Mrs. Crown," Samuel said. He turned to Marks. "What do you say, Gerald?"

"We'll do it," he said, holding out his hand.

Samuel shook his hand. "I'll come out there the week after next and we'll begin to make a few changes in the salon." He smiled. "I can see it in the ads now. 'Paul, the Furrier of Beverly Hills.'"

"Not Paul," Motty said.

"Why not?" Samuel asked. "It works at Hudson's in Detroit."

"That's Detroit," Motty replied. "This is Beverly Hills. They need something more impressive."

Samuel stared at her. "You want Revillon, maybe?"

"No," she laughed. "Just call it Paolo of Beverly Hills. The ultimate in furs. Los Angeles is a hick town. They're always impressed with foreign names."

"Paolo of Beverly Hills," Samuel repeated smiling. "The ultimate in furs. I like it. Let's have a drink to it."

It took almost an hour before they closed the door behind Samuel. Motty leaned back on the couch as Marks turned to her. "I'm exhausted," she said. "I thought he would never stop talking."

He looked at his watch. "It's nearly seven," he said. "Why don't you take a relaxing bath and then get dressed, and we'll go out for dinner?"

"Do we have to go out?" she asked.

"No," he answered. "We can have dinner in the suite."

"I'd like that," she said. "I'm a a little tired of having to go out for dinner with people."

"We'll have dinner here, just the two of us." He bent down and kissed her. "I've been wanting to do that all afternoon," he said.

"I did too," she said, putting her arms around him. She kissed him again. "Happy?" she asked.

"Very," he answered. "We're a good team. I think we have a good deal with Samuel."

"Yes," she said. "I only wish that all our problems could be solved as easily."

He smiled, looking at her. "One of them is solved," he said.

She looked at him questioningly.

"I'm a free man," he said. "My lawyer called me. My

wife has completed her six weeks in Reno, the divorce has gone through, and now she's my ex-wife."

She stared at him silently.

"You don't seem happy about it," he said.

"I am happy," she said. "But I'm also a little frightened."

"You'll have to tell him sooner or later," he said.

"I know," she said. "But he's been going through such a bad time right now. I just wish he had something to do."

"There'll always be a problem," he said. "From what you tell me, he has enough girls to console him. And since you're not asking for any alimony, child support or community property, he'll recover."

She was silent.

"The divorce should be easy," he said. "You could do it in Tijuana in one day if he'll sign the papers."

She remained silent.

He looked into her eyes. "That is, unless you don't want to marry me?"

She pulled him close to her and slipped her hand over his crotch. She felt his penis growing in her fingers. "Of course, I want to marry you," she whispered.

=21=

HIS PRE-WAR Chrysler Airflow seemed out of place among Rollses, Cadillacs and Continentals parked on the street in front of A. J.'s house at the corner of Rodeo and Lomitas in Beverly Hills. The red-jacketed parking attendant gave him a ticket and drove the car away. Joe stood there for a moment before walking to the entrance of the house. He saw the car being driven far down the street, away from the more important cars in front of the house. He smiled to himself. Even automobiles were victims of the caste system.

A Chinese butler in a tuxedo opened the door for him. "Your name, sir?"

"Joe Crown," he answered.

The butler glanced at a list in his hand, then nodded. He gestured toward the living room already crowded with guests.

Blanche Rosen, A. J.'s wife, stood next to the entrance of the living room. She was an attractive woman, looking much younger than her fortyish years. She smiled, holding out her hand. "Joe," she said in a warm voice. "I'm so happy that you could come."

He shook her hand. "Thank you for inviting me, Mrs. Rosen."

"Call me Blanche," she said. She gestured toward the

179

room. "I'm sure you know most of the people here. You just make yourself comfortable. The bar is set up at the far end."

"Thank you, Blanche," he said, but she had already turned away from him to greet the next guests. He moved toward the bar. He recognized many of the guests, but very few he really knew or had met. A black barman smiled at him. "Your pleasure, sir?"

"Scotch and water," Joe said. He took the drink and moved to the side of the room. A. J. was standing, a circle of people around him, with Judi, dressed in a black sheer see-through sequined dress, beside him. Everyone in the circle seemed to be talking at the same time.

A mild flurry of excitement came from the entrance to the living room and A. J. suddenly took Judi by the arm and half-pulled her with him toward it. Joe followed them with his eyes. He saw the woman's hat, and knew at once who she was: Hedda. Her hats were famous, her trademark. She was one of the two most important Hollywood columnists. Photographers suddenly appeared and flashbulbs popped. Even A. J. fawned over the columnist.

Ray Stern's voice growled low in Joe's ear. "I really fucked myself, didn't I?"

Joe turned to the director. "What makes you say that?"

"I could have made that picture and I blew it."

"It's not that important a picture."

Stern looked at him. "Any picture that will gross like that is important."

"I don't see what it's doing for me," Joe said. "I haven't gotten a job since."

"You'll get them now, you'll see," Stern said. "Why do you think A. J. invited you to this party? You're the writer of the biggest-grossing picture out of his studio this year."

Joe looked at him silently.

"He'll probably sign you up for a sequel before the party is over."

"He never even saw me," Joe said.

"Don't believe it," Stern said. "He sees everything."

Joe shrugged his shoulders. "I don't know." He looked at the director. "What are you working on now?" he asked.

"Nothing," Stern answered. "He let my option drop. I don't know why I've been invited. Probably I was left over on an old party list."

"Come on," Joe said. "It's not that bad."

"The hell with it," Stern said bitterly. "I'll just have another drink."

Joe watched the director move toward the bar. He heard a girl's voice behind him. "Are you Joe Crown?"

He turned. She was a tall girl with blue eyes and long auburn hair almost to her bare shoulders, wearing a soft, clinging blue silk dress. "Yes," he said.

She looked at him. "I'm Tammy Sheridan. Don't you recognize me?"

He felt as if he should apologize. "I'm sorry."

"I had the second lead in your movie," she said. "The girl that had the fight with Judi."

"Now I *am* sorry." He smiled. "I never saw the movie."

"Never?" she echoed disbelief. "Not even in a projection room?"

"No one ever invited me," he answered. "And I was off the lot by that time. I'll probably see it when it opens here in Los Angeles."

"But I heard that you were writing the sequel already," she said. "I thought that I could talk you into building up my part a little."

He laughed. "You can talk me into it. But first I have to get the job."

She laughed. He knew she didn't believe him. "Are you alone?" she asked.

"Yes."

"No date with you?"

"No date," he said.

"That's funny," she said. "I heard you were married and that you were balling Judi on the side."

"You hear a lot of stories," he said. "I am married. But my wife has gone to New York and I am not balling Judi on the side."

"I heard you got her the job."

"I didn't."

"Then how did she get the job?" she asked. "She can't act worth shit. On my worst days I can act like Garbo around her."

He gestured with his hand. "I don't know. I just wrote the script."

Tammy looked across the room at the photographers taking pictures of Judi and Steve Cochran, who had just come in. "She's a fucking whore!" she said jealously. She turned back to him. "Do you have a car?" she asked.

He nodded.

"I came by taxi," she said. "Maybe you can give me a lift home after the party?"

"Sure," he answered.

"You look for me," she said, starting to move away. "Meanwhile I'll try to con some of the photographers into taking a few pictures of me."

He watched her moving in like a bird dog, then turned to the bar and ordered another drink. It was growing warmer in the room and he moved closer to a window to get some cool air. Mr. Metaxa, the banker, came over to him. "Joe," he said jovially, "congratulations."

Joe smiled. "Thank you, Mr. Metaxa. But for what?"

"A good script. Now the movie will make a great deal of money. Maybe two million, distributors' gross. We are very pleased."

"I'm glad too," Joe said.

Metaxa took him by the arm. "Come," he said. "I have an Italian producer, a good friend of mine, who wants to meet you."

Joe followed him toward a tall, good-looking man with a distinguished head of white hair. Metaxa spoke quickly in Italian, then translated for Joe. "Joe Crown, the *scrittore*," he said. "The great Italian producer, Raffaelo Santini. Signor Santini has made the great success in Rome, *The One-Wheeled Motorcycle*."

Joe had heard about the picture. It was one of the early neorealistic films that had come out of Italy. The critics had loved it. It had almost won the Academy Award as the best foreign picture.

"It's an honor to meet you, Mr. Santini," Joe said.

"It's an honor and pleasure to meet you, Mr. Crown," the Italian said, in Italian-accented English. "I liked your picture. It is most droll and shows that you have a good knowledge of what the movie audience wants to see. We need more knowledge such as that."

"Thank you, Mr. Santini," Joe said.

Mr. Santini nodded seriously. "Maybe someday you will come to Italy with me and we could make a picture together."

"I would like that," Joe said.

A. J. spoke from behind him. "What are you wops plotting behind my back with my number one writer? Trying

183

to steal him away from me?" The smile on his face belied his words.

"Of course not," Metaxa said quickly. "Mr. Santini was only complimenting Joe's work."

"I have a three-picture contract with him," A. J. said.

Joe stared at him. This was the first he had heard of it. He remained silent.

"We have a meeting in the studio Monday morning to discuss the first script," A. J. said. He looked at Joe. "Isn't that right, Joe?"

"That's right, A. J.," Joe answered.

"And what is the title of the new film?" Santini asked.

A. J. stared at him, then turned to Joe. "You can tell him, Joe."

Without hesitation Joe answered the Italian. "*The Return of the Warrior Queen*."

"Of course," Mr. Santini said sagely. "How simple, how clever. Already the title is presold."

"Don't forget. Nine o'clock on Monday morning," A. J. said, moving away and smiling.

The two Italians eyed him. Santini muttered something in Italian to Metaxa in a low voice, then turned again to Joe. "You make a remember what I say, Mr. Crown," he said. "Someday we will make a picture together in Rome."

Out of the corner of his eye, Joe saw Tammy coming toward him. "Joe!" she called out as if they were old friends. "You must introduce me to Mr. Santini. He's my most, most favorite filmmaker."

"Mr. Santini," Joe said. "Miss Tammy Sheridan."

"I loved your film," Tammy gushed. "I voted for your picture in the Academy Awards. I felt so badly when you didn't get it."

"Thank you, Miss Tammy," the Italian said politely.

"They're announcing dinner," she said. "May I sit with you? I have many questions to ask you about your wonderful movie."

"I am sorry," Mr. Santini said apologetically, "but I am not staying for dinner. I have a previous engagement at Chasen's."

"I'm sorry too, Mr. Santini," Tammy said sincerely.

The Italian took her hand and kissed it, bowing. *"Ciao,"* he said.

Tammy sighed as she looked after him. "What fucking manners that man has," she whispered. "When he pressed his lips to my hand I could almost feel his tongue tickling my pussy."

"Shit," Joe said. "I can do that."

Tammy looked at him. "Kiss my hand like that?"

"No." Joe smiled. "Tickle your pussy with my tongue."

== 22 ==

HOLLYWOOD PARTIES FINISHED early. The usual excuse was because everyone had to be in the studio at seven o'clock in the morning. Performers usually left even earlier because they had to be in makeup between five-thirty and six. It was eleven when Tammy got into his car beside him. He gave the parking attendant a dollar bill and moved out of the driveway. "Where do you live?" he asked, looking across at her.

"In the Valley," she said. She seemed slightly defiant.

"Okay," he said easily. "Just tell me how to get there."

"Go over Laurel Canyon. I'm two blocks this side of Ventura."

"You've got it," he said, turning onto Sunset.

"It gets so cold at night," she said. "I'm shivering. Could you turn on the heater?"

Silently, he switched it on. Warm air began circulating through the vents.

"That's better," she said, turning to him. "Are you going to do the movie?"

He shrugged. "A. J. wants to see me Monday."

"You're going to do it," she said with conviction.

"We'll see," he said. "I don't know. He hasn't spoken about money yet."

"He'll take care of it," she said. "That picture is money in the bank."

He smiled at her. "You sound more like an agent than an actress."

She laughed. "I should," she answered. "I've been around this town a long time."

"You're not that old," he said.

"Twenty-six," she answered. "I've been here since I was sixteen."

"You don't look it."

"Makeup," she said, half seriously. "You can guarantee that job for yourself," she added.

"Why do you say that?"

"Mrs. Rosen, A. J.'s wife. She's got eyes for you."

"I didn't notice that," he said. "She barely spoke to me."

"But I saw her watching you. A lot." She waited until the car turned off Sunset onto Laurel Canyon. "Did you know that she used to be his story editor before they were married?"

"No."

"She still reads all the scripts. A. J. never reads. And she likes writers. Especially young ones."

"I don't see how that will guarantee me the job," he said.

"You send her flowers with a thank-you note," she said. "In a day or two she'll call you and invite you to lunch at their Malibu house during the week. That's the way she operates, everybody knows that."

He glanced at her. "You *have* been around."

She nodded. "But not that it does me any good," she

said half bitterly. "This is the third studio I've been contracted to but never gotten a lead part."

"They say the third time is lucky," he said.

"I hope so," she said, without conviction.

They remained silent until the road turned and the lights of Ventura Boulevard shone toward them. "Make a right at the third corner," she said. "Second house in."

He turned the car and stopped in front of her house. It was a small house but well kept. "Looks nice," he said.

She looked at him. "I'd invite you in," she said, "but I share the house with two other girls."

"That's okay," he said.

She placed her hand on his lap. "I can give you a little head here in the car," she said.

He smiled. "No. Thanks, anyway."

"I give great head," she said.

"I'm sure." He nodded. "But I can wait."

She leaned toward him and kissed his cheek. "Thanks for the lift," she said. "I'll give you a call at the studio."

"You do that." He smiled. "Good night."

He watched her run to the entrance door of her house then turned the car around and headed for home. He was in bed just after midnight.

"You've become an important man," Shirley said. "The word came down. We've moved you to a corner office."

"I just made the deal with A. J. twenty minutes ago," he said.

"He must have been sure of it." She smiled. "He gave me the order Friday." She picked up a set of keys from her desk. "Come, I'll show it to you."

He followed her to the end of the corridor. The door to his office was solid wood, not inset with a frosted pane of glass whose window would not allow genuine privacy. He opened the door and went in with her. The floor was covered with wall-to-wall carpeting and the walls were paneled wood. The couch and two easy chairs were old, but real leather, and the typewriter was on a separate table, not the desk.

"Like it?" she asked.

He nodded. "At least I feel I can breathe."

"Good," she said. "I've already set up writing paper, carbons, yellow pads and pencils. The telephone is connected directly to the switchboard, and you can make calls and receive calls without going through me. There's a switch next to the phone which you can turn on if you want me to answer when you go out or if you want to have the calls intercepted while you're busy working."

"Seems good," he said.

"How much time do you think the script will take?" she asked.

"Maybe a month for the first draft, another for the rewrite and polish. A. J. wants the picture on the floor in July."

"That doesn't give you much time."

"I'll manage," he said.

"I'll leave you to get settled," she said, turning to the door. "Call me if you need anything."

"Thank you, Shirley," he said.

"Good luck," she said, closing the door behind her. He walked behind the desk and sat down and looked around the office. It really was not bad. There were even several decent framed prints on the wall. He placed a package of cigarettes on the desk and lit one thoughtfully. Despite the better desk and office, A. J. was still a shit. Instead of the three scripts he had promised at the dinner party, he had contracted only this script guaranteed. He did go up to twenty thousand dollars, though. The other two scripts were on option agreements to be agreed on at a later time, after this script had been finished.

The ring of the telephone startled him. He glanced at his watch. It was only eleven in the morning. He picked it up. "Joe Crown."

It was a woman's voice. "Mr. Crown?"

"Yes," he answered guardedly.

"Blanche Rosen," the voice said into his ear. "Congratulations on your new office."

"Thank you, Mrs. Rosen," he said.

"I thought we agreed you would call me Blanche," she said lightly. "I called you to thank you for the lovely flowers. That was very kind of you."

"It was my pleasure," he said. "I really enjoyed the party, and thank you again for inviting me."

"I read many of your works," she said. "Including some of the short stories you've written. You're a very good writer, Joe. Much better, perhaps, than you realize."

"Thank you, Blanche."

"I know what I'm talking about," she said. "I used to be an editor at Doubleday in New York and then joined A. J. here in the studio as story editor and consultant before we were married. I still read all the scripts that he considers."

"I find that very interesting," he said.

"I know the idea that A. J. has proposed to you and I think I can offer some suggestions that would help you avoid several of the script problems you may encounter. Why don't we have lunch on Wednesday? I have a small house in Malibu, nothing fancy, but we could be alone there and talk."

"That's very kind," he said.

"Say twelve-thirty?" she asked.

"Twelve-thirty will be fine," he said. "I'll look forward to it."

He put down the telephone. Tammy had been right. She called all the shots.

Tammy's was the second telephone call he received. "Congratulations," she said. "I told you you had the job."

"You were right," he agreed.

"I'd like to come over," she said. "I have a welcome present for your new office. Is now convenient?"

"Come in," he said. "I haven't begun working yet."

"I'll be there in ten minutes," she said and hung up.

The telephone rang again. He picked it up. "You have a busy line," Kathy said.

"Beats me," he said. "I didn't even know that anybody knew I was here yet."

"You told A. J. that you never had seen the picture?"

"That's right," he answered.

"He told me that we're having a sneak at eight o'clock tonight at the Pacific Palisades Theater for the Coast Circuit. He thought you should catch it there. You'll get a better feel of it with an audience in a theater than in a projection room."

"Tell him I'll be there," he said.

A moment later the telephone rang again. This time it was Laura, from New York. "Congratulations," she

191

said. "I hear you're writing a sequel to the Amazon picture."

"News travels fast," he said. "It was just set this morning."

"The studio sent us a teletype with a contract for you. Did you agree to it?"

"Of course," he said. "Twenty grand is pretty good."

"What will that do to your novel?" she asked.

"Slow it up, but only for a month. This script is a piece of cake."

"I hope so," she said. "What you have now is very good, I wouldn't want you to lose your momentum."

"I'll be okay," he said. "I did another fifty pages since you left. I'll send them to you."

"Do that," she said. "I'll be anxious to read them. If it's as good as what I've read so far, you're halfway home."

"I'll do the book, don't worry about it," he said. "But right now twenty grand straightens me out real good."

Her voice softened. "Are you all right?" she said. "I heard you're having domestic problems."

"Where did you hear that?" he asked. "I haven't heard anything like that."

"Some people from the Coast told me that your wife spends a great deal of time away from home."

"That's the fucking rumor factory. That's her job. She's the head buyer and has to travel because of her work."

"Okay," she said. "As long as you're all right."

"Don't worry about me," he said.

"If there's any way I can ever help you, just call me. I'm on your side."

"Thank you," he said. After saying goodbye, he stared

at the telephone. People are shitty, all they want to do is make trouble. What business is it of theirs what anyone else does?

There was a knock at the door. "Come in," he called.

Tammy came in and closed the door behind her. She was wearing a tight-fitting cotton sweater and a short skirt. All he could see was tits, ass and long fine legs. She had it all together like a billboard above Sunset Strip. She glanced around the office. "This is as nice as some of the producers' offices I've seen."

"It's fine," he said.

She placed a small rectangular gift-wrapped box on the desk in front of him. "It's for you."

He opened it quickly, then began to laugh. It was a special dozen pack of lubricated Rameses. "I hope you got the right size," he said. "Usually they're too small."

"Showoff. One size fits all."

"I'll treasure these," he said. "But when are we going to get a chance to use them?"

She turned and locked the door of the office. "I thought it would be nice if I gave you your first fuck. Afterwards you can take me downstairs to lunch."

The first man he saw when he returned to the theater lobby after having seen the movie was Mickey Cohen. They nodded and shook hands. "I liked it," Mickey said.

Joe looked at him to see if he was serious, but he was straight. Joe remained silent.

"The audience loved it," Mickey said. "They were screaming all the time, especially the high school kids in the balcony. I bet it was a three-jerk-off-time movie for them. Judi came off like all pussy."

"I don't get it," Joe said.

"You don't have to," Mickey said. "Just do it again."

"I don't know if I can," Joe answered. "I don't know if I can ever write that badly again."

"For the twenty grand you're getting," Mickey said flatly, "you'll write shit and like it."

=23=

IT WAS ELEVEN o'clock in the morning, and Judi stormed into his office without knocking. "A. J. said you're giving me a lot more lines in the new movie," she said without even a greeting.

He looked across his desk up at her. "If A. J. said that, that's what you'll get."

"I'd like to see some of the pages," she snapped.

"Don't be a fucking star, Judi," he said. "I've only been working two days on the treatment. I haven't written any dialogue yet."

"I don't believe you," she said.

"Check with A. J.," he answered. "First I have to do the treatment, then the script. That's where the dialogue comes in."

"You're not going to fuck me," she said angrily. "A million-dollar gross tells me that I'm the star. I don't have to suck anybody for a fucking job now."

"That's right," he agreed.

"I've got a contract."

"So have I," he said.

"I can get you off the fucking picture!" she snapped.

"Okay," he said. "Get me off the picture. Then you'll have no movie to be a star in. I'll get paid either way."

She stared at him. "Is that true?"

"Screenwriter Guild rules," he answered.

Suddenly she calmed down. "Then how do I protect myself?"

"Why don't you wait until I finish the script? Then you can bitch all you want."

"You've been fucking Tammy and she's telling everybody that you're giving her more lines than me."

"Everybody believes that you fucked me to get the part in the first picture," he said. "This isn't a movie studio, this is a rumor factory."

She stared at him silently for a moment. "Then how come you never ask me out to dinner?"

He smiled. "I can't afford you. The last time I took you out it cost me two hundred bucks, and A. J. never reimbursed me."

"I'm out of that business now," she said. "You can take me out to dinner for free."

"Then I'll take you out," he said.

"How about Friday night?" she suggested. "Maybe Chasen's or Romanoff. Afterward we can go to the Mocambo."

He shook his head. "That's way out of my league, Judi. I don't make that kind of money. The Brown Derby is the most I can handle."

"Cheap," she sneered.

"I work for a living," he said. "I'm not on any expense account."

"What if I get Publicity to pay for it? They're always hustling me for pictures."

"Just get me the voucher and we'll party all night."

"I'll call you," she said, and she left as she had come in, without a greeting or a goodbye.

He pulled the string to ring the bell inside the door, which was set in a long closed slatted wood fence. Blanche's voice answered from behind it. "Who is it?"

"Joe Crown," he said. He glanced at the sun. It was blazing hot.

The door opened and she hid behind it as she let him in. She was wrapped in a large beach towel and every part of her was covered with suntan oil. "You're early, it's only twelve o'clock," she said. She didn't sound angry.

"I'm sorry," he said. "But I've never been out this way before and I didn't want to be late."

"That's all right," she said agreeably.

He followed her through the small garden off the road, then through the small house outside to an open wooden sun porch built over the beach. She turned to him. "Would you like to take a swim before lunch?"

"I don't think so," he answered.

"We have swim trunks, I'm sure that you can find your size."

He apologized. "I'm sorry. I never learned to swim."

She laughed. "At least you're honest. Most people find another way to get out of it." She glanced up at the sun. "But you should slip on a pair of trunks. The heat will cook you in all that clothing—even if you stayed in the shade."

He found an old straw hat to protect his head from the sun. The swim trunks were all small sizes. He found one that fit over his hips, but even then, his pubic hair could be seen over the top. He saw her looking at him and he knew that was the way she arranged it.

"I made vodka tonics," she said. "That all right?"

"Perfect," he said.

She sat down on a mattress on the wooden floor. She held a glass out to him. "Welcome to Malibu."

"Thank you," he said, sipping the drink. It was icy cold and good.

They clinked glasses, and at the same time her beach towel fell partly away from her and uncovered one side of her from her breast to half of her curly, oily, sun-sparkled pubis. She saw him looking at her. "You're not a prude, I hope."

He shook his head.

She let the rest of the towel fall, then leaning her arms back to the mattress she offered herself up to the sun. "I'm a naturist, a real sun worshipper," she said.

"Beautiful," he said.

She turned to him. "Let me spread some of the suntan oil on you. It will keep you from burning."

"I don't think so," he said.

"Why?" she asked.

"I have a very low boiling point," he said. "I'm having enough trouble right now trying to keep myself straight."

"I'm not blind," she said, looking up at him. "Your prick is sticking out from under your trunks. You've probably got the quickest draw in the West. I just hope you don't shoot as fast."

He laughed.

She reached for his penis and pulled him down beside her. "I just want to get in some licks first." She pulled the swim trunks from him and closed a hand around his penis. She looked into his eyes. "Do you know that I heard the way Dolores Del Rio had such perfect skin was that she had a dozen young men jerking off all over her and rubbing it in?"

"I never heard that." He laughed. "You know, you're really a crazy lady."

She laughed with him. "But also really nice. After all, the boss's wife is entitled to some advantages."

"And I thought we were meeting for a story conference," he said.

"This is the story," she said, pulling his penis into her mouth.

Motty walked through the living room of the hotel suite and picked her way through the racks of dresses brought in for them to select. Quickly she calculated there were at least two hundred garments. She looked at Gerald. "We'll never go through all of these by tomorrow," she said.

"Maybe we should stay another week," he suggested.

"We can't," she answered. "Paul the Furrier will be in L.A."

"Maybe we can rush through them by Saturday," he said.

"Even so, we can't make the train until Sunday. That will bring us to L.A. on Wednesday morning. Then we'll be in trouble. You know Paul the Furrier, he'll start without us and we'll be screwed."

"I have an idea," Gerald said.

She looked at him.

"Plane," he said. "TWA, United and American all fly to L.A. from New York. They leave at nine o'clock New York time, make two stops en route, Chicago and Denver, and land in L.A. at eleven o'clock at night the same day. We can do that on Sunday."

"I don't know," she said. "That's scary. I've never been on a plane."

"They say it's great," he said. "Free drinks, dinner, good service. They say it's just as if you were in your own living room. And the whole flight is only fourteen hours—you'll be in your own bed by midnight."

She looked at him. "I'd rather be in your bed. After all, I'm not expected home until Monday morning."

"I'd rather you would too. But there's always press at the airport, just as at the train terminal. It'll wind up in the papers. That might mean more trouble for you, because my divorce was already in the papers."

She thought for a moment. "I guess you're right," she said, depressed.

"You'll have to settle things with Joe as soon as you get home," he said. "Until then we'll never be free to do what we want."

She nodded slowly. "You're right, I guess." She paused for a moment. "Do you really think the plane is safe?"

"I wouldn't suggest it if I didn't think so," he answered.

She stared at the rows of garments. "Okay," she said. "You can get the tickets."

"I'll take care of it." He looked at her. "Are you planning to have dinner with your in-laws?"

She nodded. "I promised."

"Okay, if you have to," he said. "But try to return early. I'll miss you."

"I love the matzo balls, Tante," Motty said. "You still make the best chicken in the pot."

Marta nodded, satisfied. "You have to pick out the right chickens, not too much fat."

Phil, as usual, was silent. Then he burped. "It's not that easy anymore," he said. "During the war chicken was king, now everyone wants meat. Steak is king. Good chickens are not easy to buy anymore."

"But we're doing all right," Marta said. "Our customers

are loyal. They remember that we took care of them during the war when they couldn't get anything."

"I know that," Motty said, pushing her plate away half empty.

Marta noticed. "You're not feeling well?"

"I'm tired," Motty said.

"Maybe you should give up your job," Marta said. "Taking care of a child is hard enough."

"Rosa takes care of Caroline," Motty said. "I don't have to do anything about her."

Marta looked at her shrewdly. "Joe is working?"

"He just began a new script," she said.

"What about his book?" Marta asked. "The one that he always said he was going to write."

"He's not been able to get into it," Motty said. "He spends most of his time trying to get scriptwriting jobs."

"He doesn't have to do that," Marta said. "The reason you took your job was so he would have more time to work on his book."

"It didn't work out like that," Motty said.

Marta peered at her. "He still runs around?"

Motty didn't look at her. She remained silent.

Marta picked up the plates from the table. She spoke over her shoulder as she placed the plates in the kitchen sink. "He'll never change," she said flatly. "He'll never grow up to face his responsibility as a normal married man."

"That's not true," Phil said, defending him. "He's just not like other boys. We always knew that."

"Boys are not men," Marta said. "Now, my Stevie is a man. He's finished his residency and soon he'll be opening up his own office."

"Fine," Phil said. "But that has nothing to do with Joe. He's creative, not practical."

Marta returned to the table with three glasses of dark brewed tea. She placed a glass before Motty. "Whatever you do," she said, "don't have another baby."

Motty met her eyes. "I don't plan to."

"What are you planning to do?" Phil asked.

Motty didn't answer.

Marta was clever. "Motty has a very good job. She already makes more money than Joe. She doesn't need his money. Maybe she'll divorce him and find another man that is more suited for her."

Phil was angry. "What kind of way is this to talk? Jewish people don't get divorces. It would be a *shanda*."

Marta was smart. She met Motty's eyes evenly. "Not in California," she said. "Lots of Jews get divorced in California. It's no shame there. Read the papers. Everybody gets divorced in Hollywood. Even Motty's boss, Mr. Marks, got his name in the papers when he got divorced."

Phil looked from one to the other and then back down to his glass of tea. His voice was low. "Just remember one thing," he said quietly. "Don't throw out your dirty water until you get fresh."

=24=

THE POSTMAN STOOD in the doorway. He handed Joe the package, marked as usual, "rejected manuscript." He held the delivery book for Joe to initial. "Another one, Mr. Crown," he said sympathetically. "I'm sorry."

"Writers are used to rejection," Joe said philosophically as he returned the delivery book.

He sat down at the coffee table in the living room and opened the package. Jamaica had added an extra in the package. A tinfoil bag of pungent Jamaican ganch, as well as the usual forty envelopes of cocaine. He shook his head. Once again he had forgotten to rent a post-office box.

Rosa came from the kitchen, bringing him a cup of coffee. She placed it on the coffee table in front of him, then glanced at him. "Marijuana." She smiled.

He looked up at her. "You know about it?"

"*Sí, sí.*" She laughed. "*Marijuana mexicana es la mejor.*"

"You smoke it?" he asked curiously.

She nodded. "Even the children from five, six years. *Para tranquilidad.* Good to sleep."

"Would you like some?" he asked.

"I have," she answered. "If you like, I can bring for you from my family. *Tengo mucho.*"

He laughed. "Thank you. One day I'll take you up on it." He picked up one of the small white envelopes and opened it so that she could look at the white powder. "Do you know this?"

She nodded. *"Cocaína."*

"Do you use that too?"

She shook her head. "No, *señor.* Too nervous, no sleep."

He laughed. "You're smart," he said. "But sometimes for *amor* they say it is very good."

"For *amor,*" she said, "in Mexico we make a tea mixed with peyote and marijuana. Makes many dreams."

"I never knew that," he said.

"It is old Indian *medicina.* My father uses it all the time. *Muy bueno.*"

"How old is your father?" he asked.

"Cuarenta y tres años," she said. "Like you he has many girlfriends."

"What does your mother say?"

"Nada. That is the way with *hombres.*"

He picked up the cup and sipped at his coffee.

"Desayuno, señor?" she asked.

"I don't think so," he answered. "I have to get into the studio."

"Will the *señora* be home on the weekend?"

"Not until Monday," he said.

"Will you have dinner at home those days?"

"Yes," he said. "I plan to work at home on the weekend."

"Bueno, señor," she said.

A shaft of sunlight moved into the window behind her. "I gave you money to buy underwear to wear under your dress," he said.

"I was just going to after I brought your coffee, *señor*," she said without expression.

He stared at her. "You're a teasing bitch!"

"No, *señor*," she said without defiance. "I was going to wear it."

He knew she was lying. "Turn your back to me," he said angrily.

Silently she turned around. He raised the back of her skirt over her hips and gave her two stinging slaps, one on each of her buttocks. She made no outcry as his handprint turned white and then bright pink on her skin. "Maybe this will help you to remember."

She looked back at him over her shoulder. Her face was completely expressionless, the skirt still draped over her hips. "You are like my father, *señor*," she said quietly. "But my father hits me harder and more."

He stared at her. "You like it, you bitch!"

"It is part of a woman's duty, *señor*," she said.

He had no answer for her. It was just another way of life.

Keyho came into his office and glanced around. "Very fancy," he said jocularly. "You're becoming a big man. Moving up in the world."

Joe laughed. "You're so full of shit."

"Come on," Keyho said. "This is one of the best of the writers' offices."

"I got lucky," he said.

"Million-dollar grossers do that for you," Keyho said.

"I'd rather they gave me the money," Joe said. "I can do without the office."

"You'll get the money too, in time," Keyho said. "All you have to do is play your cards right."

"Horseshit," Joe said. The telephone rang and he picked it up.

Judi's voice sounded metallically in his ear. "Publicity won't okay a voucher for you," she said. "They said your name don't mean nothing for the papers or the photographers. They want me to go out with other stars. You know, like Van Johnson, Peter Lawford, even Mickey Rooney."

"I could have told you that," he said. "Then did you get a date?"

"They're working on it, they said," she answered.

"Okay, we'll try it next time," he said.

"You're not angry with me?" she asked. "I don't have any choices. I have to protect my own star status. You understand, don't you?"

"Of course I do," he said, putting down the phone. He looked across the desk at Keyho. "That was Judi," he explained. "Now that she's a star she can only date other stars. The bitch."

"That's Hollywood," Keyho said. "That's what I told you, you'll have to play your cards right."

Joe looked at him. "I'm listening."

"You have to hire a PR agent."

"What for?" Joe asked. "I'm a writer, not a star."

"Writers can be stars too," Keyho said. "Think about it. Dashiell Hammett, Faulkner, Scott Fitzgerald, Hemingway. They're all writers. And they're stars too."

"I'm not in their league yet," Joe said. "They have a body of work behind them."

"So what?" Keyho said dryly. "A good PR man will make you as well known as any of them. This is a bullshit business but don't underrate it. Bullshitters themselves are the easiest mark for bullshit. They see you in print enough times, they'll believe you're Shakespeare reincarnated."

"I don't know," Joe said dubiously. "Besides I don't even know a PR man."

"I do," Keyho said. "My sister's son. He works at Columbia Studios as a column planter in the publicity department. He also free-lances for other clients on the side. He's planning to open his own independent office."

"Is he expensive?"

"It depends on how much you want him to do. Five stories a week, twenty-five dollars; ten stories, fifty bucks; unlimited, a hundred a week."

"That's a lot of money," Joe said. "How do I know he can deliver?"

"How about a line in Winchell's column on Monday?"

"If he can do that, I'll kiss his ass in Macy's window."

"You don't have to do that," Keyho said. "Suppose he slips in a few words on Winchell's Sunday broadcast as well? Go for a hundred up front?"

"You got it," Joe said. He placed the parcel-post package on the desk. "Now how about the merchandise?"

"The same price as the last time," Keyho said. "I'll take a hundred down for my nephew."

"I'll throw in a bag of Jamaican ganch big enough for a hundred five-dollar sticks. You give me the same money. That way we all make a little."

"It's good stuff?" Keyho asked.

Joe opened the tinfoil bag. "You'll get high just smelling it."

Keyho sniffed at it. "You got the deal." He reached for the package.

"When do I get to meet this nephew of yours?"

"How about Monday for lunch? I'll bring Gene over here. You'll like the kid."

"If he doesn't score," Joe said, "don't bring him over. Just give me the extra hundred."

"He'll score," Keyho said definitely. "Another aunt of his is Winchell's number one secretary."

"A. J. wants to talk to you," Kathy said into his phone. "Hold on, I'll put you through to him."

A. J.'s voice sounded pleased with himself. "How's the work going, Joe? When am I going to see some pages?"

"Soon, A. J.," replied Joe. "I'm working on it."

"I know you are," A. J. said. "But that's not the reason for this call. We just got a shipment of New York delicatessen from Barney Greengrass in Manhattan. I thought you might like to come out to our Malibu beach house for brunch about two o'clock Sunday. There'll be some good people there."

"Thank you, A. J.," he answered. "I'd really like that."

"Kathy will give you the address," A. J. said. "See you then. Maybe we can talk some more about the script. I have a few new ideas."

"That's better for me than the deli," he answered. "See you Sunday."

He put down the phone and checked his watch. Twelve-thirty. Time for lunch. He started for the door and the telephone called him back. He picked it up. "Joe Crown."

"What are you doing at your desk?" Blanche asked.

"Working," Joe answered. "That's what I'm supposed to do here."

"I thought you'd be doing something more interesting than that," she said. "Like playing with your prick for example."

"Not in this fishbowl," he said. "I have the feeling that all the phones coming through the switchboard are tapped."

"Impossible," she said. "A. J. invited you for Sunday?"

"Yes."

"What are you doing for lunch now?"

"I'm going down to the commissary."

"Why don't you go down on me for lunch?" she said.

"I'll never make it back to the studio," he said.

"Don't be crazy, this is Friday," she said. "Nobody ever comes back to the studio after lunch on Friday."

He felt the rush in his loins. "I'll be there in an hour," he said.

=== 25 ===

IT WAS THREE o'clock in the afternoon and A. J. was on his second bottle of Scotch whiskey. If it hadn't been for the fact that his voice was somewhat louder than usual and he had the tendency to repeat his sentences a number of times, one wouldn't realize that he was drunk as a lord. He sat sprawled on a deck chair, looking down at the beach from the deck.

Joe sat on the deck rail beside him. On the beach just below, several tables shaded by sun umbrellas and directors' chairs were occupied with guests wearing swimsuits who were going to and from the surf. The sun was still hot.

"Good party," A. J. said, holding his drink and gesturing toward the beach. "Good party."

"Very good party," Joe agreed.

"Nice people too," A. J. said. "Nice people."

Joe nodded. He recognized several of the executives from the studio, and there was a sprinkling of film people, actors, actresses, two directors and a producer. Though A. J. had mentioned that Errol Flynn was coming to the brunch, Joe hadn't seen him.

A. J. got up from his chair and leaned over the railing. "Did you see Blanche?" he asked. "Where's Blanche?"

Joe looked down at the beach. "I just saw her a few moments ago," he said. "But I don't see her now."

A. J. sipped at his whiskey. "Bitch!" he said. "Bitch!"

Joe remained silent.

A. J. peered out to the surf. "She's nowhere around," he said. "Nowhere. That happens every time we have one of these beach brunches. Suddenly she's gone. Disappeared. Every time."

Joe still remained silent.

A. J. stared at him. "She thinks I don't know what she's doing. But I know. The bitch!" He sipped again at his drink. "She's got some guy in a corner and she's sucking his cock. She's a fucking nymphomaniac." He looked at Joe's face. "You know that, Joe? She's a fucking nymphomaniac."

Joe didn't know what to say. He didn't think it was his place to agree with him.

A. J. shook his head unhappily. "You can't know how a man feels when he knows his wife has probably fucked every man at this party and there's nothing he can even say about it." He looked at Joe. "You haven't fucked her yet, have you?" he asked, then answered the question himself. "Of course not, you haven't been around here long enough. But give her time, she'll get around to you."

He sank back into his chair, refilled his glass and drank morosely. "The fucking problem is there's nothing I can do about it. I can't even divorce her because everything I have is in her name because of taxes. If I divorce her, I'd be wiped out. Not a penny to my name. Not a penny."

Joe felt he had to offer some solace. "It can't be as bad as that, A. J."

"You're nothing but a dumb kid," A. J. said, slurring his words. "How the hell would you know?"

Joe was silent again.

"The whole fucking studio knows about her," A. J. said. "The whole fucking town knows about her. But nobody gives a shit. They all think that I'm getting my share of pussy too. What the hell do they know? I can't even get it up anymore."

"I can't believe that, A. J.," Joe said sympathetically. "You're still a young man. Have you seen a doctor?"

"I've seen a dozen doctors," A. J. said disgustedly. "Zero. They all told me the same thing. It was because of a fever I had about seven years ago when I got a clap from some Chinese whore. That was the end of it."

"Jesus!" Joe exclaimed. "I never heard of anything like that. But now, since the war, they came out with a whole new batch of medicines."

"Not for what I got," A. J. said. "But that isn't the reason she acts like she does. She's been like that all the time. She's always been cock crazy. When I could handle it, it was great, we even used to party together, *ménage à trois* and all that kind of thing. Now I get nothing but shit."

Joe, still sitting on the railing, saw her coming from around the side of the house. She had changed from a swimsuit to a beach caftan. "I just saw her," he said. "She was probably just changing out of her bathing suit. She was probably feeling cold. The sun's going down."

A. J. came over to the railing beside him and looked down. "It wasn't the sun going down," he said sarcastically. "It was her."

Joe looked at him silently.

"I'm not crazy," A. J. said emphatically. "Look at that satisfied look on her face. I know that look. It's like that every time she gets it off." He went back to the deck chair. He leaned back for a moment then turned up to Joe. "Don't pay attention to me," he said. "I'm a little drunk."

"That happens to all of us sometimes," Joe said.

"We won't talk to anybody about it, will we?" A. J. asked, slightly ashamed.

"I don't talk," Joe said. "It's none of my business."

"Good boy," A. J. said, then added in a harsh angry voice, "But if by any chance you get to fuck her, give her a good one for me. Bust her ass!"

Joe didn't answer.

A. J. got out of the chair. "I'm tired," he said, his voice suddenly weary. "I think I'll go inside and take a nap."

"I think I'll be going home too," Joe said.

"Have you been working on the treatment over the weekend?" A. J. asked.

"Yes," Joe said. "At home."

"Good." A. J. nodded. He shook Joe's hand. "I'll see you at the studio tomorrow."

Caroline was having her dinner as he came through the door. "Daddy!" she cried, waving her fork and dropping a forkful of spaghetti on the table. "Pasghetti," she exclaimed.

He laughed. She never could pronounce the word. "Good?" he asked.

"Very good," she said seriously. "But I like Tootsie Rolls better."

"After dinner I'll give you some Tootsie Rolls," he promised.

"Good." She lifted another forkful of spaghetti. "When does Mommy come home?" she asked.

"Tomorrow," he answered.

She smiled. "Mommy always brings presents."

"Yes," he said.

"I like Mommy's presents."

That was true, he thought. He wondered why he never thought of bringing a present for her. But then, he never knew what to get her except Tootsie Rolls. He watched her eating. It was strange. He knew that she was his child, of course. But other men always talked about their children and carried their photographs around. He never did. In a way he never thought about her as a child. She was more like a doll or a toy. Maybe it was because he had no way of communicating with her. Perhaps when she grows older and could say more, maybe then he would understand more about her. He loved her, he knew that. But exactly why, he didn't know. Maybe that was one of the things about being a father—not understanding his feeling but only the responsibility she placed on him.

"I went to the park with Rosa," she said.

"Was it nice?" he asked.

"We saw fish in the pool," she said.

"That was nice." He looked across the room at Rosa. "Did she enjoy it?"

Rosa nodded. *"Mucho."*

"Mucho," Caroline echoed. She pointed to the empty plate with her fork. "All empty," she laughed. "Now, Tootsie Rolls?"

Joe took them from where he always kept them in his pocket. He placed three Tootsie Rolls on the table. "One extra."

"Good." She laughed, already unwrapping one.

"What do you say?" he asked.

She looked up at him. "Thank you, Daddy."

"You're welcome, darling," he said, kissing her on the cheek. He straightened up and looked over at Rosa. "I'll have dinner at eight o'clock, after she's gone to sleep."

"Sí, señor."

He kissed Caroline on the cheek. "Daddy's going to have a little nap, sweetheart. You have a nice night's sleep."

"Nighty-night, Daddy," she answered, already chewing on the first Tootsie Roll and unwrapping the second.

He went upstairs to his small study and looked down at the typewritten pages of the treatment. Thirty pages. Not too bad. Now that he was getting into it, it was coming easier. Maybe he could have it finished in two weeks.

He turned and went into the bedroom. Quickly he undressed and took a shower. The afternoon in the sun had made him tired. The hot water felt good against his skin. He dried himself with a large bath towel, then stretched out on the bed. It was warm in the apartment. He threw the towel to the floor, rolled over on his stomach and fell asleep.

Then he was in the midst of a strange dream. First, Blanche was sucking him and almost swallowed his testicles in her mouth, and then he was fucking her, ramming into her as if he were an animal and all the while A. J. was standing over them, screaming at him. "Bust her ass! Bust the bitch's ass!"

A tentative soft hand touched his shoulder. He awoke. Rosa was looking down at him. "It is already nine o'clock, *señor*," she said softly. "Would you like to have your dinner?"

He shook the cobwebs from his head and began to roll over, then stopped. He felt the urging of his erection against his belly. "First, give me the towel," he said, pointing to it on the floor.

Silently, she handed it to him. He wrapped it around his waist, still conscious of the impression against the towel. *"El señor tiene muchos sueños de amor,"* she said with a faint smile.

He ignored her comment. "Turn on the big radio downstairs," he said. "I'll have dinner on the small table in the living room. I'll be right there."

215

"Sí, señor," she answered and left the room.

He went into the bathroom and stepped into the shower again. This time, ice-cold water. He dried himself quickly and slipped on his bathrobe and started downstairs.

Walter Winchell's program was already on by the time he sat down at the table. He sat there silently as Rosa placed the salad in front of him. "Beer, *señor?"* she asked.

"Yes. Beer." He listened to the rapid speech of Winchell. The effect was exciting, as if everything the man said was of life-and-death importance.

It was almost at the very end of the program that Winchell gave the plug that Joe was awaiting.

From Triple S studios, usually better known as producers of B movies and quickie pix, comes the sleeper hit of the year—*Warrior Queen of the Amazons—* with Steve Cochran, known only as the poor man's Clark Gable, and Judi Antoine, known only as the star of pinups—*Warrior Queen* has garnered a million and a half dollars in just two weeks . . . that's one and a half million simoleons, Mr. and Mrs. America, and that ain't hay. . . . The genius behind this money-grabbing movie is a little up-to-now-unknown writer, Joe Crown . . . Joe Crown, who has written two short stories published in the Foley collection of great American short stories, has now written the script of the movie that blends fantasy and adventure that the cognoscenti compare favorably with such box office giants as *King Kong* . . . *The Lost World* . . . *Tarzan of the Apes* . . . Even though helped by the most scantily clad beauties of the silver screen, the triumph belongs only to the genius of Joe Crown . . . Remember that name, Mr. and Mrs. America, Joe

Crown . . . You'll be hearing much more about him . . . At this very minute every studio in Hollywood is trying to sign the man to a multimillion-dollar contract. . . .

Almost the moment he had gone off the air the telephone began ringing. A. J. was the first call. "Just remember, Joe, we have a contract. Don't let anybody fuck your head around."

"That's right, A. J.," Joe said. "I know that you are always in my corner."

"You bet your ass, son," A. J. answered. "I want to see you in my office first thing tomorrow morning."

"I'll be there, A. J."

The moment he put down the phone it began ringing again. A. J. must have redialed immediately. "In case I forgot to tell you, son," he said, "I meant to tell you this afternoon at the beach. I'm doubling the figures on your contract to forty thousand instead of twenty."

"Thank you, A. J.," Joe said. He put down the telephone once more. Keyho was right. Bullshitters are the first to believe the bullshit.

For the next two hours the telephone kept ringing. Almost everyone who knew anyone in Hollywood and many who didn't know were calling to congratulate him. It was finally past eleven o'clock when the telephone calls subsided; Joe had never got around to eating his dinner. He walked to the couch and stretched out.

"You didn't eat your dinner, *señor*," Rosa said.

He turned to her. "It's been too hectic," he said. He sat up and looked up at her. "You don't like to wear underwear, is that it?"

"No, *señor*," she said, the secret smile in the corners of

her mouth as she looked down at him. "I was getting ready for bed, *señor.*"

"Okay," he said. "Just bring me a cup of coffee and you can go to bed."

"*Si, señor,*" she said. She looked down at him again. "I have some *cigarillos Mexicanos, señor.* Perhaps one would calm you down and you will sleep better."

"Marijuana?" he asked.

She nodded.

He thought for a moment. "What the hell," he said. "Okay." Maybe it would work. He was still too excited to go to bed.

She was back in a moment with a cup of coffee and a thinly rolled cigarette. "Thanks," he said, lighting it. He dragged it deeply into his lungs. It was sweet and soft, not like the Jamaican, which sometimes was harsh and bitter. He dragged on it again. He began to feel better almost immediately.

"*Es bueno, señor?*" she asked.

"Very nice, thank you," he answered. "You can go to bed now."

"I can make you even more calm, *señor.*"

"I feel perfectly calm right now," he said, feeling slightly silly.

She laughed aloud. "*Mire, señor,*" she said, pointing her finger.

He looked down at himself. His prick had never looked so large. It was amazing. He began to laugh. "That's ridiculous," he said. He tried to press it down beneath his bathrobe but the moment he let it go, it sprang up almost slapping against his belly. He laughed louder. He looked up at her. "I'm fucking stoned," he said.

"*Sí, señor.*" She smiled.

"You better go to bed now," he said, trying to be reasonable. "Or I might wind up shoving it up your ass." It was really funny. He couldn't stop laughing.

"Okay in my ass," she said. "But not in there, the other place. I am virgin until marry."

He laughed again. "That makes sense."

She pulled off her dress then backed toward him. "First I must make you wet." She spit into her hand and rubbed the saliva over his penis. "Good?" she asked, looking back over her shoulder at him.

"Very good," he said, taking another drag of the cigarette. "Really very good," he laughed.

Delicately, she took the cigarette from his fingers and placed it in an ashtray. Then she carefully spread her buttocks with both hands and backed into him. At the last moment, she grabbed him with one hand and guided him into her. *"Aiee!"* she cried aloud as she sat down completely in his lap.

"Fantastic!" Her anus was as soft as a velvet glove.

She began to spring up and down on him. He grabbed her by the hips. "Hang tight!" he yelled, "or you'll go up through the ceiling!"

There was the sound of a key clicking in the door, and she suddenly froze. In another moment she was gone and racing up the stairs. Motty stood in shock at the door.

He pulled himself to his feet, trying to be serious. "Motty!" he exclaimed. "What are you doing here? You're not supposed to be here until tomorrow."

Motty slammed the door angrily behind her. "I can see that," she said icily.

He pointed, his index finger straight. "You're not going to believe what I'm going to tell you," he said seriously.

She stood there silently.

Then he glanced down at himself. His erection was pointing in exactly the same position as his index finger. That was too much—it really was too funny to believe. He began laughing uncontrollably. He fell to the floor rolling back and forth; his sides hurt from the laughter. He tried to sit up but could not. He couldn't stop laughing—tears ran from his eyes.

"It's so funny!" he managed to gasp, between spasms of laughter.

Then the nightmare began.

=26=

"Is HE GOING to be my new daddy?" Caroline asked. She was more curious than concerned.

Joe looked at her as she stood in front of him. Children came right to the point. What's in it for them and where do they fit? He glanced across the room where Motty, Mr. Marks and the attorneys sat before the small round table, exchanging agreements as several moving men carried out the suitcases and boxes packed with Motty's and Caroline's belongings to the truck outside. He didn't know what to tell the child. "I guess so," he answered doubtfully.

Caroline was puzzled. "Don't you want to be my daddy anymore?"

"Of course I want to be your daddy," he said reassuringly. "But Mommy is moving out and little girls have to live with their mommies."

Caroline shook her head. "I miss Rosa," she said. "Mommy doesn't know how to make *huevos rancheros*."

"I'm sure she will find another girl who'll be able to make them," he said.

"I hope so," Caroline said. "And then she can take me to the park too."

Joe nodded.

Caroline stared at him. "Do you like sleeping on the couch, Daddy?"

Joe laughed. "Not really."

"Then why didn't you sleep in bed with Mommy?"

Joe shook his head. This was Friday. He had been spending the nights there since Motty came home on Sunday. The week had been hell. On Monday morning, Motty told him she wanted a divorce.

"That's stupid," he said. "I really was stoned. I never even fucked, not even a little bit."

Motty was adamant. "It was not only Rosa. There were always other girls."

"Shit," he said. "They never meant anything. If I did fuck them it was only a little bit. Friendly. Sociable."

"I don't understand you at all," she said. "You were always like that. I thought you would change once we were married."

"I tried," he said.

"You didn't try hard enough," she said. "You were screwing around even while I was pregnant, the minute you started working at the studio."

"I can't talk you out of it?"

"No."

"You'll have to get a lawyer," he said. "The whole thing's going to take time."

"I have a lawyer," Motty said. "The same one that handled Mr. Marks's divorce."

"What's Marks got to do with it?"

She was silent.

He stared at her, a light dawning in his head. "You're going to marry him?"

She flushed.

"Holy shit!" he exclaimed. "I've been really stupid. You've been fucking him all the time!"

She was angry. "You make things sound so dirty."

"You made it dirty," he answered. "At least, I didn't play angel."

She changed the subject. "Are you going to the office this morning?"

"I have to," he said. "I had a meeting scheduled with A. J."

"I'm staying home with Caroline," she said. "I'll tell the lawyer to call you there."

"I'll be home in the evening," he said. "He can talk to me here."

"You're not going to get into the bedroom," she said.

"I can sleep on the couch downstairs," he said. "But I don't see any reason for me to move out. I'm not the one looking for a divorce."

"I'll be moving by the end of the week," she said flatly and walked away from him.

A. J. stared at him across the desk. "I don't know how you did it," he said. "That Winchell plug means another half million at the box office."

"I was lucky," Joe said.

"More than luck," A. J. said. "None of our PR people could ever get a plug in Winchell."

Joe was silent. Somehow he had not felt as elated as when he listened to the man last night. The rest of the night had been a disaster.

A. J. peered at him. "You don't look like you're happy at all. As a matter of fact, you look like a truck ran over you."

"Wife troubles," Joe said.

"Serious?" A. J. asked.

"She wants a divorce," Joe said.

"You talked to her?"

"Until I was blue in the face," Joe said. "She means it. She's going to marry her boss."

A. J. stared at him. "Gerald Marks, the department-store guy?"

Joe nodded. "You know him?"

"I know him," A. J. said. "I heard he just got a divorce."

"What kind of a guy is he?" Joe asked.

"Okay, I guess," A. J. answered. "He's not like us. Very straight, serious. And a lot of money. He's the only heir of his family. Someday the whole department-store chain will belong to him. Your wife is smart."

"Fucking cunt," Joe said bitterly. "She's already lined up a lawyer. Marks's attorney."

"That's serious," A. J. said. "He's going to clean you out."

"What for?" Joe asked. "Marks has money. She'll have all she needs, she won't want any from me."

"You're naive," A. J. said sagely. "That's not the way it goes. Her lawyer will tell her to go for your throat. You better get yourself a sharp lawyer just to keep yourself alive."

"There's nothing they can take," Joe said. "The furniture cost shit. I got maybe twenty-six, seven grand in the bank."

A. J. stood behind his desk. "They'll take it. And besides that they'll hit you for child support. And wait until they find out about the new contract we're signing. Then you'll see the shit flying."

Joe stared at him. "What do I do about that?"

"First, you get a lawyer. I know a good man for you and he's not too expensive," A. J. said. "Then I suggest we delay signing any new contracts until after the divorce is completed, otherwise they will really wipe you out."

"Motty will never go along with that," Joe said.

"She has no choice," A. J. said. "I put you on week-to-week for seven fifty, no guarantee. If they get tough, we just agree to lay you off."

Joe was silent.

"Then when it's all over we'll just sign the contract," A. J. said. He looked at Joe, who was still silent. "You can trust me, Joe," he said. "Just remember, I'm on your side. I don't like the idea of a talented kid like you winding up getting screwed."

"Do you really believe she'd do that?" Joe asked.

"All women are bitches," A. J. replied. He looked at Joe. "Do you have a joint account?"

Joe nodded.

"You better grab your money out before she does."

"She won't do that," Joe said.

"No?" A. J. said pointedly. "Call your bank and put a hold on your account. You can use my phone."

Joe picked up the telephone and dialed the bank. An assistant vice president answered. Joe asked him to put a hold on the account, then waited.

After a moment, the bank officer came back on the line. "I'm sorry, Mr. Crown," he said, "but Mrs. Crown was just here this morning and withdrew all the funds and closed the account."

Joe put down the receiver and stared at A. J. "She took out all the money," he said in a stunned voice.

A. J. shook his head. "I told you."

"But all the money," Joe repeated, still stunned.

"Like I said," A. J. answered. "When it comes to money, all women are nothing but bitches and whores."

"What do I do now?" Joe asked.

"I'll make an appointment for you with the lawyer," A. J. said. "You better see him right away."

Joe pulled two Tootsie Rolls from his pocket and gave them to Caroline, then glanced over at the table where Motty and Marks sat with the lawyers. Joe's attorney, Don Sawyer, was a young man, a nephew of A. J.'s. Whether he was capable or not Joe could not judge, because everything seemed very cut-and-dried. At the end of it all, Joe had no choices. Motty held all the cards—she had been well prepared.

His attorney gathered a stack of papers and placed them on the coffee table in front of Joe. "It's simple," he said. "Only four agreements. You sign them and it's all over."

Joe looked down at them as Don pulled a chair opposite him. "What are they?" he asked, feeling stupid.

Don nodded. "First is the agreement for not contesting the Mexican divorce; second, the agreement about the community property; third, you waive your visitation rights concerning the child in exchange for no payment of either alimony or child support; and fourth, you accept the return of ten thousand dollars formerly in your joint bank account, and the furniture and accessories to the furnishings in the apartment belong to you and will be turned over to you the moment the divorce is finalized. That should be sometime next week."

"What happens if she does not go through with the divorce?" Joe asked.

"She'll go through with it," Don said confidently. He lowered his voice so that he could not be overheard. "They're hotter for the divorce than you are."

"Shit," Joe said. He stared down at the papers. "I guess I have no choices."

"Unless you want to fight," Don said. "And even if you do, you're going to lose. The California courts and laws are all against you."

Joe looked across the room at Motty. Motty kept her face turned away from him. He turned to Don. "Lend me your pen," he said. "I'll sign."

Quickly he signed the agreements, and Don took them back to Motty's attorney. Motty looked at her attorney. "Can I leave now?" she asked.

He glanced at the agreements. "Everything's been signed. You can leave whenever you're ready."

She crossed the room and took Caroline by the hand. "Come, Caroline," she said. "We're going now."

The child looked at Joe. Her face was already smeared with chocolate. "Bye-bye, Daddy," she said calmly.

Joe started to get up from the couch. "Goodbye, baby," he said, his voice strained. He turned to Motty. "Happier now?" he asked bitterly.

She didn't answer, her face flushing. She started toward the door, pulling the child along with her.

Joe stared at her. There was something in her face, something about the way she walked. It was nothing new. He had seen that before. Then he remembered. "You're fucking pregnant!" he shouted.

She rushed out the door with the child. He turned and looked at Marks, who was hurrying after her. "Asshole!" he shouted. "I'm not the only asshole in the world! That's the same way she nailed me!"

But Marks was already outside the door. Joe turned to his attorney. "No wonder they were in such a rush," he said. "We were stupid. I was stupid. I should have guessed!"

Then his anger dissipated as quickly as it had come. He smiled wryly. "I've been outfucked and outsmarted. But maybe I got away lucky."

Don nodded. "It could have been worse."

"Yeah," Joe said. "I could have been fighting over two kids, not one. And one of them not even mine!"

=== 27 ===

IT WAS NEARLY six o'clock by the time the attorney gathered up all the agreements and placed them in his briefcase. "I'll be on my way," he said. "My in-laws are coming over for dinner."

Joe nodded. "Fine."

Don looked at him sympathetically. "Would you like to join us?"

"I don't think so," Joe said. "But thanks anyway."

"You ought to go out for dinner, maybe catch a movie. It won't be much fun for you to be sitting around here alone. The first night after the divorce papers is a bitch."

Joe looked at him curiously. "You know?"

Don nodded. "I've been through it. I'm on my second marriage."

Joe thought for a moment. "I guess everyone thinks that they were the only one it ever happened to."

Don smiled. "It's almost like a way of life out here."

Joe nodded, and shook his hand. "I'll be okay," he said. "Thanks for everything."

"I'll call you at the beginning of the week," Don said. "Just as soon as they return the official agreements to me."

Joe closed the door behind the attorney and then opened

a bottle of Scotch. Quickly he drank three straight shots. He felt the liquor burning its way down his throat and coughed. "Shit!" he said, then turned on the radio and slumped into the couch. He spun the radio dial until he found a station that broadcast only music—he was in no mood for the news program that usually came on at this time. He had another drink, then leaned his head back against the cushion. Suddenly, he felt exhausted. His eyes were burning, and he rubbed them slowly. It was not tears he felt; he never cried. Then he fell asleep.

He thought he heard a baby crying and opened his eyes. The room was dark. The sound was the buzzing of the radio after the station had gone off the air. He switched off the radio and turned on the lamp next to the couch. The half-empty bottle of Scotch stated up at him from the coffee table. He shook his head, trying to clear it. He hadn't realized he had drunk that much. He checked his watch. It was after one in the morning.

He looked around the room. It was strange—not familiar at all. Then he realized that it was the silence. There always had been some sound in the apartment. Now, nothing. He lit a cigarette. The scratch of the match echoed loudly in his ear. He took a deep drag of the cigarette and let it out slowly through his nose. He stared at his hands, which were trembling. He dragged again on the cigarette. Besides his shaking hands, he had the granddaddy of all headaches.

Slowly he pulled himself to his feet and walked into the kitchen. He took a bottle of Pepsi from the refrigerator and then a tin of Bayer from the shelf. He popped three aspirin tablets into his mouth and swallowed them with the Pepsi. He finished the bottle of Pepsi and went up the steps to the bedroom.

He turned on the light and stood in the doorway looking

into the bedroom. It was a mess. Motty's closets were open, clothes hangers strewn on the floor: the dresser drawers and cabinet doors had been emptied and left open. Looking through the bathroom door, he saw that the medicine cabinet doors were also thrown open and only his shaving cream and razors remained. Inexplicably, even his toothbrush and toothpaste had disappeared.

He turned from his bedroom door to Caroline's room. Her small bed and other furniture were gone and the room seemed bare with only the narrow cot and small cabinet that had been assigned to Rosa and her few belongings. He wondered whether Rosa had taken her things with her when she had run out of the house that night. He didn't trouble to check the cabinet. It didn't matter anyway. She had not returned since.

He closed the door and walked into his study. He walked to his desk. His manuscript papers were still neatly piled on the desk top. There was a sheet of paper on the typewriter. He picked it up. It was in Motty's handwriting.

Fuck you!
    You're nothing but a fucking fake. You can't write. Not one thing you've ever done was worth a shit. You can't even write a lousy comic strip. Not only that you can't write, you can't fuck. Now that I have a real man, I really know what fucking is. You will take a hundred years to do what he can do in a minute. And if you think you have such a great big prick, forget it. His is twice the size of yours and he can do more things with it than you can ever imagine. You're a kid, not a real man, all you're good for is jerking off.

                                        Love, Motty

Angrily he crumpled it into a ball and threw it across the room. "Bitch!" he exclaimed. Then he picked it up from the floor, straightened it and placed it on the desk in front of him. Then he stared at it and began to smile. Dumb cunt, he thought. She signed it "LOVE."

He picked up the framed eight and a half-by-eleven photograph standing at the far end of the desk and looked at it. Quickly he slipped the glass off the frame and then, carefully folding the note so that it covered the bottom portion of the photograph, placed it so that her downcast eyes seemed to be looking at the note. He smiled as he replaced the glass and put the frame back on the desk. If ever he needed a reminder of how a woman could screw him, he would always have it.

He began to feel hungry. He hadn't eaten since lunch the day before. He went back to the kitchen. The refrigerator was empty; a half-empty bottle of milk, some bottles of Pepsi and two beers—Nothing else. He scratched his head. Tomorrow he would have to go to the market and stock up.

He left the apartment, got to his car and drove to the all-night drive-in on Sunset and Cahuenga. It was after two in the morning and the drive-in was almost empty. He headed the car into the curb, turned off the engine and rolled down his window.

A moment later, a cute little blonde wearing a French sailor hat with a red pompom, and a little flared-out, short-sleeved cotton shirt that barely covered her tight little shorts, came toward him in her red high-heeled shoes. She placed the clip tray over the car door. "Coffee?" she asked, the filled paper cup in her hand.

"Please."

She placed the cup with two lumps of sugar and a thin

wooden spoon on the tray. "Our special tonight is two beef dogs on a roll with chili and french fries."

"Sounds good to me," he said. "How about a beer?"

"It's after two o'clock," she answered. "Regulations. No wine or beer on the premises after that."

"Could I have a glass of water?" he asked.

"Sure. But we have Coke and any soft drink you want."

"I brought my friend with me," he said, picking up the Scotch bottle next to him so that she could see it. "Johnnie."

She laughed. "Johnnie Walker's everybody's friend. Even me."

"Bring an extra glass and I'll introduce you."

"Not on the job," she said. "They'll have my ass for that."

"We can fake it," he said. "Just bring the extra glass."

He watched her go behind the serving counter as he turned on the car radio. The only station that was on the air was playing Mexican music. Good enough; it went with the chili. There were two water glasses on the tray she brought back. The chili dogs were on a paper plate with a wooden fork, the french fries in a square paper container. A half-dozen foil envelopes held the ketchup and mustard.

He poured the whiskey into one of the glasses. As he lifted it up to the tray he knocked over the container of french fries. "I'm sorry," he apologized, holding the Scotch bottle in his hand outside the car, pointing down toward the french fries.

She smiled and knelt to pick up the container. At the same moment she took the drink and swallowed it in one gulp. She came up with the paper container. "No problem, sir," she said, the liquor flushing her face. "I'll get you another."

He had eaten half the first chili dog by the time she returned with the fries. "Very smart." She grinned.

"Where there's a will there's a way."

"I needed it," she said.

"How much time do you put in?"

"Six hours," she answered. "Another fifteen minutes, then I can go home."

"Do you have to go home?" he asked.

"I should," she said. "My husband likes me home when he gets in. He works the night shift at Hughes Aircraft and he's in by five usually."

"That's two and a half hours," he said. "Johnnie's got a twin brother at my place and he's not even been opened yet."

"I don't know," she said hesitantly. "I don't have a car. I only live two blocks from here. That's why I took this job."

"I'll get you home in time," he said. "You and me and Johnnie will make up a great *ménage à trois*."

"I don't even know your name," she said.

"I don't know yours," he replied. "But what difference does it make? Let's leave it at that."

"You're so bad." She smiled. She looked back to the drive-in and then at him. Silently, she placed the ticket on the tray. He threw a five-dollar bill on it. "Keep the change."

She took the ticket and the money. She looked at him for a moment. "What do you work at?"

"I'm a screenwriter."

"At a studio?"

"Triple S."

"Maybe you can get me in for an interview?" she asked. "I was in all my high school plays."

"Maybe," he said.

234

She stared at him again. "I'll change out of my uniform. Another girl will take your tray away. You can pick me up on the next block."

He watched her return to the serving counter and walk into the back of the drive-in. He had finished almost half the second chili dog when he saw her leave from the side door. He honked the car horn and another girl took the tray away almost immediately. Carefully he backed out into the street and followed the blonde. She was exactly in the middle of the next block. He pulled the car over to the curb and opened the door.

She got into the seat beside him. The bottle of Scotch pressed hard between them. She picked it up and laughed. "If you're as hard as our friend Johnnie," she said, "we're going to have a hell of a party."

He watched her uncork the bottle and bring it to her lips. "Good whiskey," she said, offering him the bottle. "Black Label. The best."

He waved it away. "Not while I'm driving."

"Very smart," she said, nodding owlishly. She raised the bottle to her mouth again. By the time he drove to his apartment, the bottle was empty and she was pissed drunk. When he opened the door to let her out of the car her legs gave beneath her and she slipped onto the small lawn in front of the sidewalk.

He lifted her up from under her arms and placed her back into the car. "I'd better take you home," he said.

"I'll be okay," she said. "All I need is a little food. I never eat at the restaurant, I hate the crap they serve there."

"But I haven't anything to eat in the house," he said. "That's why I went to the drive-in."

"Too bad," she said. "Too bad."

"Where do you live?" he asked.

"Two blocks from the drive-in," she said.

He got back into the car and turned on the motor. It didn't take long to drive her home; it took ten minutes to get her from the car to her door.

She leaned on her door, weaving slightly. "Thank you for a lovely evening," she said politely.

"You're welcome," he said and went home.

The apartment was still as silent as when he had left it. Crazy. He never thought he could feel so alone. He took three more aspirin and two more drinks and went upstairs to his bedroom. He looked into the study room for a moment, then took the framed photograph and letter from the study, and walked into the bedroom and put it next to the night table beside him.

He watched it while he undressed and by habit placed his clothes away neatly. Then he got into bed and turned off the light. But sleep evaded him. He tossed and turned; the strange silence was too much for him.

He turned on the radio, but found the same Mexican station. He sat up in bed, smoked a cigarette and stared at the photograph. Then he put out the cigarette and reached to turn off the lamp. The photograph still stared at him. Suddenly he was angry. "Fucking cunt!" he shouted and threw the frame and photograph across the room. The tinkling sound of the broken glass took his anger away. It was the same sound he had heard when he smashed the glass under his foot on their wedding day. It was only right that the marriage should be ended with the same ancient ceremony. He fell asleep immediately.

He heard the telephone ringing in the distance. He rolled over in bed and opened his eyes. Nine o'clock in the morning. He pushed himself erect and reached for the telephone. "Hello."

"Joe? It's Laura Shelton from New York."

"Good morning," he said.

"Did I wake you?" she asked. "I'm sorry about the news of your divorce," she went on. "But if you're feeling down, maybe a little good news will lift you up."

"Good news will help," he replied, lighting a cigarette. He thought he smelled the aroma of coffee coming from downstairs. But it had to be an illusion.

"Santini, the Italian producer, wants you for two pictures in Europe. Guaranteed pay or play, thirty-five thousand each and five percent of the net. I've already received the contract and a deposit check of ten thousand dollars if you sign."

"I thought it was cocktail-party talk," Joe said.

"He obviously meant it," Laura said. "I spoke to him in Rome, he's anxious for you to begin right away."

The aroma of coffee was not an illusion. Rosa appeared in the bedroom door, a tray of coffee and sweet rolls in her hands. He looked at her silently as she placed the tray on the bed beside him and left the room. He took a sip of coffee. It was hot, and it warmed him.

"Right away?" he said to Laura. "What about my agreement with A. J.?"

"I have a feeling that A. J. is going to pull out of it," Laura said. "Kathy tells me that Steve Cochran won't do the picture and Judi told A. J. that she would not do the picture unless she got a new contract with a lot more money. A. J. has already placed her on suspension."

"Where does that place me?" he asked. "I have the treatment almost ready."

"How long will it take you to finish it?"

"Another week."

"You have no signed contract," she said. "You can turn the treatment in and go on your way. As a matter of fact, I have a feeling that A. J. will be relieved."

He sipped at the coffee again. If he had no deal with A. J., he had nothing to tie him down here. The only life he had here was wrapped around the industry. He had no real friends. "You sound like you know something?" he said. "Have you spoken to A. J. already?"

She hesitated for a moment before answering. "I'm a good agent," she said. "I don't want you to get screwed on anything. A. J. said he wouldn't stand in your way."

He was silent.

"And another thing," she added. "I spoke to the chief editor at Rinehart. They're interested in your novel."

"You've been busy."

"I'm your agent," she said. "I was testing the waters with Rinehart. The manuscript is at Doubleday right now. They can come up with a lot more money with all the book clubs they own."

"I'm feeling better already, Laura. What you're doing is above and beyond the call of duty."

"Not duty, Joe." There was a pause. "I think you've got two good opportunities. You can take advantage of both of them. What do you say?"

He took a deep breath. "Let's do them."

"Good. I'll have the papers and tickets here in New York for you. You can sign them on your way through."

"I'll see you then, say, a week from today. Okay?"

There was another pause. "My office will handle it, Joe. Just papers to sign—everything will be in order."

"You don't *want* to be there?" he asked.

"It's not a question of wanting or not wanting, Joe. It's a tangle of feelings about you that I don't know how to handle. I'm working for you, but I sincerely believe that I'd feel safer if we don't meet just now."

He stared at the phone for a moment. "You scare me, Laura."

"You've got a fine director to work with, a new film world. You've got a book that one publisher will put up money for—it's a whole new world. Enough to scare anyone, so why add another mixed-up lady? You've had your share of them too, haven't you? Work is the answer right now, not romance."

"Now you really sound like an agent."

"Not like an agent, Joe. I really care about you—not only about your talent and the money you will make, but about you. 'Bye for now, Joe."

He put down the telephone. "Rosa!" he called.

He heard her footsteps on the stairs, then she appeared in the doorway. "What are you doing here?" he asked.

"I came for my clothes, *señor*," she said. "When I saw you were asleep and there was nothing in the kitchen for breakfast, I went to the market to bring something in."

"Thank you," he said. He looked at her closely. Her face showed several faint bruises and the remnant of a black eye. "What happened to you?" he asked.

"My papa beat me for losing my job," she said simply. "I must have another job or he will send me back to Mexico to my mother."

"I'm sorry," he said.

"It is not your fault, *señor*," she said. She looked at him. "Perhaps I could be your housekeeper. I would cook and clean as I did before and I would ask only twenty dollars a month."

He stared at her. That was ten dollars less a month than she had been paid before, including taking care of the child.

"I wouldn't change your salary," he said. "But I will not be here for long. I am going to Europe very soon to work."

"Even working for one week would help me, *señor*," she said. "Perhaps by that time I could find another job."

He thought for a moment. She would be a great help to him. There was no way he could handle the apartment by himself. "Okay," he said.

She came to him and kissed his hand quickly. "Thank you, *señor. Mil gracias.*"

"It's all right," he said.

"I am sorry for what happened, *señor*," she said.

"That part is over," he said. "Now we both must look forward to tomorrow."

PART III
1949

=== 28 ===

"BELLE STARR AND Annie Oakley," Santini said. "The title alone is worth a million dollars."

"I still can't believe it," Joe said as they came from the projection room. "The picture is not bad."

"It's a work of genius," Santini said with his Italian superlatives and enthusiasm. "And it was all your idea. You were the one who talked Judi Antoine into coming here to co-star with Mara Benetti in a Western. I don't know how you ever thought of it."

"It was John Wayne and Cary Cooper in drag," Joe laughed. "And it worked. But you were the genius. I never thought two big pair of tits like that would fit on the screen at the same time in Cinescope."

"We're Italian." Santini smiled. "We're used to big tits. All Italian women have them." He turned to the small man that always followed behind him. Giuseppe was the ultimate flunky. "Giuseppe, *il carro*." He snapped his fingers.

"*Sì, maestro*." Giuseppe bowed and ran out.

Santini turned back to Joe. "Now, my friend, what is the next project your genius will propose for me?"

"I thought I might rest a little from movies for a while and work on my novel," Joe said. "I'm hoping that you

243

will be able to give me the balance of the fees from the picture to carry me."

Santini smiled. "No problem," he said. "I will make a distribution deal for the states in another week; then I will send you the money."

Joe stared at him. That was what he had said when they finished the first movie he had written for him, *Shercules*. It had been a ripoff of *Warrior Queen*. But the Italian actress Santini had discovered was even more exciting than Judi. It was a very successful drive-in movie in the States and set up the girl for this movie. Yet, even with that, Joe had not received the balance from the first picture until he began working on the second. As far as profit shares—zero. Italian accounting was even more dishonest than American. "I could use five thousand dollars right now," he said diplomatically. "I have many bills to pay."

Santini took out his checkbook and a pen with a flourish. "I will do that immediately." He wrote the check and handed it to him.

Joe looked at the check. It was for five thousand dollars. He kept his face expressionless. They both knew that the check was made of rubber. "Thank you, *maestro*," he said politely.

"What are you doing for the month of August?" Santini asked, equally polite. "At the Lido in Venice as you did last year?"

"I haven't made up my mind," Joe said. "It's too expensive for me right now. Besides, last year, I met this beautiful girl, unbelievable. She stayed with me all three weeks I was there. Then when I was ready to leave, her father showed up and shook me down for a bundle. I thought the girl was at least twenty—she was fourteen. Not only that, she left me with the clap."

Santini laughed. "Summer romances. It's always like that. Love and disillusionment." He looked at him. "Was she good in bed at least?"

Joe laughed. "The best."

"So it was not so bad," Santini said. Looking toward the street through the glass doors, he saw his car pulling up to the curb. "I have an appointment." He waved to Joe as he left. "I will call you at the beginning of the week. *Ciao.*"

"Ciao," Joe said. He watched the car move away, then looked at the check. Carefully he folded it and put it in his wallet. He knew the routine. The bank would bounce it. Then he would have to get in touch with Metaxa in New York to collect it for him. If he was lucky, he might collect it in three or four months. Slowly he left the building and walked up the side street to Via Veneto.

It was six o'clock, and the heavy humid heat of Rome pressed wearily against the pavement. The tourists were already returning from the museums, the Vatican and other sightseeing attractions. Now they were looking in the shop windows or seating themselves at the tables beside the sidewalk cafes for ice cream or coffee and pastries. He stopped at his usual table on the sidewalk in front of the Café Doney. He glanced at the entrance of the Excelsior Hotel and then across to the newsstand on the opposite corner of the street where they sold all the foreign magazines, newspapers and books. Someone once said that if you sat here long enough you would see everyone you knew in the world walk by. Maybe not in the whole world, but at least everyone you knew in Rome.

His usual waiter suddenly appeared. Old, thin-haired, with old-fashioned gold-rimmed glasses. He placed the usual espresso before Joe and took the "reserved" card away.

"Buon giorno, Signor Joe." He smiled with his nicotine-stained, crooked teeth.

"Buon giorno, Tito," Joe answered.

"I heard you saw the new movie," Tito said. "Is it good?"

Joe looked up at him. There were no secrets in this town. Especially from waiters. He shrugged. *"Così, cosà."*

Tito nodded. "I have a friend who works at the laboratory. He said there is one scene where the two girls fight in the mud of the street and that it was just as if they were both *nuda."*

"That's right, Tito," Joe said. He put a cigarette in his mouth. Tito held a light for him. "They both have great bodies."

Tito smacked his lips. "I would like to see that."

"As soon as they have prints made, I will invite you to a private screening," Joe said. "But that will not be until September. All the laboratories are closed for the month of August."

"Italy, Italy," Tito sighed. "No one wants to work. But I will be patient, *Signor* Joe, and I thank you for your invitation."

Joe pressed a thousand-lire bill in the waiter's hand. "Thank you, Tito."

A group of tourists came toward a table next to Joe. Quickly, the little waiter moved them away to a further table. *"Scusi, reservato, reservato,"* Tito said and then took their orders as they sat down.

Joe glanced at the Excelsior entrance. There were the usual hustlers and guides standing there, but also a number of paparazzi, their cameras slung around their necks and shoulders. One of them, a young man, glanced back over his shoulder at Joe. Joe gestured his arm in invitation.

The paparazzo nodded and came toward him. *"Ciao, Joe,"* he said.

"Ciao, Vieri," Joe answered. "Have a drink with me."

The young man looked back at the hotel entrance but the offer of a drink was too much for him. He slipped into a chair. "Cognac, *francese,"* he said.

Joe nodded. That was normal—the most expensive drink he could order. He signaled to the waiter, who had already heard. Joe turned to Vieri. "What's all the excitement about?"

"You haven't heard?" Vieri asked. "Ingrid Bergman and Rossellini had just returned from shooting their film on Stromboli and they are in the hotel."

"You saw them?" Joe asked.

"Not yet," Vieri answered. The waiter placed the snifter containing the cognac on the table along with a glass of water. Vieri swirled the cognac and held it under his nostrils. He breathed its scent lightly. "The perfume of the gods," he said.

"Salute," Joe said.

"Salute," Vieri replied and took a sip of the cognac. "My friend saw them when they came out of the airport. He said she was pregnant as a house."

Joe didn't understand the simile. "I thought Rossellini had a home in Rome."

"He does," Vieri said. "But his wife is living in it."

"Oh," Joe said.

"You saw your picture today," Vieri said; then without waiting for an answer, "Did Santini pay you your money?"

Joe laughed. "Of course not."

"The prick," Vieri said. "He owes me for some photographs I made for him five months ago."

"It's a way of life for him," Joe said.

"For all the Italian producers and directors," Vieri said

sarcastically. "They think they are above all things like that. But not above their own money. That they get first."

Joe shrugged and sipped his espresso.

"What are you doing this summer?" Vieri asked.

"I don't know," Joe said. "I thought I'd go back to the States and work on my book. There are no jobs over here."

"The Americans," Vieri said. "The big companies are planning important movies. There's a lot of building going on at Cinecittà and the money is coming from the States. And I also hear that many American stars are coming over. Audrey Hepburn, Gregory Peck, Elizabeth Taylor, Robert Taylor. Production costs are less than in Hollywood."

"It doesn't do me any good," Joe said. "Nobody contacted me."

"Maybe they will," Vieri said. "After all, you've been here almost two years already. You have the experience and know how things are done here."

"I can't hang around without money," Joe said. "I have to produce."

"Are you going to the Contessa Baroni's party tonight?" Vieri asked.

"I haven't made up my mind yet," Joe answered. "I don't know whether I'm up to dressing in a tuxedo tonight with this heat."

"You should go," Vieri said. "It's her annual event. Always on the last Friday in July. Everyone will be there. Then she spends the month of August in her villa at Cap Antibes on the French Riviera. She always invites five or six people to stay with her."

"She didn't invite me," Joe said.

"She never does until the night of this party," Vieri said. "But I hear they have a ball over there. That's where all the action is. She has a yacht and there's a gala every night. Monte Carlo, Nice, Cannes, Saint-Tropez. The most beautiful girls from all of Europe flock there next month. And they're all looking for a good time and a place to stay."

"That leaves me out," Joe said. "The contessa is very possessive."

"She swings both ways, I hear," Vieri said.

"So?" Joe shrugged. "Then she'll get the girls, not me."

"You'll get seconds. That's not too bad."

Joe laughed. "She'll never invite me. I'm not important enough for her."

"You've been out with her a number of times," Vieri pointed out. "You fucked her, didn't you?"

"She's fucked everybody," Joe said. "That doesn't mean anything."

"She's got it all," Vieri said. "Money, dope, champagne, parties. You should go tonight. Maybe you'll get lucky."

"Are you going?" Joe asked.

"I'm not invited, but I'll be there," Vieri answered. "Outside. Trying to grab a few pictures. If you go, I'll take a few shots of you."

"Don't waste your film," Joe said. "You won't be able to sell any of the pictures."

"You hang around until a pretty girl or a star shows up, then get next to them, and I'll get the shot."

"That's not my style," Joe said.

"Go to the party anyway," Vieri said, standing up. "I've got to get back to work. Thanks for the cognac. *Ciao.*"

"*Ciao,*" Joe said, watching him walk to the hotel entrance. He held up his hand for the check. Then he went back to his hotel near the foot of the Spanish Steps.

His small apartment seemed cool, protected from the heat outside by the louvered wooden window shutters. Quickly he pulled off his shirt damp with perspiration and dropped his slacks across a chair. He bent over the sink and splashed water over his head and face, then took a deep breath. Slowly he dried himself with a coarse face towel. He looked at himself in the mirror over the sink and shook his head. It was no wonder people ran away from Rome in the August heat. It was a real bitch.

The telephone began to ring. He walked to the little desk in the living room and picked it up. *"Pronto,"* he said.

It was Laura Shelton, calling him from New York. "How are you?" she asked.

"Hot."

"It's hot here too," she said.

"Nothing can be as hot as heat in Rome."

"Have you seen the movie?" she asked.

"Today," he said.

"What did you think of it?"

"It's okay," he said. "If you like big tits on a big screen and a lot of them."

She laughed. "I thought that was your thing."

"Not in movies," he said. "Seeing is not always believing. A little more story would have helped."

"Did Santini pay you?"

"One rubber check for five thousand, if you can count that. Otherwise, he said he'll pay me the rest when he makes his distribution deal in the States. He said the picture will gross a million dollars."

"I heard from the Coast that several companies are interested in it. Apparently, he shipped two prints out there before he showed it in Italy. Kathy told me that A. J. might take it on."

"Good," he said. "Then I may get my money."

"You'll get your money," she said confidently. "I'm turning your account over to Paul Gitlin, he's an attorney who will act as your agent as well. I've known him a long time and he's very good."

"What are you going to do?" he asked in surprise.

"I said I wanted to be an editor and I finally got a job at Doubleday. So we'll still be in touch, only I'll be your editor, not your agent."

"How does the agency feel about that?" he asked.

"Okay," she said. "They never liked you as a writer anyway. You were not genteel enough for them."

"How did you wind up with that job?"

"Doubleday likes you," she said. "They were satisfied with the sales of your first book. They told me that they will come out with between thirty and forty thousand books, the Doubleday Book Club pushed out one hundred and twenty five thousand copies, and they made a paperback deal with Bantam for forty thousand dollars—that's not so bad. They get half of it, that's twenty thousand."

"Where does all that fit in with you?"

"You're one of my authors. All you have to do is turn out another book in a year or so. They already are willing to up the terms for the second book."

"I haven't started to write it yet," he said.

"Then start now while you have time," she said. "I know you have the story, you told me about it."

"I'll need help," he said. "You're my editor—meet me here and we'll block out the novel together."

She laughed. "I still have work to do."

"What work?" he asked.

"It will take me about two weeks to clean up my desk here. Doubleday wants me on the first of September."

"You can still spend the last two weeks of August with

me," he said. "I'll pick up a car and we'll travel along the French Riviera. I hear that it's fantastic."

She laughed again. "You're really crazy. Do you know how much money that would cost?"

"I can afford it," he said. "Besides, I would like to see you."

"I don't know," she said hesitantly.

"Look, you don't have to worry about that goddam agency spying on you all the time. You're the boss now. We'll have a real ball. I'll send you the ticket."

She was silent for a moment. "Would you give me a little time to think it out?" she asked.

"How much time?" he asked.

"Call me on the tenth," she said. "Maybe I'll feel better about it then."

"I'll call you on the tenth, but I'll send the ticket now," he said.

"Where will you be?" she asked.

"I'll be traveling but the ticket will be open. I'll be wherever you are when you give me the okay."

"Don't send me a ticket. I can afford my own," she said. "And call me at home, not at the office."

"Gotcha. Have you ever been to Europe before?"

"I spent two years in college in Paris."

"Then you speak French?"

"Yes," she said.

"Then you have to come over," he said. "You'll be able to take me around."

She laughed. "Just call me on the tenth and start thinking about the new book."

"I can think of more fun things than a new book," he said.

"Don't play games with me," she said. "I'm a very serious person."

"I'm being very serious," he replied. "You just tell me that you're joining me and you'll find out just how serious I can be."

He stared down at the telephone for a moment, then placed his monthly call to his parents. He put down the receiver and checked his watch. It was six hours earlier in New York than it was in Italy. The chances were that there would be no answer on their end. But he was wrong. Miraculously, the call went through in ten minutes.

His mother answered. "Hello?"

"Mama, how are you?" he asked.

"Where are you?" she asked suspiciously. "You sound like from the corner."

"I'm still in Rome," he said. "How's Papa?"

"Papa's all right. He takes care of himself and he is all right. When are you coming home?"

"I don't know," he said. "There is another job on the way and I'm taking a month's vacation in France."

"In France," she said. "You're becoming so fancy-shmancy. France has nothing but the most expensive whores."

He laughed. "You'll never change, Mama."

"What should I change? When your book came out I thought you had some respect. But instead, all our friends that read it said they never read so much filth like that. I don't understand, it was on the best-seller list for fifteen weeks."

"Did you read it?"

"I should read filth like that?" she asked. "I don't even tell anybody that you're my son, I'm so ashamed."

253

"You're never going to change," he repeated. "Is Papa home?"

"No," she said. "He went to the market today, just for a few hours."

"Then tell him that I called." He put down the phone.

It was no use. He could never win with her.

== 29 ==

HE LEFT THE bathroom door open so that he could hear the telephone ring as he slid into the comfort of the large, deep Italian bathtub filled with lukewarm water. He lit a cigarette and leaned back in the curve of the bathtub. It was almost nine o'clock and still bright daylight. He hadn't yet made up his mind about the party tonight. There was no rush. Italian parties didn't start until midnight.

He heard a knock from the living-room door. He shouted from the bathroom. "Who is it?"

"Marissa," the girl's voice came through the door. "I've brought all your files from the office."

Marissa was the black girl who had acted as his secretary while he worked on the scripts for Santini. She was the daughter of an Italian consulate attaché in New York who had married a black American woman, and when he was recalled to Italy in 1940, he brought his wife and daughter, Marissa, then fifteen, to Rome with him. She had worked as an interpreter for the American Army when they came to Rome during the war, and afterwards she had worked at various jobs, winding up as secretary-interpreter for various Italian film producers.

"Come in!" he yelled, from the tub. "The door is open."

He looked into the small living room. She was carrying a large olive-drab canvas army surplus duffel bag, which she dropped on the floor. "What the hell have you got in there?" he called.

"My clothes," she replied. "I need a place to stay for a few days."

"What happened?"

"Santini closed the office for August without paying me. My *pensione* is very strict about the rent. I'm out of money, so I thought I would get my things before they locked me out."

"The cheap bastard screwed you too!" he exclaimed.

"Did he pay you?" she asked.

"You gotta be joking," he answered. "He said he'd pay me as soon as he made a distribution deal for the States."

"I also brought over your files," she said.

"Thanks," he said.

She came to the bathroom doorway. "Do you have a cigarette?"

He gestured. "On the shelf under the mirror." He watched her light a cigarette. There were sweat stains under her armpits and the silk blouse seemed glued across her strong breasts. "How long would you need to stay here?"

"Just the weekend," she said. "My girlfriend will give me her apartment for the month of August. She's going to Ischia with her boyfriend."

He looked up at her. "Okay."

"You're wonderful!" She bent over to kiss his cheek. "I won't be any problem," she added. "If you have anybody over I can sleep on the couch."

"I don't have any plans," he said, glancing down the open neckline of her blouse. Her nipples were dark lavender against the lighter tan of her breasts. Beads of perspiration rolled down the valley of her chest. "You're sweating bullets," he said. "Why don't you get into the bathtub with me?"

She dragged on the cigarette. "I stink that bad?"

"No." He laughed, holding his erection out of the water so that she could see it. "I just want to fuck."

She began taking off her clothes. "Great!" she said. "I'm always horny." In a moment she was naked. She stepped into the tub, standing erect over him. Quickly she masturbated her vulva, then spread her vagina with two fingers so that the small purple clitoris peeked out between her labia. "How about that?" she laughed, looking down at him.

"Fantastic!" He held his erection and arched his back to meet her. "Get on it."

"In a second," she said, reaching for a bar of soap. Quickly she soaped and rubbed his phallus until he thought every nerve was burning through to his testicles, then she held him tightly and, sitting on her haunches, brought him into her.

He gasped for breath. It felt as if he had been dipped into a vat of burning oil. He grasped her buttocks to bring her closer to him as she leaned over his face, her breasts smothering him.

He felt himself slipping back down into the tub, the water beginning to reach his face. "You're going to fucking drown me."

"Don't worry." She laughed. "I'll save you. I have a lifeguard's certificate." She began writhing and bringing him more inside her, never letting him slip out. "Just relax." She smiled, sure of her power. "Let me do all the work. Just think as if I'm a propeller spinning on your shaft."

He looked up at her. "I never knew you could fuck like this when we were in the office."

"Office fucks are never the best," she said. "They're always quickie duty fucks. You can never be creative. Just get your rocks off and run."

"Hallelujah!" he cried.

Suddenly she held him still. "Don't move!" she ordered.

He glanced up at her. "What's wrong?"

"Nothing," she said. "I'm starting to pee. Ooh," she whispered ecstatically. "Now you do it inside me."

"I can't pee through a hard on," he said.

"Yes, you can," she said. "I'll show you." Quickly she placed a finger under his testicles and pressed a nerve. His urine came pouring forth like a spout. At the same moment, she took his phallus from her and lifted it still urinating onto her face and gulped as much of it as she could catch in her mouth. When the urine had stopped she replaced him instantly inside her. She moved her face close to him. "I love the taste of your pee," she said. "It's like sweet sugar."

He felt her exciting writhing again. "Where did you ever get into that?" he gasped.

"From the American soldiers during the war," she said huskily. "They all wanted to give me golden showers, and after a while I really got into it."

"Christ," he said.

"That wasn't all," she said. "The Americans were more fun than the Germans. The Boche were straight fuck and suck. The Americans even loved to stick Mars Bars and Baby Ruths up my ass and cunt."

"Then what did they do?" he asked.

"Either they ate it or I did," she said.

"Shit," he said.

"That, too," she answered. "When you're on the losing side you do what they tell you. Otherwise you're out. Nothing to eat, no jobs, no favors."

"Is it that way now?" he asked.

"In a kind of way," she said. "You don't get any kind of job unless you fuck for it."

"You didn't have to fuck me for the job."

"You didn't hire me," she said. "Santini did." She looked down at him. "You're losing your hard," she said. "That's what happens when you think too much and talk too much."

He stared up at her silently.

"Don't worry about it," she said. "I'll get it back for you in a moment." She moved slightly to one side and passed her hand under his buttocks. A moment later she had slipped two fingers into his anus and began lightly pressing and massaging his prostate. His erection was instantly resurrected.

"Now, you motherfucker!" she cried. "Do it! Do it hard!"

He was half dozing on top of the bed when the telephone began to ring. Sleepily he looked across the room toward Marissa. Nude, she was moving around the living room, unpacking her clothes. She glanced at him questioningly.

"Answer it," he said.

She picked up the telephone. *"Pronto."*

He could hear an Italian woman's voice in the receiver. She listened for a moment, then called to him. "It's Mara Benetti," she said. "She wants to know if you are going to the contessa's party?"

"I haven't made up my mind yet," he said.

"It's after ten o'clock," she pointed out.

"So what? Nobody ever gets there until midnight," he answered.

Marissa spoke to the actress in Italian, who then fired a number of words at her. "She wants you to escort her," she told him.

"What happened to Santini?" he asked. "He was supposed to take her."

More words spewed from the telephone. "Santini screwed her," Marissa explained. "He's taking the American actress instead. Her boyfriend said he'd give her a limousine to use tonight, if you'd take her."

"Why doesn't *he* take her?"

"He's a Mafioso," Marissa said flatly. "He's maybe got other things to do."

"He'll blow my fucking head off after the party," he said.

"Not if you bring me along with you," Marissa said shrewdly. "That will show him that you respect him."

"You'd like to go?" he asked curiously.

"Of course. It's the big party of the season," she answered. "And I stole a great dress from the wardrobe in the studio just for a chance like this."

Joe shrugged. "Ask her if she would mind if I brought you along?"

"I'll explain it," she said. "After all, you don't speak Italian, I'm your secretary and you need me to interpret for you. Also, she knows me."

"Okay."

Marissa turned to the telephone again, spoke quickly in Italian. "She said okay. The car will be here to pick us up."

=== 30 ===

HE WAS JUST taking his white dinner jacket from the closet when she came from the bathroom. He stared at her.

She smiled. "You like?"

"Beautiful," he said. "But you look naked under your gown."

"I *am* naked," she answered. "Flesh-colored sheer form-fitting chiffon sprinkled with bugle beads."

"I can see your pussy and the crack of your ass as you turn around. Even the purple-red color of your nipples."

She laughed. "That's makeup. I also dusted some silver sprinkles over me. I think it's exciting."

He looked at her. She was completely made up with mascara, blue and gold eye shadow, rose rouge highlighting her cheekbones, and scarlet lips. A soft black curled long-haired wig covered her own tightly crinkled hair. "You look like a Harlem hooker I used to know."

"Sexy?"

"Very," he answered. "Mara's going to blow her mind. I don't think she expected this kind of competition."

She laughed. "I told her what I was wearing. She said it would be okay. She's wearing a black dress, lace, open-cut down between her breasts to her pussy in front and down her back to the middle of the crack of her ass. She said that between us we'd put the American actress away."

"I'll never understand you women," he said.

"You don't have to," she said. "Just enjoy it."

The paparazzi were having a field day. Vieri came over to Joe. "How did you manage it?"

Joe held out his hands. "It just happened."

"You're fucking both of them?" he asked.

Joe smiled without answering.

"Lucky bastard," Vieri said. "These have to be the best pictures of the night. I'll be able to sell them all over Europe."

"Good," Joe said. He looked at the photographer. "Did Santini show up yet?"

"Yes. About a half an hour ago. The American girl is stupid. She wore a simple white organza dress. Nothing but big tits and ass, not sexy at all, and the white doesn't photograph well."

Joe laughed.

"Mara's boyfriend know you took her out?" Vieri asked.

"He arranged it," Joe said. "It's his car that we're using."

Vieri nodded. "Good," he said. "I was worried that you might get into trouble. He's a tough man."

"It's okay," Joe said. He walked toward the girls still standing at the steps posing for the photographers. "I think we'll go in now."

"Just stop a moment at the top of the steps," Vieri said. "That way I can shoot up and get a shot of the girls with their pussies showing right through their dresses."

"You've got it," Joe said. He walked up with the girls, held still for a moment, then turned as the footman opened the door.

The foyer of the house was almost as large as a ballroom and crowded with people. Joe vaguely recognized many of them but didn't know their names. Whispering behind her hand, Marissa identified them for him. He looked at her gratefully. She was a perfect secretary.

Slowly they moved through the foyer; the girls' hands were kissed again and again. He handed his card to the butler, with both their names beneath his.

The butler called out, *"Dottore* Joseph Crown and *Signorina* Mara Benetti and *Signorina* Marissa Panzoni."

They walked down the steps to the ballroom. A waiter walked toward them with a tray of champagne glasses. Joe handed a glass to each of the girls. *"Salute."*

Mara was smiling. She felt good. She knew that everyone had been looking at them. *"Salute,"* she said to Joe, and in her accented English, her eyes glancing across the room, "Have you seen that son of a bitch yet?"

"Not yet." Joe smiled.

"I will tear his eyes out," Mara said sweetly. "And that *putana* with him."

Joe laughed. "You don't have to worry about them. Everyone has already forgotten them, blinded by the dazzle of your beauty."

Mara nodded seriously. "I am much more beautiful than her?"

"Without question," Joe said quickly. "You're the most beautiful woman in this party."

Marissa nodded in agreement. "If I were a man I would throw myself at your feet."

"You're so sweet." Mara smiled. "And Joe, too. I am so glad I invited you both to this party."

Marissa and Joe glanced at each other. Who invited who,

who was invited by who? They smiled. "I am happy too," Joe said.

At the far end of the ballroom an orchestra played and people began dancing. The cool night air was coming in through the large French doors. In the next room was a long buffet table laden with food and a long line of guests queuing up for dinner.

Another uniformed footman came toward him. *"Dottore* Crown?"

Joe nodded.

The footman spoke to him in Italian. Joe glanced at Marissa, who translated. "The contessa would like you and your guests to come to her private apartment."

Again Joe nodded and they followed the footman through the dining room and a narrow hallway, then up a staircase and through another corridor. He opened large double doors and closed the doors behind them as they entered.

The contessa was seated on a large thronelike chair at the head of a table also laden with food. The contessa was a beautiful woman with an imperious manner. She gestured for Joe to come to her. "Joe," she said, laughing. "My brilliant American writer."

Joe kissed her outstretched hand. *"Eccellenza,"* he murmured. He straightened up. "You know my friends. *Signorina* Mara Benetti, the star of my movie, and my assistant, *Signorina* Marissa Panzoni."

The contessa nodded. "Very beautiful children," she said, then turned back to Joe. "You are fucking with both of them?"

Joe laughed.

"Don't be embarassed. You should be proud. I would love to see the three of you making love. It would be most exciting." She leaned from her chair and ran her hands across each girl's body. "Beautiful, beautiful," she murmured. "So firm and strong and sexual."

The two girls were used to it—but then, they knew the contessa better than Joe did. "Thank you, *Eccellenza,*" they answered in unison.

The contessa snapped her fingers. A footman came toward them with a small covered silver sugarbowl, which he opened before them. Quickly the contessa picked up a tiny gold spoon and took two big snorts in each nostril. She then offered it to them.

Joe took it first. The coke exploded in his head. It was top quality. The coke that Joe bought on the streets in Rome was like shit next to this. This was a real buzz.

Mara snorted it cautiously, but Marissa was like a steam shovel—four heavy snootfuls in each nostril. Her eyes lit up like electric bulbs. *"Mamma mia!"* she laughed. "I think I'm coming already."

The contessa laughed and put her hand under Marissa's dress. "It's true!" she shouted, taking out her fingers and licking them. "You're soaking wet."

Mara looked down at the contessa. "Pardon me, *Eccellenza,* have you seen Maestro Santini this evening?"

The contessa gestured with her hand. "He is downstairs with his American girl. She has no class, very common. I left them downstairs with the hoi polloi." She turned to Joe. "Do you think his movie will make some money?" she asked. "I have invested one hundred thousand of my dollars into it."

"I think you have a good chance," Joe said loyally. After all, he had a stake in that movie too.

"Has he paid you?" she asked shrewdly.

"Not yet," he answered.

The contessa laughed. "He is such a crook, not even a

charming scoundrel. He told me that he had paid everybody off."

Joe was silent.

The contessa turned to Mara. "And you? Has he paid you?"

Mara nodded. "My gentleman friend arranged that."

"That makes sense." The contessa nodded. "He will not have any trouble from your friend."

"He even owes me twenty thousand lire," Marissa added.

"Cheap," the contessa said. "Cheap." She turned to the footman. "Give the *signorina* ten thousand lire."

"No, *Eccellenza*," Marissa protested. "It is not your responsibility."

"You are my friend," the contessa said firmly. "And also you have a very sweet pussy."

Another footman brought a tray of champagne and they all took one, while still another footman came with a tray of cigarettes. As Joe lit the first cigarette, the heavily perfumed hash oil laid on the tobacco came through the room.

The contessa laughed. "It's a lovely party." She turned to one of the footman. "Lock the doors to my suite. We'll have our own party."

Mara hesitated. "*Eccellenza*, I must beg your pardon, but my gentleman friend would not approve of this for me."

The contessa laughed. "He will not object, my dear. After all, I am his sponsor in Rome. He knows that you were joining me. Wasn't it his idea that he give you his limousine?"

Mara stared at her.

The contessa smiled. "Enjoy a cigarette and relax. Then we will all have dinner together. I will have your breasts for dessert. I will lick them as if they were the sweetest Devonshire cream."

Joe glanced around the room. So far only themselves and the contessa were in the private apartment. A moment later two couples entered from a rear door. The men were dressed in Indian turbans, short brocaded vests and blousy harem cotton pantaloons tied by a string around the waist. The girls were wearing harem-type softly twisted brassieres and beribboned, flared silk skirts that revealed their bodies from legs to waist. Soft music came from between the curtains, and the room lights began to dim.

"We can change our clothes here," the contessa said huskily. "We have more costumes for all of us." She looked at Mara and Marissa. "Each of those men have cocks at least twenty centimeters large, and all of them, the men and the women, are trained in the eastern arts of pleasure."

She reached for the sugar bowl and took two more snorts from the golden spoon, then rose from her chair. Her dress had not been fastened, and it fell to the floor as she moved forward. Her body was large and firm. Slowly one of the men began to wrap a costume around her.

Joe turned to the two girls. They returned his glance silently. Then he picked up the sugar bowl and helped himself before he began to undress. Marissa followed suit immediately, and a moment later Mara began to slip her dress from her shoulders.

The contessa raised her champagne glass. *"A la dolce vita!"*

=31=

IT WAS ALMOST eight o'clock in the morning when they left the contessa's palazzo and got into the car. "We can have some coffee at my hotel," he said. "The kitchen is already open."

Mara looked at him. "I think I'd better go right home."

"We could all use some coffee," Joe said.

"I'll drop you off," she said. She lit a cigarette. "It's been a long night."

"As you like," Joe said.

Mara looked at them. "You won't tell my friend what we did?"

"I don't know anything," Joe said. "I don't even know him."

"He is very jealous," Mara said. "If he thought that I had been with another man he would kill me."

"And what about the contessa?" he asked.

"He knows about her," she said. "Besides, women don't count."

"Okay."

The limousine pulled up in front of his hotel and he and Marissa got out. "Thank you," Joe said.

"It's nothing," Mara answered. "Will you stay in town this month?"

"I don't know yet."

"I will call you," she said. *"Ciao. Ciao,* Marissa."

The limousine drove off, and they went into the hotel. He placed his order for breakfast with the concierge before he went up to his apartment. Marissa was out of her dress and into an old army surplus T-shirt before he had even taken off his jacket.

"Jesù Cristo!" she said. "That contessa is too much."

He took off his shirt and threw it on a chair. "She's something else."

"I never knew anyone could eat pussy like that," she said. "One time I thought her tongue would go through my cunt to my asshole."

He looked at her. "You liked it?"

"She was the best. I heard that lesbians were the best, but I never believed it until now."

There was a knock at the door and the waiter brought in the tray with coffee and rolls. She waited until the waiter had gone. "She left me forty thousand lire, not twenty."

"Not bad," he said.

"She gave you something," Marissa said. "I saw her."

Joe laughed and took out a small wax-paper bag. "Cocaine."

"She's a real lady," Marissa said. She filled the coffee cups. "Was she a good fuck?"

"I'm not complaining," he said.

"My cunt is so sore," she said, "it burns when I pee."

He laughed and sipped his coffee. "It'll get better."

She looked at him. "Do you want me to sleep on the couch?"

269

"You can sleep in the bed," he said. "Just don't wake me up if you have to move around."

"I'll be quiet," she said. "Do you have any plans for tomorrow?"

"I might look for a car in the afternoon," he answered. "There's an Alfa convertible I have an eye on."

"You'd better take me with you," she said seriously. "You're American, they'll steal your eyeballs. Let me do the talking and it will cost you less."

"I'll think about it when we wake up," he said. He dropped the rest of his clothing and crawled naked into bed.

She looked down at him. "Do you mind if I shower? I have to take off my makeup and get the shiny sprinkles off me, or they stick all over the bed."

"Go ahead," he said. "But turn out the lights in here. I want to sleep."

"Okay," she said. The lights went off and she closed the bathroom door behind her. A moment later he heard the soft running of the shower. He closed his eyes.

La dolce vita, he thought. The contessa was right when she called it that. It would make a good title for a movie, but not for him. It really was another world. He could enjoy it, but he could not begin to understand it. Then he was asleep.

The sound of voices came through the closed bedroom door. Slowly, he opened his eyes. Marissa was not there. He heard her voice from the living room. He sat up and put on his wristwatch. It was four o'clock in the afternoon. He lit a cigarette and listened to the other voices—a man's and another woman's.

Quietly he went into the bathroom, splashed cold water

on his face and slipped on a bathrobe. Still barefoot, he opened the bedroom door.

Marissa, Mara, and a man he didn't know were seated at the small table; the waiter had just served coffee. *"Buon giorno,"* he said.

The man sprang to his feet. He was a strong-looking man of medium height, his black hair slicked back in the fashion of the time, with dark brown eyes, a large Roman nose over full lips, and a square chin. He bowed, smiled to Joe. *"Signor Dottore,"* he said.

Joe looked at him, then at Marissa. Mara spoke quickly. "This is my friend, Franco Gianpietro. He has much honor and pleasure to meet with you."

Joe nodded and held out his hand. "It is my honor."

They shook hands European style, pumping hands up and down twice. The man said something quickly in Italian. Marissa translated. "Signor Gianpietro apologizes for the intrusion. If you want to return to bed, he would be pleased to come back at your convenience."

"It's okay," Joe said. He gestured. "Please sit down."

The Italian nodded. "My English is not too good," he said. "But with *permesso*, I will try."

Joe smiled. "It's very good." He took the coffee that Marissa had placed before him and leaned back in the couch. The coffee was strong and black. That woke him up. "What can I do for you?" he asked.

"You are a very important *scrittore*," Gianpietro said. "Mara tells me that you are the best in America."

"She is very kind," Joe said.

She smiled. *"Vero.* True."

"Santini is a prick," Gianpietro said.

"I won't argue about that." Joe laughed.

"Mara thought that you perhaps write a movie for her.

271

She feels that Santini screwed her in this picture, he gave all the good scenes to the American girl." Gianpietro looked at him.

"It would be an honor," Joe said. "But there are some problems. One, I have no producer; two, I have no story suitable for her."

"The producer I can obtain," Gianpietro said. "And maybe there is a magazine story that she read might be good for a movie. It is a well-known story in Italy, has been very well received. *La Ragazza sulla Motocicletta*."

"I know the story," Marissa said. "It's good. It's about a girl from a poor family who steals a big motorcycle, then runs all over Rome fucking and stealing in order to feed her family. It has an exciting ending where the police chase her through the streets in the city, and she is killed because she will not run over a little child that was crossing the street."

"It sounds interesting," Joe said. "But I'd have to read the story. Is there a translation around?"

"I can do one for you in a day," Marissa said.

Gianpietro nodded. "With me, you would get all your money. I am a man of honor, not like Santini. Also, I have heard that you would like to spend August in the south of France. I have a large villa just outside of Nice where Mara and I will be. There is a nice guest house, and you could live there in comfort. I even have a car for your personal convenience."

"That sounds good," Joe said. "But I would have to read the story first. Perhaps I am not the right writer for it. I don't know that much about the people here."

"Mara and Marissa can tell you everything you need to know," Gianpietro said. "And I know how much fees you command. I will pay you the thirty-five thousand and expenses in full when you've finished the script. You don't have to wait for the movie to be made."

"You are more than generous," Joe said. "But I do think I should read the story first. I don't want to cheat you and say I can do it if I can't."

Gianpietro looked at him for a moment, then took a roll of bills out of his pocket. Slowly he counted out a number of one-thousand-dollar bills. "That's twenty thousand dollars," he said as he finished counting and replaced the roll in his pocket.

"What's that for?" Joe asked. "I haven't agreed to do the script yet."

"This has nothing to do with the script. This is the money I collected from Santini for you."

Joe stared at him.

"It's okay," Gianpietro said. "The contessa asked me to take care of it."

"But Santini wouldn't give it to me," Joe said. "He said he did not have the money."

Gianpietro smiled. "It's surprising how quickly a man like this finds that he has the money, especially when you squeeze his balls a little."

Joe looked at him, then picked up the money and put it in his bathrobe pocket. "Thank you."

Gianpietro nodded. "I have given a copy of the story to Marissa, and perhaps Tuesday night after you've read it we could have dinner and discuss it."

"It will be my pleasure," Joe said.

Gianpietro rose and Mara joined him. She looked at Joe. "You will make a very big star of me. More of a star than that *putana*."

He kissed her on the cheek and shook hands with the Italian. "Tuesday night for dinner," he said.

He turned to Marissa after they had gone. "Did you know anything about this?"

"I heard Mara and the contessa speaking, but we were all kind of spaced out so I didn't think anything about it." She laughed. "Maybe we got lucky."

He looked at her silently. "You sure you didn't put them all up to this?"

"I'm just nothin' but your nigger secretary. Nobody would pay any attention to me."

"I'm not that sure," he said.

She changed the subject. "The American Express office is still open," she said. "We better get over there and you can turn your money into traveler's checks. It's too much cash to carry around."

It took Marissa almost two days to translate the story and only two hours for Joe to read it. He threw the manuscript on the table and stared at it. Then he looked at Marissa. "It's pure shit," he said. "There's no way I can write this script."

Marissa lit a cigarette. "There must be some way you can save it."

He shook his head. "No way. It's pure pulp. On top of that, it's not even entertainment. It's childish."

"Gianpietro will be disappointed."

"I'd rather he be disappointed with the truth than lead him down the garden path. He's not stupid. Sooner or later he would figure out that I took him for the money. I would not like him to get angry with me. I don't think I'd like him squeezing my balls a little."

"You'll have to be very diplomatic," she said. "He's got his mind set on making Mara a star."

"I'll explain it to him. We have to find a better vehicle for her."

"You know what you're doing," she said, disappointed. "There goes our spending the month on the French Riviera."

"I'm going anyway," he said. "My agent is coming over in a couple of weeks."

"I'm going to have to sweat it out here in town," she said, meeting his eyes.

Joe smiled at her. "You're a fucking hustler. I guess you think I'll feel sorry for you."

"Don't you? Just even a little?" Her eyes were wide. "How would you feel if you were stuck here?"

"Hustler!" Joe laughed.

"I have an idea," she said.

He looked at her.

"Why don't you tell him that we'll spend the two weeks with them and try to come up with a story that would be right for all of us?"

"That's a real con," he said.

"Not really," she said. "Who knows? You might come up with something that will work."

"You've gotta be joking, you know that cunt can't act. I wouldn't know what would work for her," he said.

"You said you don't need the money," she pointed out. "Tell him it's for free, all you promise is to try for two weeks. All it will cost him is the house expenses, which he is spending anyway."

"And you get your vacation?"

"Of course," she said. "And it wouldn't cost you anything. Also, you don't have to pay me any salary."

He laughed. "You want it that bad?"

She met his eyes. "Yes. For a girl like me, the French Riviera is the top of the world. Who knows what opportunity

I may find? All the rich people are there. I might get very lucky."

Joe looked at her seriously. After a moment he said, "Okay. I'll suggest it to him. But if it doesn't work, don't blame me."

She kissed his cheek. "I won't blame you. And I'll get off your back at the end of the two weeks, but you'll have to be careful."

"Careful of what?" he asked.

"Mara," she said. "She's got the hots for you and he has to stay in Rome during the week and only comes over on the weekends."

"What makes you think that?" he asked in surprise. "She's not stupid. She knows on which side her bread is buttered."

"True," she answered. "But she wouldn't mind a little partying with you on the side."

=32=

IT WAS A typical old-fashioned Mediterranean villa situated on a small knoll above the sea in Villefranche. Just slightly in front of the main house was the small guest house that Gianpietro had offered him. It was not decorated in the same manner as the main house—in former times, Joe thought, it had been assigned to the servants. But it was comfortable despite the tiny rooms, and it was far enough away from the villa so that sounds did not carry. There was a private staircase that led down to the pebble beach.

Joe placed his typewriter on a table in front of the large window through which he had the view of the whole bay of Villefranche across to the end of St.-Jean Cap Ferrat. He looked toward the villa. He could see a corner of the staircase that a guest in the main house could use to go down to the beach. In front of the beach there was a dock to which was tied a small Riva.

Late in the same afternoon Joe had arrived, Gianpietro came down to the guest house. "You like it?" he asked.

Joe smiled. "It's perfect, thank you."

The Italian smiled. "I thought you would like it. Here you have the privacy you need to work. No one will disturb you."

"Thank you again."

"I have a favor to ask of you," Gianpietro said.

"Just ask," Joe answered.

"Mara wants to speak American," he said. "It is difficult to find a tutor for just a month here. Marissa said that she could help her and stay for the month even when you leave."

"That's okay with me," Joe answered.

"Thank you, Joe." Gianpietro smiled. He waved his hand out, gesturing to the bay. "What do you think of the Côte d'Azur?"

"What I see right now is beautiful."

"It is the garden spot of the world," Gianpietro said. "Get yourself organized, then come up to the villa at six o'clock. We will have drinks, then at nine o'clock we will have dinner at the Hotel de Paris in Monte Carlo. After that we'll go to the casino and maybe to a night club."

Joe laughed. "You're not wasting any time."

"I only have the weekend, then I must go to Rome and work. I will return here every Friday night."

"You should spend more time here," Joe said.

"I can't." He shrugged expressively. "Even on the weekend here I have business. This evening I have some associates, Frenchmen from Marseilles, who will be joining us for dinner."

Joe nodded. "I understand."

He looked at Joe. "Do you think Mara has the talent she needs to become a star?"

Joe returned his gaze honestly. "Nobody knows. She has the look, but the rest of it is in the lap of the gods. She has one thing going for her in any case. She is not afraid of hard work."

Gianpietro nodded seriously. "That is true. But I would

prefer that she relaxes and we have a baby. That is what I really want."

"Then why doesn't she do it?"

"She said not until we marry. She does not want the reputation of being a *putana* like many other actresses we know."

"Marry her then," Joe said.

Gianpietro smiled wryly. "It's so easy for Americans but not for Italians. I am already married, and even though I have not been with my wife for more than ten years I cannot obtain a divorce."

"I'm sorry," Joe sympathized.

Gianpietro laughed. "It's not that bad. Being married, I cannot become married. And in the last ten years, Mara is the fourth girl I have fallen in love with. Perhaps next year I might fall in love with another girl. It is easier to get rid of a girlfriend than a wife."

"I didn't think about that," Joe said. "But I guess you are right."

"I am right," Gianpietro said. "Think of the problems that Rossellini and Bergman are having. And, now, Ponti and Loren. His wife will not allow him a divorce either. And Vittorio De Sica, with one legal wife and another illegal wife, each living on the same grounds, one house behind the other, each with her own family of his children."

"Do they know about each other?"

He shrugged. "Who knows? Probably they do but no one ever discusses it. No wonder sometimes he seems as if he is going crazy and spends his spare time gambling all his money at the casino."

"Do you know De Sica?" Joe asked.

"Very well," he answered.

"Do you think he would do a picture with Mara?"

"He always needs money," Gianpietro said.

"If I had an idea for a story," Joe said, "not a script—he could select his own scriptwriters—could you give it to him?"

Gianpietro nodded. "Of course. And if he likes it, he would make it with Mara."

"You're sure of that?" Joe asked.

Gianpietro laughed. "There are many ways a man can get his balls squeezed. De Sica already owes me almost seventy thousand dollars." He paused for a moment. "You have an idea for him?"

"I'm not sure," Joe said. "De Sica is a classy director. I don't know whether he would work with a writer like me."

"He owes me seventy thousand dollars," Gianpietro repeated. "For that kind of money he'll work with a monkey in the zoo."

"I'm feeling a different kind of love story. Usually the American soldier has a baby and leaves the baby with the girl. This asshole wants the baby for himself and takes it to the States. The girl fights her way by hook or crook and tracks him to a small town in the Midwest. Finally, when she sees that the child is really having a good life, one better than she could have given him, she leaves the baby with the father and returns to her home in Italy."

"De Sica will do it. Of course, he will want you to collaborate with his own writers, but that is nothing. He will feel more secure with their Italian idiom. Within a few days I will arrange for him to meet with you."

"And if he doesn't like it?" Joe asked.

"Fuck him. There's always Ponti or Rossellini plus a dozen others who owe me a lot of money." He walked to the door. "Just leave it to me. All you have to do is get dressed for dinner tonight."

The Hotel de Paris restaurant extended outside the huge great French doors to a terrace on a carpeted platform that reached almost to the edge of the sidewalk. The outside walls were a bank of beautiful flowers that prevented the tourists and hoi polloi from looking at the crowds of shapely ladies and the men who exuded riches and power. Each table was covered with beautiful linen and crystal and centered with artfully arranged flowers.

Gianpietro had reserved a table seating for ten placed against a corner in a secluded location. Besides himself, Mara, Marissa and Joe, three Frenchmen and their ladies were his guests. Unfortunately, none of them could speak, or pretended not to speak, English. They made the usual French handshakes of introduction, and after that, it seemed as if Joe did not even exist. The men spoke always in monotone, the women never at all. There was no laughter, and it did not take long for Joe to see that this was a business meeting, not a dinner. Joe smiled at Marissa and paid attention to his dinner for the food was superb. Joe was not unhappy.

Dinner was served quietly and quickly. Joe had the feeling that it had been arranged in advance because when the dinner was completed, the Frenchmen and their ladies said their goodbyes.

Gianpietro stood at the table until they had gone, then returned to his chair. "The French are always the same. They have no manners."

Mara spoke to him in Italian. She sounded angry.

Gianpietro shook his head. "It's business," he said.

She was still angry. "You're not going to leave me alone here this summer while you run around doing your business."

"Just two weeks," he said. "Then I'll be back." He called

for the bill and turned again to her. "We can do our talking in the car on the way home. This is no place to allow anyone to hear what we speak about."

"We're not going directly home," she said. "I thought we were going to the casino."

"I have no time for that just now," he said. "I'm leaving at six in the morning on the Rome Express from Nice."

═ 33 ═

JOE AND MARISSA headed down the path to their small bungalow. It was almost one-thirty in the morning when they closed the guest-house door behind them. He asked Marissa what was happening.

She began slipping out of her gown. "It was simply business," she answered. "The French want Gianpietro to get two hundred tons of raw untreated heroin from Sicily and deliver it to Marseilles, where they have just set up laboratories. If he can do this for two weeks, his share will be two million dollars."

"Then what is Mara so pissed off about? She should know that Gianpietro will take good care of her."

"She wants to show herself around the Riviera playing the star. He won't be around, so who is there to show her off? She's simply a selfish bitch."

Joe had taken off his jacket and thrown his black tie and shirt on a chair when there was a knock at the door of the bungalow. "Come in," he called.

Marissa had just slipped on her dressing gown when Gianpietro came into the room. He turned directly to Joe, not even looking at her. "I need your help, my friend," he said.

"How can I help you?" Joe said.

"As you probably realize, I have to go away for several weeks on business. Mara became very angry, but I have finally been able to calm her down. First, and most important, she wants you to continue the script for her. Second, she doesn't want to stay alone in the big house. She said that she would feel more secure if Marissa moved up there with her. I also arranged for her to have enough money so that she could shop and go out several times during the week for dinner and amusement. She also wants to speak only in English with Marissa so that she becomes very expert and fluent."

Joe looked at him. "I agree with you, of course, but don't you think it would be more discreet if I returned to Rome with you? After all, Mara is a very attractive lady and people will talk, as they always do."

"Let them think what they will, fuck them. You are my friend and a gentleman. I know in my heart that there will not be any improper behavior between you."

Joe turned to Marissa. "What do you think?"

"I agree with Franco," she said. "This is, of course, the correct way to handle the situation."

Joe held out his hand. "Then it will be done."

The Italian embraced him. "Thank you, my friend. Thank you."

Despite the heat in the small room, he slept as though he were dead. But then a strange new aroma filtered to his nostrils. It was a new scent, not Marissa's—he was familiar with hers. Slowly he opened one eye and looked at his watch. It was one o'clock in the afternoon. Then he opened the other eye and looked across the bed.

Mara was seated on a chair next to the bed, naked, her

legs apart. She smiled at him. "I thought you would never wake up."

He stared at her. "What did you do? It looks like you shaved off ninety percent of your pussy."

She laughed. "You have a good eye. But this is the big style in the south of France. The new bikinis are so tiny that any hair will make you look like you're wearing a beard down the sides of your thighs."

Suddenly he was completely awake. "You're speaking English?" he questioned. "I thought you knew only a few words."

She met his eyes. "It makes more sense this way. People prefer it, they think that you are more stupid, and because of that they say many things that they expect you not to understand."

Marissa came in from the bathroom. She was drying her naked body with a towel. She laughed at Joe. "How do you like it?" she asked. "I did a pretty good job on Mara. Maybe I should become a cunt coiffeuse."

"I could do it better," Joe laughed. "And I wouldn't need scissors, I could nibble at it with my teeth."

"Don't be a wise guy," Marissa said. "Grab yourself a shower, then throw some shirts and slacks into a valise. We're on our way to Saint-Tropez for a few days."

"Saint-Tropez? Where the hell is that?"

"About fifty miles down the coast," Marissa told him. "It's the fun place of the Riviera. Not with old people like Monte Carlo, but all the young rich and fun people. All day on the beach and parties all night long."

"And Franco left me with money," Mara added. "He already knows that an old friend of mine invited us to his house. He has one of the biggest homes near the beaches."

"I don't know," Joe said cautiously. "Franco never told me about a setup like this."

"There'll be nothing wrong," Mara said. "He knows my friend is a *peole*. As long as Marissa stays with me teaching me English and you keep writing, it's okay. Besides, we'll be home long before he returns."

Joe looked at her. "But how are you going to explain the trimmed pussy?"

"My hair grows fast enough," she said. "Besides, he's a true Italian. He wouldn't go down on a pussy even if he had a nose as big as Pinocchio's."

"I still don't know," Joe said doubtfully. "I wouldn't want Gianpietro to be angry with me. He's a tough one."

Mara laughed. "That's just his act. He's really a sweet man."

Joe stared at her quizzically.

She rose from her chair, and went to the bed and pulled his hand to follow her to the bathroom. "Get into the shower," she said. "You'll feel better, especially when I wash your prick and balls with my own perfumed soap."

A two-hour drive in the small Renault brought them to Saint-Tropez. Mara and Marissa took turns driving. Joe scrunched into the rear seat among the luggage. Most of the drive was interesting, Joe thought, as they passed along the RN 7, the coast road through Nice, Antibes and Cannes. After Cannes the road became uncomfortable, but the narrow asphalt-and-dirt trail was the only road between the mainland and the peninsula that connected Saint-Tropez to the mainland. That road was the only passage on land— there was neither railroad, bus service nor taxis, although during the day there were several sixty-passenger ferries that traveled from eight in the morning until eleven at night.

Saint-Tropez was in the process of changing from a small village surrounded by vineyards that produced cheap table wines to a fashionable resort for the young, playful, monied French and other knowledgeable Europeans.

Mara turned the car away from the port of the village, where the lights allowed them to see that many people were still in the streets and the restaurants were still busy. She took the car up a dirt road and turned finally into the driveway of a large villa whose lights were shining.

Joe got himself out of the car feeling very much like a sardine pried from its can. Mara led them to the large open doors. The house was silent but in a moment a majordomo arrived.

He bowed politely. "I am sorry, mademoiselle, that Monsieur Lascombes and his guest have gone out."

"I would guess that." Mara spoke in French. "But he has invited myself and my friends to join him here in the villa." He glanced down at the sheet of paper and read out Mara's name.

"Correct," Mara said. "The lady and the gentleman are my guests. I will arrange it with Monsieur Lascombes in the morning."

"*D'accord,* mademoiselle," he said. "For the moment, I will assign the two ladies to room twelve and the gentleman will occupy room nine across the hall from you. Each room is on the second stage."

"Thank you," Mara answered.

"I apologize," said the majordomo, "that the porters have already departed for the night, but we will bring the luggage in first thing in the morning."

"I understand," she said. "We'll take the things we need for the moment and we'll manage." She opened her purse and handed him a five-hundred-franc note. "Meanwhile, if you would be kind enough to show us to our rooms, we will be content."

The second floor in a French house is two flights up—this equal to the third floor in the States. The girls' room didn't seem too bad; there was a large bed and a private bathroom. Joe's room was a horror. It had to be a maid's room. A small uncomfortable bed, and in the corner there was only a bidet and a washbasin. But he was too tired to complain. Quickly he got out of his clothes and passed out bare-assed on the bed.

He felt he had slept less than an hour when Marissa touched him on the shoulder. "Joe," she said in a low voice, "wake up."

"I'm sleeping," he said. "Wake me in the morning."

"It *is* morning," she said. "Get up. We have a problem."

He opened his eyes and rubbed them as he sat up in the bed. The gray morning light came through the window. "What's happening?"

"You'll have to get out of here," she said.

He stared at her. "How can I do that?"

"I'll drive you over to Saint-Raphael. You can get a taxi there to take you back to the villa."

"That doesn't make sense," he said. "Mara said everything would be arranged."

"She fucked up," Marissa said.

He got out of bed and pulled on his pants. "Let me talk to her."

"It won't help," she said. "She took two Nembutal and she'll sleep until the middle of the afternoon."

"How did you find out I have to go?"

"Lascombes came into our room. He said this room has been promised. Mara never told him that you were joining

288

us. He doesn't want any hassle from Gianpietro, so you have to go."

"Shit!" he exclaimed. "I might have figured that she was a nut. I wanted to stay at the villa. I'm sorry I let her talk me into it." He looked at her. "Can't I move into a hotel in Saint-Tropez?"

"I checked all the hotels. They're booked up. There's not a room in the town."

He looked at her. "Then you're staying here?"

"If it's okay with you," she said. "Gianpietro is paying me for the month to stay with Mara. But I'll go back with you if you want."

He thought for a moment. "No, it's okay, I'll manage."

"You'll be more comfortable at the villa anyway," she said.

"Sure," he said. "How much time to get ready?"

"I'm ready right now," she said.

He nodded slowly. "Give me ten minutes. I'll meet you downstairs."

She looked up at him. "I'm sorry, Joe."

He smiled wryly. "That's the way it goes. You can't win them all."

=34=

IT WAS FOUR days later that he waited in the Nice Airport for Laura to arrive on her connecting flight from Paris. An airport announcement bell echoed before a girl's voice came from the loudspeakers, first in French, then in English. Laura's flight would be delayed by two hours because of weather conditions in Paris.

Joe looked up at the flight departure and arrival board below the giant clock. It was nine o'clock. The flight arrival that had been scheduled for nine-thirty was now posted for eleven-thirty. He swore to himself and headed for the small restaurant and bar and sat down at a table. Carefully he placed the two dozen roses he had brought for her on the table and looked up at the waiter. "Scotch whiskey and water," he said.

The waiter shook his head. "Sir, at the tables one must always order food."

"I had breakfast already," Joe said. "What do you suggest?" Automatically he gave the waiter a hundred-franc note.

"In that case, monsieur," the waiter said, "I will bring you a double Scotch and water."

"Beautiful." He looked out at the airport. A crowd was

already waiting for the Paris flight to arrive. They waited patiently, apparently always used to delays.

The waiter brought his two Scotches and waters, and placed them on the table. Joe stared at them. He lifted one of the glasses and tasted the Scotch. It was strong. By the time Laura arrived, he would be completely bombed. He decided to nurse the drinks as he reflected upon his last few days.

It had been two o'clock in the afternoon when he returned to Gianpietro's villa from Saint-Tropez. The houseman came out as he descended from the taxi. *"Bon jour,* Monsieur Crown," he said in greeting. "Monsieur Gianpietro is on the telephone for you."

Joe paid off the taxi and followed the houseman to a telephone in the hall of the main house. "Franco," he said.

"Joe, my friend," Gianpietro said. "The houseman said that you had gone with the girls to Saint-Tropez."

"It was not my cup of tea," Joe said. "There was no way I could work there."

"You will be more comfortable at the villa," Gianpietro said.

"Probably," Joe said. "But I have been thinking about your kind offer and I feel I can't give you the kind of story you need for Mara. So I have decided to leave and begin work on my next book."

"You are probably right," Gianpietro agreed, a note of relief in his voice. "Mara is a cunt. She is not serious about her work. All she wants is people to do it for her."

"You don't sound very happy with her," Joe said. "I hope I am not the reason for that."

"Not at all," Gianpietro said reassuringly. "As a matter

291

of fact, there is another girl I have had my eye on for a long time. I think that Mara will have a surprise quite soon."

"I'm sorry," Joe said. "May I have your permission to telephone my editor in the States? Also, I will be leaving the villa tomorrow."

"Anything you want, you know that, my friend," Gianpietro said. "If there is anything you need, please call on me."

"Thank you, Franco. *Arrivederci*." Joe put down the telephone and turned to the houseman. *"S'il vous plaît,"* he asked, in about all the French he could speak, "would you place a telephone call to New York for me?"

The houseman nodded. *"Avec plaisir,"* he said, handing a small paper pad and pencil to Joe. "Write the number for me, please," he said as he picked up the phone.

Joe wrote Laura's telephone number on the pad and returned it to him. Quickly the houseman spoke to the operator and waited for a reply. Joe heard the scratch of a girl's voice from the receiver. "The circuits are occupied just now. It will take about two hours to place your call."

"That's okay," Joe said. "I'll wait."

The houseman spoke a few words into the telephone, then replaced the receiver. "Is there anything else, monsieur?"

"I'm leaving the villa tomorrow," Joe said. "What is the best hotel in Nice?"

"The Negresco, monsieur."

"Can you get me a double room there for a few days?"

"It will be difficult, monsieur. This is the height of the season and they're usually *complet*."

"Damn," Joe said. "Is there any way you can help me?"

"My brother-in-law is in the conciergerie. Perhaps he can arrange something?"

"Talk to him," Joe said. "Tell him that I will give him fifty dollars if he can get a room for me."

"I will try my best, monsieur," the houseman said.

"Thank you," Joe said, pressing a ten-dollar bill into the man's hand. "I'll be down at the guest house and begin my packing. When the New York call comes through, call me there."

By the time he had gone into the guest house, the telephone rang. It was the houseman. "I have already spoken to my brother-in-law and your room is confirmed."

"That's wonderful," Joe said. "Thank you very much."

"It is my pleasure, monsieur," the houseman said. "I will be pleased to drive you to the hotel tomorrow."

"Thank you again," Joe said and put down the phone. He went to the large armoire and took out his valise. He carried it to the bed, then stared at it. Suddenly he felt very tired. It was a long drive from Saint-Tropez and the heat had already dragged him down. Almost automatically he stretched out on the bed and went to sleep.

The sun flooded in from the west window opposite his bed, awakening him. He looked at his watch. He had been sleeping almost an hour and a half. He splashed some water on his face and began to feel better. He picked up the telephone. The houseman answered. "Any reply on my New York call yet?" Joe asked.

"No, monsieur." The houseman was polite. "Would monsieur like something to eat or drink?"

Suddenly Joe realized that he had not had lunch. "Yes, I would like something."

"I have prepared several sandwiches, one chicken, one *rosbif*. What do you prefer to drink, wine or beer?"

"Do you have any Coca-Cola?"

"Of course, monsieur." The houseman sounded slightly surprised.

"That's great," Joe said. "With lots of ice. Very cold."

"I will bring it immediately, monsieur."

Joe put down the telephone and began unbuttoning his shirt. It was damp with perspiration. Before he had the shirt off, the telephone rang.

"La Contessa Baroni, monsieur," the houseman said.

Joe was puzzled. "For me?"

"She asked for you, monsieur."

"Okay," Joe said. He heard the click in the receiver as the call was transferred. "Hello?"

"This is Anna Baroni," the contessa's voice echoed in his ear. "What are you doing living with that gangster down there?"

"I was trying to think of a movie idea for his girlfriend," Joe said. "But I can't make it so I'm leaving in the morning. I'm planning to meet my editor so that I can begin working on my next book."

The contessa laughed into the telephone. "Is your editor a man or a woman?"

"A woman." Joe smiled.

"I might have guessed," the contessa said. "Is she pretty?"

Joe thought a moment. "More than that," he said. "She has style."

"Spoken like a writer," she said. "By the way, in case you don't know it, I am your publisher in Italy. I own the company that is putting out your novel in Italy."

"Have you read it?" he asked.

"No," she answered honestly. "I do not have the patience. I called to invite you on my yacht for a long weekend."

He hesitated. "I would love to join you, but my editor is very conservative."

The contessa laughed again. "There is a quiet group on the boat. Your editor might even enjoy it. The managing director of my publishing company and his wife will be along."

"Thank you," he said. "But I haven't received her arrival date yet. It might be too late for you. She's expected either the day after tomorrow or the weekend."

"Either way, call me," she said. "You can reach me on my yacht, just telephone the captain's office at the Port d'Antibes. They will transfer the call to my boat."

"Okay," he said. "You will hear from me on Friday. And thank you again."

"*Ciao*," she laughed and hung up.

It took two hours for the call to Laura to go through. By that time he had everything packed and his valises closed. Laura's voice sounded half asleep.

"Did I wake you?" he asked.

"Yes," she said. "It's after midnight here." Now she was awake. Her voice sounded concerned. "Is there anything wrong?"

"Nothing is wrong," he answered. "Yes, everything is wrong. You're not here."

"It's not the tenth yet," she said. "I told you to call me on the tenth."

"It's the fifth," he said. "I'm sure you know what you want to do. I'm in Nice and it's taken six hours for the circuits to clear so I could make this call to you. I want you to come now. The tenth will turn to the fifteenth before you get here, then before we know it, we'll have no time together."

"Have you done any work on the book?"

"No," he answered. "I've been farting around with an Italian producer. Finally, I decided there was nothing in it

295

for me. I'd rather work on the book, but I need your help to get it started."

She was silent.

"Besides, I want to be with you," he said.

She took a deep breath. "I don't want to be just another girl with you."

"You're not just another girl," he said. "You're someone special to me. I know that now. All the others were yesterday, I was playing with myself. I called you because I need you. I don't know what I can do, but I do know that I don't want to write any more scripts. I want to be a real writer. And I need you, not only for myself but to help me work."

"You really mean that?" she asked softly.

"Yes," he said.

"When do you want me to be there?" she asked.

"I'd like tomorrow."

"This is Tuesday," she said. "How about Friday?"

"I'll settle for that," he said. "I'll pick you up at the Nice Airport. I'll be at the Negresco Hotel when you get the tickets. Hurry."

"Joe," she said. "I don't want to make any mistakes."

"You won't," he said. "I promise."

The houseman's brother-in-law had the right connections. Joe was given one of the best rooms in the hotel, on the fifth floor, with two wide glass doors leading to a narrow balcony over the broad expanse of the beaches and the Mediterranean. Joe looked at the twin beds.

The room clerk who had ushered him to the room smiled. *"A l'Américaine,"* he said. "Most of our American clients prefer twin beds."

Joe smiled. "Doesn't bother me." He gave the clerk a

hundred francs and nodded as the clerk thanked him. The clerk had just gone when the porter came in with the valises, and right behind him came the valet, who unpacked everything. Joe watched his twenty-franc notes flying like paper airplanes. But he had a good feeling. The service was great, even if it cost.

He opened his portable typewriter and placed it on the desk near the window. He took several sheets of paper from his brief case. He had an idea for the novel. He didn't care that everyone said there were too many novels about Hollywood; this would be a story that no other writer had written—a story of booze, dope and broads. It had nothing to do with the movie business.

The telephone rang. It was Laura. "Friday morning okay with you?" she asked.

"Perfect," he said.

"What are you doing?" she asked after she had told him about her flight.

"I'm trying to have something on paper to show you," he said. "I didn't want you to feel that I was screwing off."

"That's good," she said.

"This is the height of the season," he said, "and everything is filled up. But I was lucky. I got one of the best large rooms in the hotel, looking out on the sea."

"Sounds beautiful," she said.

"Only one problem," he said. "It has twin beds."

She was silent for a moment. "Remember, I spent two years in France; I can handle it."

He laughed. "I hope I can. But I'll be at the airport waiting for you. I'm really very excited."

"So am I," she said.

He put down the phone and then looked at the typewriter. He had already written four pages. He looked at his watch.

It was eight o'clock at night and the sun was still shining. Suddenly he felt hungry. He hadn't eaten any lunch. He called down to the concierge.

The concierge recognized his voice. "Monsieur Crown, this is Max. We met when my brother-in-law brought you here."

"Max, of course," he said. "What restaurant do you suggest for dinner?"

"The restaurant in the hotel is very good, monsieur," Max answered.

"Fine," Joe said. "Can you reserve a table for me at nine o'clock?"

"Of course, monsieur. You will be alone?"

"Yes," Joe answered.

"Very well, monsieur. Thank you." The receiver clicked off and Joe put down the telephone. He showered and dressed and was ready to go downstairs when the telephone rang.

"Joe?" It was Marissa.

"Yes," he said.

"Mara wants you to return to the villa."

"Tell her to fuck herself," he said.

"She said Gianpietro will be angry," Marissa said.

"She's lying," he said flatly. "I already spoke to him and he said it was okay for me to leave."

She was silent for a moment. "What are you going to do?" she asked.

He lied a little. "My editor will arrive from New York tomorrow morning, then we're beginning to work on my next book."

"I'm sorry, Joe," she said. "I really like you. I'm sorry that it's ended like this."

"I still like you too," he said. "But we had a good run. Maybe there'll be another time."

"I hope so," she said sincerely. "Good luck."
"And good luck to you," he said. *"Ciao."*
He went down for dinner.

The airport announcement bell echoed. Quickly, Joe paid for the Scotches. Laura's flight was on the ground.

==35==

SHE WALKED THROUGH the hotel room and walked out on the narrow balcony while the porter placed her valises on the luggage racks and left. Joe stood in the middle of the room watching her. She turned back to him. "I still can't believe that I'm really here," she said.

"You can believe it," he said, moving to the small table on which there was a bottle of champagne that stood in a silver ice bucket. Quickly he popped the cork out and filled a glass for each of them. "Welcome to the Riviera," he toasted.

She tasted the champagne. "It's lovely," she said. She met his eyes. "You've done everything. Roses at the airport, champagne in the room. Do you know that you're a romantic?"

He laughed. "I never thought that. I was just happy that you came."

"I'm happy too," she said. She came to him and kissed him lightly. "Thank you."

He shook his head silently.

"I've got to take a shower," she said. "I have a feeling that my clothing is stuck to me. Eighteen hours on the plane isn't the most relaxing way of traveling, only the fastest."

He held up his glass. "To modern speed," he said. "You take your shower. You'll feel better then."

She looked down at the beds. "Which one is mine?"

"Take your pick," he said. "It doesn't matter to me."

"I'll take the one nearest the bathroom," she said. She placed the champagne glass down. She opened one of her valises and took out a small box that held her cosmetics. "Is there an extra bathrobe in the bathroom?"

He nodded.

"Good, she said, going to the bathroom. "I won't be too long."

"I'll be here," he said. He sat at the desk and looked down at the pages he had written. Twenty-seven pages, single-spaced. That was pretty good. She had to be pleased. Then he heard the water running in the shower. He closed his eyes. In his mind he could see her nude body, the water pouring over her. He felt the excitement throbbing through his erection. Quickly, he walked out on the balcony and looked out toward the sea. He cursed to himself at the way the Italians cut their slacks—all that was needed was a half hard, and it showed against the material.

A few minutes later, she was beside him on the balcony. "What are you watching?"

"Nothing," he said. "It's just that it's warm and there's no fan in the room."

"I think it's great," she said. "We had nothing but rain the last few weeks in New York."

He turned to her. She was wearing the terry bathrobe supplied by the hotel. "How was the shower?"

"I feel a lot better," she said. "But I'm still tired."

"That's normal," he said. "Why don't you have a siesta? There's no rush."

She looked up at him. "What are you going to do?"

"The same thing," he said. "I was too excited to sleep well."

He followed her into the room and hung a "Do Not Disturb" sign outside the door. Then he took down her bedcover and threw it on a chair. *"Voilà,"* he said.

"That looks good," she said, turning back the blanket. She stretched out on the bed and covered herself with the sheet.

He sat at the end of his bed and took off his shoes. "Okay if I undress and rest in my undershorts."

"Don't be silly," she said. "It's too warm to try to sleep with your clothes on." She wriggled under the covered sheet. A moment later she had the bathrobe out from under it and at the foot of the bed. She looked at him. "I'll just rest a little while. Then we can talk."

He undressed with his back to her. He still had his wet hard and didn't want her to see the wet spots on his shorts. He pulled the drapes across the window and the room turned dark. He stretched out on his bed and closed his eyes. But he couldn't sleep; he was listening to the soft breathing from the other bed. He became annoyed at himself because his erection wouldn't relax. He turned on his side, away from her, and tried to clear his mind. Then the telephone rang.

Quickly he rolled over and picked up the telephone before it could ring again and wake her. "Hello," he said in a low voice.

"Joe." It was the contessa. "Did your editor arrive?"

"Just this moment, Contessa," he said.

"I wanted to remind you that you are both invited for a long weekend on my yacht. We will be sailing at noon tomorrow."

"May I call you at seven o'clock this evening?" he asked. "I will be able to let you know by then."

"Okay," she said. *"Ciao."*

As he replaced the receiver, Laura turned on the lamp on the night table between them. She was unaware that the sheet had slipped half away from her. "Who was calling?" she asked.

"The Contessa Baroni," he said. "She's invited both of us for a long weekend on her yacht." He felt himself growing more erect and rolled over on his stomach to cover himself.

"Contessa Baroni?" she said reflectively. "I know that name."

"Baroni—that's the name of the publishing company that bought the Italian rights to my book. She owns the whole company and many other things I don't even know about." He tried to burrow deeper into the bed. "She also financed the last picture I did for Santini and arranged for me to collect all the money he owed me."

"How did you meet her?" Laura asked. "At one of her parties? She also has a reputation for being a great hostess."

"Santini introduced us and for some reason she seemed to like me. I have a feeling that she gave her publishing company orders to buy my book. She told me that the managing director of her book company will be on the yacht on the weekend with his wife."

She met his eyes. "Did you have an affair with her?"

"Jesus!" he exclaimed, automatically sitting up. "I'm not her type. She's into young girls."

She stared at him, her eyes looking at his erection, the front of his shorts bulging, a large wet stain half covering the fly. "But she did that to you on the phone?"

"That's stupid," he snapped. "I've had this hard on from the moment you came off the plane. Besides, looking at you half naked right now doesn't make it any easier for me."

She glanced down at herself, the sheet falling off. She didn't pick it up. "I did think, several times, that you were looking uncomfortable."

"You were right," he said.

"Take off your shorts," she said suddenly, "before you get a hernia."

He swung himself off the bed and dropped his shorts to the floor. His phallus slapped up against his stomach.

She looked at him. "You have a large penis, almost up to your bellybutton," she said softly. "Like eight or nine inches."

"I never measured it," he said.

She took a deep breath. "I love big pricks. That's why I kept away from you. I wanted it to be only business. I had a feeling that you would be like that."

"Is that what you want now? Only business?" he asked.

She looked up at him and laughed, "Now you're the one who's crazy. I didn't fly half across the world only to help write a book."

"I don't get it." His surprise echoed in his voice. "You were always so cool. What made you change your mind?"

"Eight years in that damn agency with all their stupid rules." She looked up at him. "And you know something? It would be the same in the new job so I quit it before I started."

"What are you going to do then?"

She reached and clasped his phallus in her hand. "This," she said. "And I want to live free. Like you. You do anything you want. You seem to always be having a ball. What I read in the papers, you are always where the action is. People. Parties. My life is just boring."

He sat down on the side of the bed and placed his hand between her legs. "Your cunt is soaking," he said huskily.

"I want you to kiss it," she said. "I was engaged to a lawyer for almost six years and he never did anything but fuck me, and that was always with a condom. I never had a man kiss me there."

"You came to the right man," he said. "Eating pussy is my thing." He bent his face into her. He could hear her moaning as he moved around and into her. He felt her clitoris grow larger in his mouth. "My God!" he exclaimed. "You've got the biggest clit I've ever seen. It's like a little prick."

She grabbed his hair and pulled his face tighter into her. "Stop talking when I'm coming in your mouth!" she said gasping, shaking her head wildly from side to side.

He glanced up at her. Her eyes were tightly closed. Quickly he pushed her legs back, his hands under her knees until she was opened wide to him. He slammed himself deep into her. Her mouth gaped open as she half screamed. "Is this prick large enough?" he growled.

"I feel it in my throat," she cried. "I love it! I love you! Just love me like this, forever and ever."

$=36=$

THE SOFT SOUND of the ship's engines awakened him. He checked the radium dial of his wristwatch. It was just past seven o'clock in the morning. Carefully he slipped out of the small three-quarter-size bed in the cabin and glanced at Laura. She was fast asleep, with the bedsheet draped over her head. Quickly he stepped into his bermuda shorts and pulled on a shirt. Quietly he left the cabin and closed the door without making a sound.

He walked up the small circular staircase past the main deck and made his way to the dining salon. Already there was a small buffet set out for breakfast. He picked up a glass of tomato juice and sipped it slowly. Through the windows he saw the land slipping behind them as the ship moved forward.

"The girl is going to marry you," the contessa said behind him.

He turned in surprise. The contessa was wearing a silk robe over a tight bathing suit. "What makes you think that?" he asked.

"There are some things I know," she said. She held out her cheek for him to kiss. *"Buon giorno."*

"Buon giorno," he said, kissing her. "Are you psychic?"

"No," she said. "But we have been together three days now. That's enough to tell. But do not be afraid. She will be very good for you."

He was silent.

"Is she a good fuck?" the contessa asked.

Joe nodded. "Very good."

"I thought so," the contessa said. "I felt she was a woman who had kept her sex bottled inside for a long time. And now this is the first time she feels free with herself."

"What else do you have to tell me, O wise lady?" He smiled.

"I would like to eat her pussy," the contessa said. "And I am sorry that will never happen. This kind of sex is not a part of her. She loves you, Joe. That is the simple truth of it."

"Where is your little Danish girlfriend?" he asked.

"Still asleep," she said. "But I am bored with her. She has no imagination. I am also bored with Enrico and his wife. So much discussion of business does not make for a good time. This has to be done once a year. It is important to keep in touch with my business affairs."

"You have many," he said.

"My father didn't have a son so I had to take care of all his business after he died." She pulled a cord to summon the steward. "Would you like some American breakfast?" she asked. "Eggs and bacon?"

"That would be nice."

The steward in his immaculate white jacket appeared. She spoke to him in Italian and he left the salon. She gestured for Joe to follow her to the breakfast table. She sat at the head of the table and placed him to her right. Silently she poured a small cup of coffee for herself from the silver carafe and poured another cup for Joe. She drank the coffee slowly. "Dull," she said. "Nothing but dull."

Joe was silent.

She looked at him. She took out a vial of cocaine and a small gold spoon from the pocket of her silk robe. "I need a lift," she said, taking two deep snorts and holding it out to him.

He shook his head. "It would make me crazy in the morning."

She laughed. "Then let me put some on your fingers, and stick your hand in my cunt."

He broke up. "Anna," he laughed, calling her by name for the first time. "You really are too much. We're here in the dining salon. The steward is bringing breakfast, and who else do we know that might show up?"

"Nobody will see even if they came up," she said. She lifted the edge of the tablecloth and spread open her legs. "It will only take a moment. My cunt is on fire. Cocaine will cool it off."

"What about your bathing suit? You can't take that off?"

"Let me worry about that." She said, taking his fingers and sprinkling the cocaine across them from the vial. "Now put your hand under the tablecloth."

He looked at her and did as she had suggested. He felt her hand grasp his hand and pull it toward her pussy. Surprised, he felt the seam under the bathing suit open. She slid forward in her seat and then strongly pulled his hand into her already soaking pussy, her cunt almost covering his knuckles. "Now!" she said, gasping. "Twist it twice then pull it out!"

He could feel the juices running over his hand as he took back his hand. He looked at her. For a moment she was flushed, then the perspiration broke out on her forehead.

She let her breath out in a slow sigh and smiled slowly at him. "You can wash your hand in the fingerbowl on the table next to you. It is scented with fresh lemon."

Quietly he splashed the water over his fingers, then wiped himself with a napkin. "Better now?" He smiled.

She dabbed her face with her napkin. "Didn't ruin my makeup?" she asked.

"You look just perfect," he said.

She leaned across the table and kissed his cheek. "You are a very sweet man," she said. "Believe me, that girl is very lucky."

He was staring in wonder at her as the steward came into the salon with his breakfast. He waited until the man had left. "Anna, tell me. Why?"

There was a strange sadness in the back of her eyes. "Life is so fucking dull, darling," she said, sounding almost angry at herself. "Sometimes you have to do something crazy."

The last day of the weekend on the yacht ended with the fireworks display in the bay of Cannes on Tuesday night. The contessa's yacht was surrounded by boats, large and small, as the fireworks exploded above them. Joe and Laura had gone up to the sun deck to look at the sky. The others had remained on the afterdeck close to the buffet dinner placed on a long table. The contessa had invited about thirty guests to join her on the yacht.

"I've never seen fireworks like this," Laura said, staring up at the exploding lights in the night sky.

"Neither have I," Joe said. "Last summer I spent at the Lido in Venice. They never had anything like it."

She glanced over the railing toward the afterdeck. "I don't think any of them down there are even watching."

"They are more interested in drinking and eating," he said.

"I thought I caught a sniff of marijuana near some guests."

Joe laughed. "It's not marijuana, it's hashish. They don't have any ganch here. But the contessa has everything. Cocaine, hash, absinthe, opium. All you have to do is ask."

"Kathy told me you always had coke and ganch," Laura said.

"I did in Hollywood," he said. "But here I don't have any connections."

"I've smoked with Kathy a few times," she said. "But I never had any cocaine. Sometime I think I would like to try it. What does it do for you?"

"It's a big high," he said. "Goes right through your head. But you can't use too much of it. Then it's a big downer."

"It might be fun if we could try it together."

"I'll check with the contessa," he said. "Maybe she'll give me a little."

She looked down again over the railing. "I don't know how the contessa got all these people together at one time." She turned back to Joe. "I saw Ali Khan and Rita Hayworth and Rubirosa and Zsa Zsa Gabor. There were also a lot of faces that I recognized but I couldn't connect their names."

"The contessa collects them all," he said. "She can afford it."

An explosion of white Roman candles turned the night into day. "Do you like my dress?" she asked.

"Beautiful," he said. The black silk dress clung softly to her lush figure.

"I bought it in a store on the Rue d'Antibes today," she said. "When I heard there would be a party I realized I didn't have an evening dress with me that would be appropriate."

"It's just great," he said.

"It was two hundred dollars," she said. "I never spent that much money on a dress."

He laughed. "I'll pay for it. It's worth it just seeing you in it."

She kissed him quickly. "I had another idea while I was walking around in Cannes. It's a much smaller and quieter town than Nice. I found a small one-bedroom apartment on La Croisette, just across from the beach. The hotel would cost like fifty, sixty dollars a day. I can get the apartment for two hundred dollars for two weeks. It has everything. Bathroom. Kitchen."

"You planning on cooking?"

"I'm a good cook," she said. "And we can save some money while you're working."

He was silent.

"I've already gone through your twenty-seven pages. You have the whole book there. I can help you block it out into chapters, then I will write a few pages of outline I know would sell if you write five chapters to go with it. I know I can get this book sold, for a crazy deal."

He stared at her. "Then what's going to happen to our fucking?"

She moved closer to him. Quickly she opened his fly and held his phallus. It went hard almost immediately. She squeezed him. "I always know where to find it." She laughed.

He held up his hands in mock surrender. "You win. I'll tell the contessa that we'll get off here in the morning."

She took his handkerchief from his jacket pocket. She wiped her hand, then handed it to him. "You'd better dry yourself. Your cock is dripping like a leaking faucet."

$=37=$

IT WAS ALMOST two o'clock in the morning when he finished the last page of chapter three. He pulled the page from the typewriter and read it, then glanced down at the table that he used as a desk and studied the chapter block-out that he and Laura had worked out. He needed two more chapters to submit to a publisher in New York. Laura had finished the outline of the book and he had to admit to himself that she, with her experience as editor and agent, had written a better outline than he could have done.

A look at that last page, and he realized that it worked well. But it was not going as quickly as he would like. The two chapters he had to finish would take more than the two days left of the two-week lease of the apartment, and they had already been notified that the apartment would not be available after the lease expired.

He rose from the table and turned off the light. He walked into the darkened room and looked out the window. Across La Croisette he saw people entering and leaving the casino. Near the other corner he watched the whores offering their wares. The way he had it figured, business was not very good. But then, the end of the season was approaching.

He heard the rustle of silk and turned. Laura had come

from the bedroom in a short silk robe and joined him at the window. "Finish the chapter?" she asked.

He nodded. "But it's only the third. I'll never make the five chapters in the two days we have left here."

"We can find another apartment," she said. "The season is over and there are plenty of vacancies."

He shook his head. "I've had enough of these places. The French aren't very cooperative with their tenants. Besides the rent, they charge you for towels and sheets, they murder you with a deposit on the telephone—which you'll probably never collect once you're gone."

"What do you want to do then?" she asked. "Do you want to go back to Rome?"

"That won't help," he said. "I have nothing there except some trunks in storage."

She looked up at him. "I know you," she said. "You have an idea."

He nodded. "Our lease is over Wednesday. Every Wednesday an Italian liner stops at Cannes to pick up passengers on the way to New York. The trip takes eight days. I can finish the next two chapters on the boat. And we'll be home."

"An ocean voyage is very romantic," she said. "But it's also very expensive. Could we afford it?"

He laughed. "If it's good it's automatically expensive."

"But you have to wear an evening dress at dinner every night. I have only the one I bought for the contessa's party," she said.

"So buy a few more. They should be cheap enough, it's the end of the season."

"Are you sure you'll be able to work on the boat?"

"I'll be able," he said. "We should have everything together so that you and the lawyer can work out a deal for the book."

"Then what are you going to do?" she asked.

"Write the book and get rich."

She looked up at him. "And what plans do you have for me?"

He took her in his arms and bent down to kiss her. "You come with me," he said.

"I don't believe it," she said angrily. "They told me the boat is completely booked up. Not a stateroom or cabin available. Maybe next week they might be able to accommodate us."

Joe glanced at his watch. It was just after eleven in the morning. "Who did you talk to?" he asked.

"There are only two people in their offices—the manager and his secretary. They were polite, but that's all."

"Money talks," he said. "Did you offer them a gratuity?"

"I'm not stupid," she said. "Of course I did. It didn't help."

"Okay," Joe said. "We have friends. Let's see what they can do. Let's get the contessa on the telephone."

Laura picked up the phone and gave the operator the contessa's number. She spoke quickly in French then put the phone down. "The contessa is on her yacht on her way to Capri and cannot be reached."

"I have one more chance," Joe said, reaching for the phone and calling Gianpietro's villa. The houseman called Gianpietro to the phone.

"Joe, my friend," Gianpietro said. "I am happy to hear from you. Are you well?"

"Okay," Joe said. "And you, Franco?"

"Much better," the Italian said. "I have a new girl. She

is Swedish and a model, and best of all she does not want to be a movie star."

"What happened to Mara?" Joe asked.

"I have sent her back to Rome with your former secretary. Mara cried a lot but when I gave her money, her tears were dried." Gianpietro laughed. "I was lucky—everything went well."

"Congratulations," Joe said. "I wonder if you have any connections at the Italian Lines? I'm trying to board the Wednesday voyage to New York, but they tell me they are all booked up."

"What do you need, my friend?" Franco said.

"A good double cabin, large if possible, because I plan to write on the voyage."

"Your editor is with you?"

"Yes," Joe said. "We rented an apartment in Cannes."

"Give me your telephone number," Franco said. "I will call you back in less than a half-hour."

"Thank you," Joe said.

"*Ciao,*" Franco said.

Laura looked at Joe as he put down the phone. "Who is he?"

"Gianpietro," he said. "I guess we could call him a banker. He has financed many Italian pictures, and he partnered with the contessa the one I did for Santini. As a matter of fact, he was the one who brought me the money from Santini."

"Why would he do all of that for you?" she asked.

"He had an idea that I could write a script for his girlfriend. He offered me good money, but I didn't have any ideas for them. Besides, I wanted to be with you."

"He sounds like Mafia to me," Laura said.

"He probably is." Joe smiled. "But then, all Italians seem like Mafia to me."

"What if we don't get on the boat?"

"Then, plane," he said. "I've had enough of these French apartments. I can get a good hotel apartment in New York and work there."

She looked at him. "What would be wrong with my apartment?" she asked.

"What about your mother?"

"My mother passed away two years ago."

"I'm sorry, I didn't know."

"I kept the apartment," she said. "There's plenty of room."

"That's what we'll do then," he said. The telephone rang and he picked it up. "Hello."

"Joe," Gianpietro said. "You have your stateroom, first class, very good. Can you go immediately to the office of the Italian Lines? It is all arranged."

"That's wonderful, Franco," he said. "I'm sure that no one but you could do that. I don't know how I can thank you."

"You are my friend," Gianpietro said. "That's what friends are for. To help each other."

"I don't know what to say," Joe said.

Franco spoke quietly. "You have nothing to say. Only good luck to you. And bon voyage." The phone clicked off.

Joe put down the phone and looked up at Laura. "We have reservations and we have to get over to the Italian Lines office right away."

She stared at him. "I can't believe it."

Joe laughed. "Let's get our ass over there and grab our tickets before someone else gets them."

* * *

Second dinner sitting was at nine o'clock. This was for the first-class passengers. Second-class passengers were served in the same dining room but they were seated at seven o'clock. The maitre d' turned to Joe and Laura as they came to the dining-room entrance. He bowed. "Mr. and Mrs. Crown?"

Joe smiled. "That's right," he said. The ship's personnel had everything organized. The maitre d' knew that they were not married but he was schooled in old-fashioned diplomacy.

"We have several tables that you might choose," the maitre d' said. "A table for two, or other tables with guests seated for six."

"A table for two," Joe said, handing him a ten-dollar bill.

"A good choice." The maitre d' bowed. "We have a lovely table for you." He gestured to a table captain. "Table sixty-nine."

They followed the captain to a side of the dining room, under one of the large portholes. He pulled the table out for them as they seated themselves on the comfortable banquette. With a flourish he placed the napkins on their laps and gave them the menu. He bowed, "I recommend the caviar most highly," he said. "Malossol gros grain and we serve it with vodka russe."

Joe turned to Laura. "I love caviar," she said.

Joe gestured approval to the captain, who bowed and walked away. Joe turned back to her. "I love this table too," he said. "Sixty-nine is my favorite number."

It was more than an hour and a half before they left the dinner table. He turned to her as they stood a moment in front of the dining-room entrance. "Back to the stateroom, or would you like a walk on the promenade deck?"

317

"A little walk, please," she answered. "I've never eaten so much in my life."

Apparently many of the passengers felt the same way because the promenade deck was crowded. They made their way to the aft-deck railing and leaned against it looking down at the water sparkling in the moonlight behind the ship.

Laura looked up at the sky. "It's a full moon."

Joe nodded. "They tell me that a full moon makes women horny."

She laughed. "Who told you that?"

"I don't remember," he answered.

"You made it up," she accused.

"Maybe," he said. "But I'd better believe that all the food you ate does it. Caviar, pasta, fish, sorbet, lemon veal scaloppine, chocolate cake and ice cream."

"Don't remind me about it. This is only the first night on board and we have seven more in front of it. I'll gain forty pounds," she said.

"You'll have to exercise," he said. "There is a gym on board."

"I never liked exercise even at school," she said.

"Then let's go to our stateroom. Maybe I can suggest another kind of exercise you might like."

He held the door open for her as she entered the stateroom. "I don't believe it!" she exclaimed as he closed the door.

"What?" he asked feigning innocence.

"Look at the bed," she said. "The maid has placed a sheer black nightgown on my side. I've never owned a black nightgown."

"I bought it for you yesterday and left it with the steward when we came aboard."

Then she gestured to the small breakfast table. "Champagne and roses! No one can ever tell me that you are not romantic. Will you always be like this every time we go anywhere?"

He held up a small vial in front of her. "Cocaine." He smiled. "You said you might like to try it."

She stared at him. "Will it make me crazy?"

"Happy crazy," he laughed. He filled the champagne glasses. "Bon voyage, darling."

"Bon voyage, darling." She sipped, then put her glass down. "Let me undress quickly," she said. "I can't wait to put on my new nightgown."

"First this," he said, lifting up a tiny spoon. "It's done like this." Quickly he snorted a hit in each nostril, then held it out to her.

She looked at him apprehensively.

"It won't hurt you," he said. "Sniff hard."

She did exactly as he told her. Then she sneezed. "It burns," she said.

"Give it a moment," he said. Then he saw her eyes begin to brighten and sparkle. "How does it feel now?"

"Wonderful. Suddenly I don't feel full or tired anymore."

"Then let's get undressed," he said. He took off his tie and jacket and shirt and turned to her.

Her dress was on the floor and she lay naked on the bed, not wearing the nightgown but holding it between her breasts and down her body between her legs.

"Jesus!" he exclaimed. "You look exactly like a French whore!"

She laughed. "That's what I always wanted to be," she said. "Now get your pants off and fuck me."

=38=

"THE OUTLINE AND the five chapters of the new book are very interesting. I'm sure that we can develop a very strong deal for it. I personally know several publishers who will go all the way with it." The attorney nodded very judicially. "I must congratulate you."

Joe glanced at Laura. "It's not me alone," he said. "If it were not for Laura's editing and advice, it would not be even half as good."

Laura smiled. "Thank you, Joe. But don't forget that it was you who did the writing. I am not a writer."

"You make a good team," the lawyer said, smiling. Then he turned to Joe and said seriously. "Meanwhile we do have a real problem. According to the records that I have gone through, you have not filed your Federal income taxes for the last two years."

"I didn't think I had to," Joe said. "I've been working in Europe all that time."

"You are still responsible for filing income taxes."

"Have they called me on it yet?" Joe asked.

"Not yet," the attorney answered. "But they will soon. I know how they operate."

"Why don't we wait until they come after it?"

"If they do that, it will be too late. They'll come down on you like a vulture. They'll strip you clean. Not filing a return is a criminal offense. Filing and not paying is simply a collection job for Internal Revenue."

"Then what do I do?" Joe asked.

"I will prepare your returns and we will file them with the excuse that you were working outside the country and didn't realize that you had to file. That way, all you will have to do is pay interest and a small penalty on the tax."

Joe stared at the lawyer. "About how much will that cost me?"

"Thirty-five or forty thousand dollars," the lawyer said.

"Shit!" Joe said disgustedly. "That will almost clean me out. It's more than sixty percent of what I have in the bank."

"It's better this way than if they catch you. Then they'll lien everything you have—not only the bank accounts but the monies your publishers have to pay you in royalties." The attorney nodded emphatically. "Just pay the man the two dollars."

Joe laughed. That was the first time he realized that the attorney had a sense of humor. "Okay," he said. "I'll leave it up to you. But we better make a quick deal on the new book."

"The important thing is to get a good deal," the lawyer said.

Joe turned to Laura. "How do you feel about it?"

"He's right, Joe," she said. "Let him do his job and you continue to do yours. Write the book."

"Don't worry, darling, I'll write the book. I just hope we get the kind of deal we want." He glanced at his watch. "Jesus, it's after two o'clock already and I promised my parents I would meet them at the market before three. My father is selling his share of the market this afternoon and they want me to be there. They've already sold the house, and Saturday they move out. My brother has his practice in Fort Lauderdale and he found an apartment for them in North Miami."

"They're flying?" Laura asked.

He laughed. "You don't know my mother. She won't fly. She won't even take the train. They're going to drive down."

"Is that good, with your father's heart condition?"

"They're going to take it slow. Only five hours a day on the road, and probably she'll be driving most of it." He rose from his chair. "I'll be running now."

"Are you having dinner with them?" Laura asked.

"No," he said. "My mother said she'll be too busy to do anything except pack. I should be at the apartment by about seven or eight o'clock."

"I'll have something for dinner for us," she said.

"Don't trouble yourself." He kissed her cheek. "We'll go out for dinner."

The attorney waited until Joe had left, then looked at Laura. "I haven't heard anything about your plans."

Laura met his eyes. "I haven't made any plans."

"Is that wise?" the lawyer asked. "He can walk out on you any time. It's not as if you were married."

A secret smile lurked deep in her eyes. "I'm not worried about that. A piece of paper never kept anyone, man or woman, together if they wanted to go."

"But you *do* want to marry him, don't you?"

She laughed. "Even the wisest men are stupid when it comes to women. And I'm surprised at you, Paul. He may not know it yet, but he will marry me. Not because I want him to, but because *he* wants to."

It was just a little after three-thirty as Joe hurried out of the subway. The streets and stores were crowded as Joe turned down the block to his father's market.

His father's car was in front of the door and the Italian had parked his truck in the alley. Joe opened the door and went inside. His mother and father were closing a brown envelope and were tying envelopes in batches.

His mother looked at him. "You're late already, your father and me have been here since six o'clock in the morning."

"But I'm here now," Joe said. "What do you want me to do?"

"Take these batches of envelopes, we're putting them into the trunk of the car," she said.

"Okay," he said. He saw his father sit down in his desk chair. "Are you all right?" he asked.

"A little tired," his father said. "But I'm all right."

"When is the Italian bringing over your money?" Joe asked.

"He's out of it," his father said. "The Mafia wanted him out too. They are going to change the place into an auto-mechanic yard and garage."

"I thought he wanted it for himself."

"He did but the others have the right connections. He's loading his chickens and going down to his brother-in-law's stall in the market on Atlantic Avenue. He's going to be only in the wholesale business. He'll get along."

Joe was silent. He began to load the car. It took only a half an hour to get everything out. He looked at his father. "What about the furniture and fixtures?"

"It's all old junk," Phil said. "They can have it." He took out his pocket watch. "They should be here any minute. They're supposed to be here at four o'clock."

"You have the papers?" Joe asked.

"I have them ready to sign," Phil said. "They're giving me the money right away. All in cash—no check."

"That makes me feel a little more comfortable," Joe said.

The buyers were exactly on time. Of the three men two seemed really tough; the other was introduced as their lawyer. Quickly they signed the papers and one of them handed an envelope to Phil. Phil opened it and checked the bills. He looked up at them. "I was supposed to get five thousand. This is only four five."

"Five hundred for the lawyer's fee," one of the men said.

"But I was never told about that," Phil protested. He began to get angry.

"That's normal," the man said. "The seller pays all the bills."

Joe looked at him and then at his father. "That's right, Papa," he said. "Let it go. It's done now. You already signed the papers."

Phil was silent for a moment. "Okay." Then without saying another word, he walked out of the store and got in the car.

Joe stood next to the window of the car and looked at his father. "Do you mind if I drive?"

"No," Phil said.

Joe opened the rear door for his mother. She looked up at him. "Before we go home," she said, "stop at the East New York Savings Bank on Pitkin Avenue. I want to put this money in the bank right away."

"Okay," Joe said. He slipped into the driver's seat, started the car and moved out into the traffic.

When she returned from the bank, Joe asked, "What about your plan for Florida?"

"We took the offer of thirty-five thousand for the house,

but you know your father, he says we should have gotten forty."

Joe looked at his father. "Thirty-five is good."

"Moving the furniture down there would cost five thousand, along with other things," his father said.

"You're planning to move into an eight-room house there?" Joe asked.

His mother spoke from the back seat. "No, Stevie has found for us a four-room apartment near the beach. My friend Rabinowitz who moved there six months ago told me everything is dirt cheap. You can buy enough furniture for a whole apartment for fifteen hundred dollars."

"It doesn't make sense to move your furniture," Joe said. "You ship only your linen and kitchenware. You'll probably get more than a thousand dollars from a secondhand furniture dealer."

Joe stopped the car to allow the traffic on Pitkin Avenue to pass so that he could turn into the lane. He glanced in the rear-view mirror and saw the sign on the fence around his father's market. They were already taking it down. He looked at his father. His father's face was sad and it seemed as if there were tears in the corners of his eyes. Joe reached over and touched his father's hand. It was trembling. "Don't feel bad, Papa," he said. "You did the right thing. Life will be a lot more comfortable from now on."

"I remember when we made that sign. It was almost thirty years ago, just after you were born. We had such great hopes then," Phil said.

"You made them all happen, Papa. You have enough money in the bank to live comfortably. It's time now that you leaned back and took it easy."

"That's what I mean," Phil grumbled. "I don't know what to do with myself."

Joe looked at his father. He smiled. "What does Rabinowitz do?"

"He goes to the beach and looks at the girls."

Joe laughed. "There's nothing so bad about that."

"I'll kill him," his mother said. But even she was laughing.

He pressed the bell of Laura's apartment. She opened the door for him. He was carrying two cardboard boxes, which he placed on the foyer floor. He bent over and kissed her.

"What's in the boxes?"

"Books," he said. "My mother gave them to me. I have had them since I began to read. She saved them for me because she thought I might want to keep them."

She looked up at his face. "Are your parents all right?"

He nodded. His face was tight and hurting.

"You need a drink," she said quickly.

He followed her into the living room and sank into the couch. She poured a heavy Scotch on the rocks. "Drink it," she ordered.

Silently he swallowed half the drink, then looked up at her. "You know, sometimes you see people but you never really see them. It's like they have always been there. They always look the same."

She said nothing.

"Suddenly I saw my father, and I realized I'd never really seen him. And my mother too. Suddenly, overnight, they had grown old. They were not the young and angry parents I had always known. They were old and apprehensive people moving to a world they've never known, facing dangers they could never imagine." He felt the tears welling in his eyes and tried to hold them back. "I don't know if they really know how much I love them. Maybe I haven't told them enough times. Usually we were so busy arguing that we didn't have the time."

She said softly, "They know, just as you know. Sometimes you don't have to say the words. Love is just there."

"I watched my father's eyes when they tore down the sign over his market. He put it up there when I was born. Thirty years ago. And I saw thirty years of his life blow away." He looked up at her. "Is that the way it's supposed to be? Thirty years from now, will I see my life blowing away like that?"

She knelt before him and placed her hands on his cheeks. "It won't be like that," she said, gently. "Thirty years from now, the book you wrote two years ago, the book that you're writing now, and all the books that you will write in the future will still be there. Just as your father will live always in his world, you are a writer and you will always live in your world."

She drew him down to her breasts and cradled his head against her. "Don't be afraid to cry, lover," she whispered. "Tears are part of loving."

EPILOGUE

I WAS FIRST in line to debark from the 747 as the passenger hatch rolled open. I had to wait for a moment for the immigration officer to take the passenger list from the chief steward and then step out onto the ramp. An Air France service manager came toward me. "Welcome home, Mr. Crown." He smiled as he took my attaché case from my hand and led me into the terminal. "Was it a good flight?"

I shook his hand, even though I did not know his name. "Very good, thank you." I followed him quickly, not using the cane I always carried. It was more than a year since I had been in the hospital with a broken hip.

"If you would give me your baggage claim checks," he said, "I'll take you through customs quickly. Your car and chauffeur are already waiting."

"No baggage," I said. "I keep a complete wardrobe here and in France. It saves time."

"Very wise." He nodded. "Then I'll take you directly to customs."

The customs officer was a woman. I passed my declaration card and passport to her. She glanced at me. "You're Joe Crown, the writer?"

"That's right," I said.

"I'm happy to meet you," she said. "I just finished your new book. It's number one on the best-seller list already." She laughed. "It's wild, really wild!" she added.

"A little bit," I answered.

Then she turned serious. "Where's your luggage?"

I placed the attaché case on the counter and opened it. "Here it is."

"Nothing else?" she asked.

"No," I said. "I have all the clothes I need here at home."

She was silent for a moment, then punched some numbers in the computer in front of her. "Nothing else to declare?" she asked. "Gifts, jewelry, perfume?"

"Nothing." I said. "I travel light."

She punched the computer again, then turned to me, returned my passport and initialed the custom declaration. "Leave the declaration at the door as you walk out. I love your books, really I do. They're very exciting."

"Thank you," I said.

She looked at me. "Didn't I read in the papers that there is a party tonight to celebrate your silver anniversary on the best-seller list?"

"That's right," I answered.

"It must be wonderful," she said. "You go all over the world, with parties and exciting happenings."

"It could be worse." I laughed.

"Good luck," she said.

"Thank you again," I said and walked out. I thanked the Air France service manager. I looked for my car. LAX air was never the best, maybe 80 percent carbon monoxide on a good day. This was a good day. I choked only a little.

The silver-and-blue Rolls convertible cut into the traffic and stopped in front of me. Larry jumped out and ran around the car to open the door for me. "Welcome home, boss."

He smiled. "I would have been waiting here for you, but one of the cops chased me away from the curb. But it wasn't bad. Only twice around the airport."

I got in the seat beside him. "Close the convertible top and turn on the air conditioner," I said. "The air stinks and it's as hot as a bitch."

Larry had it together in a moment; then we moved out into the mainstream of traffic. He looked at me. "You're lookin' good," he said. "How's the walking?"

"I'm doing good," I said. "No problems now."

"That's good," he said.

"Where's Mrs. Crown?" I asked.

"She's down at the restaurant putting the finishing touches on the party," he said. "Then she'll be home. The hairdresser and the makeup man are due there at five-thirty."

"That figures," I said.

"Your doctor called you. He wants you to call him the minute you get in," Larry said.

"Okay." I picked up the telephone and called. The nurse answered. "Joe Crown returning his call." There was a click as Ed came on the phone.

"How the hell are you?" he asked.

"I'm alive. And I don't know how but I made it."

"You home already?" he asked.

"No," I said. "I'm calling from the car. We're just leaving the airport."

"I'll meet you in half an hour," he said. "I want to have a quick look at you."

"Good enough," I said. "I'll be there."

"And by the way," he said, "congratulations on the new book. I see it's number one already."

"I got lucky," I said.

"Great," he said. "See you."

I put down the phone and looked over at Larry. "How've you been doin'?"

"Okay," he said. "There's not much going on when you're away." He glanced at me as he moved the car onto the freeway. "I read in the *Enquirer* that the girls dancing in the French discos are all topless, that true?"

"That's true," I said.

"Jesus!" he exclaimed. "How can you stand it? If'n I walked on the floor to dance I'd have such a big hard on I'd pop the zipper on my pants."

I laughed. "I don't have any problems. Don't forget, I can walk pretty good but I'm not up to dancing yet."

Traffic was heavy on the freeway and Ed beat me to the house. He was in the bar nursing a Scotch and water. He watched me as I walked toward him. "You're walking real good, sport," he said, standing up and hugging me.

I hugged him too. "I feel good," I said.

"Why the cane?" he asked, taking it from me and studying it.

"When I get real tired, I ache a little."

"That's normal," he said. He felt the metal head of the cane. "Real gold?"

I nodded. "What would you expect me to have? Stainless steel? It would ruin my reputation."

"Where did you get it?"

"A girl gave it to me in France," I said.

"Laura?" he asked.

"Who else?" I answered.

He handed the cane back to me. I walked behind the bar and mixed a Scotch and water for myself, then sat down behind the bar opposite him. "Cheers," I said.

"Cheers," he replied. "How was the summer in France?"

"Okay," I said. "I thought you were going to come over."

"I couldn't make it," he said. "Too busy."

"I heard you got a divorce," I said. "Divorces keep you busy."

"Shit," he said. "I'm not lucky with women."

"Maybe you were lucky to get rid of this one," I said. "Look at it that way."

"I'd like to find a nice lady and just be happy," he said.

"That's easy," I said. "But you don't have to marry them."

"You're still married. How do you manage with all the trouble you get into?"

I smiled at him. "I always go home to Mama," I said. "And she knows it."

"You're wheezing," he said.

"Eighteen hours in planes, and the shit they call air at LAX is enough to croak anybody. Especially me with my asthma."

He took his stethoscope from his pocket. "Take your shirt off and let me listen to your chest."

"Playing doctor again?" I grumbled.

"I am a doctor," he said deadly serious. "Now do what I say."

I took off my shirt and we played the breathing-in-and-out routine. "And by the way," he said, "I keep telling you it's not asthma, it's emphysema. And that you don't get better. You still smoking?"

"Yes."

"Stop now and you pick up five years more of living. "I'll guarantee it."

"Five years or fifty thousand miles?" I laughed.

"I'm serious," he said. "You're just getting along now. From here on it can get worse."

"I'll think about it," I said, putting my shirt back on. "But whenever I begin writing I reach for a cigarette."

"Relax," he said. "Work less. You don't have to do all that. The money isn't that important now. I know that you have everything straightened out."

"You don't understand," I said. "There's no way a writer can stop working—not as long as there is an idea in his head. And I will never live long enough to write every story I want to write. Not even if I lived to be a hundred and fifty."

His face softened. "You know you're crazy, don't you?"

"Yes," I said. "But there's always another mountain I have to climb. Thank you for trying, though."

"Come into my office on Friday," he said. "Just for a regular checkup."

"Okay."

"And I'll see you tonight," he said, getting up. "Try to get a little sleep before the party. You've already had a long day."

I looked through the window and watched his car go down the driveway. Then I went upstairs to the bedroom, lay down and closed my eyes. Sleeping wasn't bad at all, but I could hear the jet engines roaring in my ears.

I felt a light hand on my shoulder. "Hi, baby," I said without moving. "I'm sleeping."

Her soft cheek pressed against mine. "I'm sorry, lover, I didn't want to wake you, but it's six o'clock and you've been sleeping for four hours. I have the barber and manicurist waiting for you. We have to be at the party before eight o'clock when the guests arrive."

"Fuck 'em," I said. Then an unfamiliar scent came to my nostrils. "Jesus!" I said. "I wound up in the wrong house."

She laughed. "I was trying out a new perfume. Now,

336

stop faking it and get your ass out of bed." She took my hand and placed it between her legs. "Now, tell me that you're in the wrong house."

I pulled her down and kissed her. "Hello, Mama."

"You awake now?" she asked.

"Yes," I said.

She got up. "Then get started. After all, it's your party."

I followed her into her bathroom. She was nude. I stared at her. "What did you do to yourself?" I asked. "I saw you only three days ago in France and suddenly you got skinny."

"I didn't get skinny," she laughed. "I got bloated in France from eating too much and drinking too much. So I had a couple of body wraps. It's magic—I sweated out nine pounds of water. Do you like it?"

"Do we have time for a fuck?" I asked.

She laughed. "After the party," she said. "Now get over to your bathroom and let the barber and manicurist work on you."

Upstairs at the Bistro all was silver and white. Even the flowers were sprayed silver. The place cards at the tables were embossed in silver, and silver-and-white ribbons covered the ceiling. In the large barroom outside the dining room silver letters were painted on the mirror behind the bar. SILVER ANNIVERSARY—JOE CROWN—25 YEARS ON THE BEST-SELLER LISTS.

Gene, who directed my public relations, smiled at me. "It's going to be the best of all of your parties. We've got two bands, one rock, one middle-of-the-road. After dinner we have a show with a dozen girls we brought in from the Casino de Paris in Las Vegas. And we've got the best guest list in town. All A's. From movies and TV to politicians and socialites. One hundred guests. And I even squeezed in two tables of press. We'll be covered all over the world. Newspaper, radio and TV. Laura and I broke our asses to set the place cards at the right tables. Do you like it?"

I laughed and hugged him. "Don't you even say hello?"

He looked at me and laughed. "You look great," he said. "What did you do to yourself?"

I smiled. "Makeup," I said. "But you are right. It's just the greatest."

Three-quarters of the way through dinner I looked across the room. Gene was right—everyone was there. And my voice was hoarse and almost gone, what with the greetings and all the interviews I had hurried through. But I was getting tired. The long day was catching up with me.

Across the room I could see Kurt Niklas whispering into Gene's ear, then Gene came toward me. He bent close and in a low voice said, "Kurt tells me there's a very distinguished old black man downstairs. He said he was an old friend of yours. He also said that the old man is wearing a beautiful tuxedo and the largest diamond rings and cufflinks this side of Sammy Davis. He said he was from Jamaica or something."

"Jamaica?" I asked curiously.

Gene nodded.

"Bring him up," I said.

"He's got a wild black chick with him," Gene said.

"Bring them both up and have the waiter bring two chairs over here beside me," I said.

"What is it?" Laura asked me as Gene walked away.

"A very old friend of mine," I said. "I don't remember whether I had ever mentioned his name to you."

The waiters were placing dessert and coffee on the tables as Gene led Jamaica and the girl to our table. I was on my feet already. We hugged each other. I looked into his face.

Scarcely anything about him had changed—not a wrinkle showed. But the full head of kinky black hair had turned to white. I looked into his eyes. He was crying. "Jamaica," I said.

"Joe," he said softly. "Joe, my man. I didn't even know if you'd remember me."

"Crazy bastard," I said. "How could I not remember you?" I turned to Laura. My voice was really almost gone. "Laura, this is my old friend, Jamaica. Jamaica, this is my wife, Laura."

She stood up and held out her hand. Gently he took it in his and bent to kiss it. "Laura, thank you for doing good for my man. He was a good boy an' I loved him truly."

"I'm happy to meet you," Laura said. "Please sit down with us."

"No, no," Jamaica said. "I don't want to butt into your party. I just wanted to see my man once again and tell him how proud I was of him."

"Please, sit down," Laura insisted. "Besides the lights are going out and the show will be starting. Sit right down there right next to Joe."

Jamaica bowed. "Thank you, Laura." He gestured to the girl with him. "This is my youngest girl, Lolita."

"Hi," the girl said.

I remembered the edge in Jamaica's voice. Time hadn't robbed it from him. "Now, Lolita," he said softly, "you say a polite how-de-do to my friends, just like your mama taught you."

"How do you do, Mrs. Crown, Mr. Crown," Lolita said. She made almost a half-curtsy.

I was smiling as they sat down. All the lights in the room went out. Then a young man in white-and-silver tails came out on the small stage. "Ladies and gentlemen, since Mr.

Crown has just arrived this day from France, the Casino de Paris of Las Vegas has the pleasure of bringing their girls here tonight to perform a genuine version of the Can-Can."

The orchestra struck up the music and the girls came flying out on the stage. Joe whispered to Jamaica, "Where the hell did you come from?"

"I retired to Cleveland," the old man whispered back. "I have an apartment in Honolulu for the winter. These old bones cain't take the cold weather. I jes' heard about your party on the television in the hotel. I was here on the plane layover."

"I'm happy to see you," I said.

"I read all your books," he said. "When I retired I had the time to read them. Even the first one when you wrote about me."

"Watch the show." Joe laughed. He found Laura's hand and held it tightly. "I was working for him when you sold my first short story."

"Then he was the—"

"Yes," Joe whispered. "The one in the book."

Then the fanfare sounded and the standard finale of the dance began. The girls locked arms on the stage and kicked in precision twelve times, then suddenly they turned around, their backs to the audience and flounced their skirts back up over their derrieres. The audience began to applaud wildly. Each bared bottom was imprinted, one letter on each cheek— and a twinkling exclamation point on the last bottom—in sparkling silver. Together they spelled out the words CONGRATULATIONS JOE CROWN! Then the stage went dark as the girls ran off.

The applause was still ringing as the lights came on. He leaned over and kissed Laura. "Thank you," he said. Then he turned to Jamaica. But the old man had gone.

He started to get up and go after him. Laura held his hand. "Let him go," she said softly. "He wanted to share a memory with you, and you both did. Now you can let it go."

"But—"

Laura interrupted. "It was another world then. Don't spoil it for him. This is not his world."

Joe was silent. "Is it mine?" he asked.

"Your world, lover," she said, "is whatever you want to make it be."